THE AMERICAN AU PAIR

FILTHY RICH ROYALS

M. S. PARKER

BELMONTE PUBLISHING, LLC

Copyright © 2019 Belmonte Publishing LLC

Published by Belmonte Publishing LLC

FREE BOOK

Get a book for FREE! Click Here to subscriber to my newsletter and start reading the exclusive 200 pages stand-alone Erotic romance, *The Billionaire's Sub*.

FREE BOOK!

FILTHY RICH ROYALS

Thank you for reading *The American Au Pair*, the third book in my Filthy Rich Royals series. Each book can be read stand-alone but I do recommend reading them in this order:

- **1. The Perfect Guy (Liechtenstein)**
- **2. The Dukes Virgin (Luxemburg)**
- **3. The American Au Pair (Monaco)**
- **4. Filthy Rich Royals 4 (Belgium)***
  ****Release summer 2019***

ONE

KITT

"Got you!"

The little blonde child shrieked as I swooped down and caught her up in my arms. From behind, I swung her around in a wide circle before depositing her on the ground and smacking a loud kiss on her cheek.

Karol, the blue-eyed little bundle of mischief, spun around and tipped her head back to glare at me. She planted her hands on her hips and gave me an imperious look. It was one I'd seen before, and it never failed to amuse, but I bit back my smile.

"Josef told me that was a *good* hiding spot," she told me.

"He was right." Linking my hands behind my back, I bent down until we were eye-level. "It was a very good hiding spot, and it took me almost ten minutes to find you."

"Really?" Her brow crinkled.

"Yes." Okay, I was hedging a bit. It had been a bit over five, and I'd walked slowly through the large manor house, but she was only three, and I was twenty-two. I had to make some accommodations. Besides, her brother used to hide in this very spot. In fact, for almost a month, we couldn't go more than one or two rounds of hide-and-seek without him choosing this very spot under his mother's desk in the pretty library with its soft blue walls and floral accents. But when the hider is all of three or four years old, what is a nice au pair to do?

You let them hide under the desk for the hundredth time.

Her frown of distress melted away, and she slid her hand into mine. "Come on, Frau Kitt. I'll help you find Josef."

The girl could give a sled dog a run for its money, I decided, as she hauled me along behind her pint-sized body with determination and a strength that didn't seem possible considering she didn't even reach my hip.

"Josef!"

I bit back another smile. "I don't think he'll *tell* you where he is, honey."

She let go of my hand and darted into the laundry room, checking the hamper and giving out a disgusted sigh when he wasn't in there. She looked in the closet and spun around, flinging her arms wide. "He isn't anywhere!"

"Oh, that's not true. He has to be *somewhere*." I winked at her. "He didn't disappear."

She looked like she wanted to argue, but her eyes narrowed, landing on something behind me. I stepped aside, watching as she all but pounced on the front-loading dryer. Clearly, I was no longer looking for him. She was.

It suited me fine.

I was worn out.

An early-morning thunderstorm had woken me. Actually, it had woken Josef up, who'd knocked on my door and crept inside to tell me that Karol was in his room crying because the thunder scared her so could we please watch *Avengers*?

I'd been working as an au pair for the Weiss family for

almost two years. Normally, such contracts were limited to twelve months, but Anne Weiss, my employer, had contacts with the German government, and it hadn't taken much work or discussion for her to extend my contract.

The list of movies my charges were allowed to watch was fairly short and mostly consisted of Disney cartoons, some German-produced pieces that were geared toward children... and just about every movie from the *Marvel* Cinematic Universe, *Star Wars* and the *Harry Potter* series. Well, perhaps it wasn't really that short.

Karl Weiss, my host father, had sheepishly told me that he was counting down the days until the children were old enough to enjoy *Lord of the Rings* with him.

He was one of the few adults I thought I could have related to just fine, even if he hadn't been a parent, simply because we would have bonded over a shared love of all things geek.

His wife, Anne, had laughed when I told her. "He keeps that inner geek tucked away for the most part. He loves having somebody to talk *Iron Man* and *Thor* with."

They were out of town for a few days, and I was in charge of the children. Knowing it wouldn't do much good to try and convince them to go to bed, we'd settled down in the entertainment room with cereal, chocolate milk, and *Avengers* on the oversized television. They'd drifted off to sleep before Hulk smashed New York, and I'd gotten another half hour or so of rest before giving up on the idea of sleeping.

Maybe they'd be tired enough to nap.

Karol usually still laid down for a while after lunch, but it was a rare day that her older brother bothered.

She closed the dryer with a flounce and turned around, face

puckering up with an uncharacteristic display of grumpiness. Oh, yes. She was going to need a nap.

"Come on." I held out a hand. "He's not in here. Let's see if he's found a secret spot in the kitchen where he can eat all the food."

That teased a smile to her lips. "Josef is *always* hungry."

I could have pointed out that she was too, but I didn't.

It took another five minutes to find him.

The little sneak had wormed his way under the coffee table somehow, and I had a few seconds of panic when he couldn't get out.

"My head!"

Hefting the end of the heavy piece up, I asked, "Now?"

He scrambled out, gaping at me wide-eyed. "Wow. You're strong."

"Thank you. Let's not hide under there again, okay, Josef? I think you're getting to be a bit too big."

He rubbed his head with a sheepish look. "It wasn't so hard to get under there. It was getting out."

I lifted a warning eyebrow. "Josef..."

"I won't."

I hugged him and ruffled his golden brown, downy soft hair. "Good. All right...whose turn is it to hide?"

AFTER ANOTHER TWO ROUNDS, they were bored, and Karol was getting crankier. She stood at the big bay window that looked out over their backyard. "When is it going to stop raining, *Frau* Kitt?"

"The weather report says it will clear up this afternoon." I stroked a hand down her hair in commiseration. The thunderstorm had cleared up, but the endless rain continued.

I wouldn't let on, but the dull, dreary day had me edgy.

Or something did. Maybe it was the lack of sleep. Slipping Josef a look, I saw him knuckling his eyes as he crouched over the picture in front of him. He was as tired as his sister.

If I was lucky, I could coax both of them into taking a nap. Then *I* could grab a short one myself. We might all end up staying up a bit later, but I was fine with that if it cleared the fog from my brain and chased away the unsettled feeling that lingered under my skin like a thousand burrowing insects.

I'd only felt like this twice…

Immediately, I shoved those memories into a closet in my mind. They still made me uncomfortable and not just because of what had happened after. The storm outside didn't help. A chill broke out across my skin, and I rubbed my arms out of reflex as I turned away from the window.

"How about we all go into the kitchen while I start on lunch?"

"Lunch!" Karol rubbed her belly and bolted away from the window. For one who'd teased her brother about always being hungry, she often seemed to have a tapeworm.

She beat both of us, and I wasn't surprised to find her in there, peering inside the big, glass front-fronted refrigerator. "What are we eating for lunch?"

JUST OVER AN HOUR LATER, I dropped down on the couch and sighed, exhausted.

Both of the kids were already snoozing in their beds, coaxed into naps with a promise of making cookies when they woke as long as they were well-behaved, which they always were.

The warm soup and sandwiches had been quick and simple, and after we did the clean-up—or rather Josef and I did clean-up while Karol made a mess that I dealt with along the way—we went upstairs to settle them into bed.

The rain had subsided to a lighter drizzle over lunch. To my dismay, as I settled on the couch, it picked up again, the clouds getting darker and heavier, the wind slamming the rain against the panes of glass as I dragged a blanket from the back of the couch over me.

I hated thunderstorms.

I'd never liked them. Ever since the day the barn burned down when I was eight, the fire blazing so hot, not even the rare rainstorm had dampened it.

But after my grandfather had been killed driving in one when I was fifteen, they just unnerved me even more. It was an irrational fear, and I knew that.

Knowing it didn't help.

Turning into the couch, I shoved my face against it and blocked out the sound of the rain and memories.

Or I tried.

I was tired enough that, after a few minutes, I succeeded and drifted off the sleep.

I DREAMT of a slick wet road, a big semi-truck hydroplaning and losing control, crossing the grassy median on a small highway in the Texas hill country. Screeching metal, like an awful scream, shattering glass and people screaming to get help.

But help was useless at that point.

Even in my dream, I knew it.

Rain poured down from the sky in sheets, but it wasn't enough to douse the blaze that ignited when the two trucks collided, one a big rig empty after delivering its load, the other an older model Ford F-150, but still in prime condition.

Or it had been, until the collision.

The driver of the big rig made it out.

I wasn't there the night it happened.

In my dream, I was, and he stumbled up to me much as he had at the funeral, grabbing my hand and begging forgiveness.

"I'm sorry," he said, voice thick with tears. "I'm so sorry…"

His voice turned into a cacophony of bangs, and I jolted back, staring at him in horror. He opened his mouth again, and it happened a second time.

Boom, boom, boom—

Jerking upright, the dream clinging like a sticky spiderweb, I looked around. For a few seconds, I was still back in the room where I'd lived up until I left for college. Back in the big old house with my mother and grandmother who still blamed me for my grandfather's death.

Then the banging came again.

The front door.

Swiping a hand over my mouth, I swallowed before clearing my dry throat. My face was painfully hot, my eyes too dry, although there were tears I wanted to cry and couldn't.

"Shit," I whispered.

Pushing to my feet, I looked out the window.

It was still raining, but it had settled to a steady patter again. "Just a minute," I called in German as I smoothed my hands down my shirt and jeans. My host family, the Weiss's, didn't mind if I dressed casually if we planned to be at home all day, especially on the weekends, but now I felt sort of silly in a pair of jeans and t-shirt, especially since the shirt sported a dog stretching in a version of Downward Facing Dog, with *DOGA* scrawled under it.

"Get it together, Kitt," I told myself. Pushing my fingers through tangled, rusty-brown hair, I sucked in a breath. I had no idea which family friends of the Weiss's had decided today was a good day for a visit, but it was rude of me to leave them waiting while I tried to brush off a nightmare.

Telling myself just that, I started for the door.

There weren't any more knocks, so whoever it was must have heard me. I gave one more half-hearted attempt to tug at my shirt as I muttered, "Why didn't they call first?"

Then I opened the door, plastering a smile on my face.

Two men stood there, umbrellas in hand while the deep recesses of the overhanging porch protected them from the steady rain. They both wore dark suits, although it was clear the rain had splattered them as they dashed up the walk. The sight of them immediately put me on edge, although nothing *about* them was particularly unkind.

The man on my right was the shorter of the two, although considering I was barely five foot nothing, *short* was relative. His iron-gray hair was worn in a buzz cut. At some time, the gray had probably been a deep black if the thick, straight brows were any indication. They beetled over a pair of intelligent blue eyes that raked me up and down in an accessing gaze that made me feel like he'd seen clear through me.

The man at his side, younger by several years, wasn't much better.

His gaze wasn't as cynical, and he did offer a smile.

After a few seconds, so did the other man.

But neither of the smiles helped.

Just standing there made that uneasy, crawling feeling return, and I wrapped my arms around my midsection.

Swallowing, I looked back and forth between them, my mind drifting to the two small children sleeping upstairs.

"Hello." The older one gave me a polite nod. "Is this the Weiss household?"

"It is," I said, suddenly stumbling over my German, although I spoke it well, almost as good as a native, I'd been told.

"May we have your name, *frau*?" This came from the younger man, the question voiced in English.

"It's Kitt. Kitt Bocho. May I ask why you're calling?"

"Are you the housekeeper, *Frau* Bocho?"

Frowning at the older man, I shook my head. "No. I'm the au pair. Why are you here?"

They exchanged a solemn look before the older man focused on me. "I'm afraid I have some terrible news, *frau*."

TWO

AERIC

It felt damn good to lounge on a float in the middle of the sprawling, private pool and not have to worry about a fucking thing.

All the people who mattered to me were settled and quite content, even my favorite relation, my cousin Stacia. She lived in New York, and most of the time we were relegated to communicating via Skype, text, and email, but every couple of years, we did manage to get in a visit one way or the other.

It had been a rough few months for her, but she was finally settled down with a man I kept reminding myself was a friend.

Logically, I knew that, and once I got over being pissed at how he'd upset Stacia, I knew we'd go back to being friends again. Of course, it helped that during the brief visit we'd had a few days earlier, all Luka had done was stare at her adoringly.

On principle, though, if nothing else, I had to stay on edge with him until I was certain he'd suffered enough and wouldn't transgress again. He'd been a complete dick, and for no reason.

Once I'd determined he'd suffered enough, then things could return to normal.

Logically speaking, it was more my problem than anything.

I was worried for my cousin, but I also knew her. Stacia was happy.

That was what mattered most.

She might seem sheltered to the uninformed observer, but the people who'd raised her, my aunt and uncle...well, they'd done the exact opposite of *sheltering*. They'd provided for every physical want, every material need one could desire, but they'd done nothing else.

She'd grown up with next to no affection, and while that could make some open and needy to anybody who offered it, it had made Stacia independent and determined to live her life her own way.

That was something Luka, the Hereditary Grand Duke of Luxembourg, my friend and her husband, had been forced to learn the hard way.

"Love's a bitch," I murmured, face tilted toward the sun. It shone down warm on me and added to the overall lethargy melting my muscles.

I rubbed my lids with thumb and forefinger, suppressing a yawn. As pleasant as it was to take a lazy afternoon off, I was supposed to meet with my parents tonight.

My father, the Sovereign Prince of Monaco, seemed to worry more and more about his advancing age. I was all of twenty-seven, but my father had been forty when I was born.

A few weeks earlier, a close friend of his had succumbed to a stroke, dying before he ever made it to the hospital, and it seemed like more and more, *Papa* was convinced he was staring death in the face.

I must prepare you for becoming the Sovereign Prince, Aeric...

We were having dinner tonight. Again. *Maman, Papa,* and I would be sitting with his advisers—again—as we worked on every little detail. I would be forced to plan my succession to the throne I didn't even want to consider at the moment as well as determine which advisers I wanted, even though I only had a small percentage of those I'd need when the time came. I also knew we'd discuss the one thing that plagued my father the most...

When are you going to take the time to find a wife?

Finding a wife and producing an heir—a *legitimate* one—was a chief concern. Not just for him and my mother, but for the sake of the country. Although Monaco's sovereignty no longer relied solely on the reigning monarch's ability to provide a male heir, it was...preferred.

The Nicolai family had been the ruling dynasty in Monaco for centuries. My father didn't intend to see that change with his son.

I, being the son, didn't plan on letting it happen.

However, I still wasn't all that interested in focusing on some wife-hunt. Even so, I would have to listen to my parents, respectfully, as they urged me on.

Blowing out a sigh, I opened one eye and studied the position of the sun, gauging the time. As much as I wanted a nap, I didn't have the time to indulge. Rolling off into the water, I began to swim.

I HIT twenty laps before stopping for a break. At the edge of the pool, I braced my forearms on the lip and sucked in a breath, my limbs pleasantly loose and heavy.

Another ten and I'd...

I went still, the hair on the nape of my neck prickling as I realized I wasn't alone.

Lifting my head, I saw Gustave standing ten feet away. His face was placid as ever. He'd been running affairs within the Princely Palace for longer than I'd been alive, and nothing unsettled him—except disorganization.

The younger man with him, Alain, was a different matter altogether, although Gustave told me the majordomo in training would shape up just fine.

I was yet to be convinced.

Alain didn't fidget, but it was clear he was neither placid nor comfortable. Without moving his head, he looked from Gustave to me to the other two people standing on the wide patio stretching out between the pool and the palace itself.

Their mere presence had me frowning.

It was unusual, to say the least, for somebody to arrive at the palace unannounced. But for somebody to be brought to one of the royal family without asking our permission?

Slowly, I swam to the ladder a few feet away and climbed, sliding a look toward Gustave as I did. Although his expression didn't change more than a fraction, the quick flicker of his lashes and the subtle way he averted his eyes had me frowning. A household staff member I hadn't noticed until that moment rushed up and offered me a warm towel, my robe thrown over her arm. I wanted to grab the robe and wave her off, but showing the nerves I already felt wasn't wise, so I took the pristine white towel, embroidered with the family crest, and dried my face, giving my hair a quick, rough pat-down before switching out the towel for the robe.

She hurried away without speaking, head bowed and shoulders hunched.

That unsettled me even more, and I jerked the robe on with far less grace than normal, striding over to the small party waiting. I didn't recognize the two men, but they immediately offered a polite half-bow, and after I greeted them, I was given the response expected from a Monaco native.

"We're sorry to disturb you, Your Highness. I am Remy Haget, a lieutenant with the National Police." He paused and cleared his throat, each word strained and rough. He stood with his hands clasped in front of him, and I couldn't help but notice how tightly he gripped his own hands, so tightly the knuckles jutted white against his skin. "Gustave has informed us that both of your parents are resting and..."

He stopped, looking at a loss.

Gustave moved to him, touching his shoulder.

A feeling of deep unease spread through me, turning my guts liquid. Shifting my attention to Gustave for a moment, I found him already looking at me, and the expression in his eyes was awful—gleaming wet and stark with emotion.

"What is it?" I demanded, my voice coming out far harsher than I'd intended.

Lieutenant Haget looked at me square in the eyes. The younger man with him flinched and looked away.

"I'm so sorry, Your Highness. But it's your sister, Princess Anne, and her husband, Karl Weiss."

I stared at him, not understanding.

Haget cleared his throat. "The National Police received information from authorities in Germany a short time ago, Your Highness. Your sister and brother-in-law are dead, sir. I am so sorry."

The words rose in my throat, caught there, choking me.

I wanted to yell, call him out for being a liar.

But I couldn't.

The truth of his words was in his eyes, impossible to miss.

Because I couldn't trust myself to say anything, I looked away and stared out over the glowing blue water of the pool.

"Your Highness—"

"Please leave me, Lieutenant Haget. Whatever information you have, you can give to Gustave. I'll notify my parents." Each syllable sounded like a robot. "Share this with no one. We'll handle making the official announcement to the country through public channels."

"Of course." He cleared his throat. "If I may, Your Highness, I'm so sorry. I've a sister myself."

Hearing the sympathy in his voice, I looked at him and gave a short nod.

But he'd already turned and started to retreat.

I waited until I was alone before going to my knees and covering my face.

Anne.

———

I DIDN'T KNOW how long I was out there.

It felt like a lifetime, but I doubted it was long.

I felt chilled to the bone and was shivering, staring at the elegantly custom-carved tiles beneath me while a lifetime of memories rolled through my mind.

Anne and me, spending the summer at the family chalet. Stacia was there, too, but she was too young to join us as we had our riding lessons.

"I'm terribly high, Aeric. What if I fall?"

Seven-year-old me had been so arrogant as I looked at her and informed her, "I'm here. I'd never let you fall, Anne."

Something hot and wet hit my cheek.

"Your Highness."

I flinched.

Gustave wrapped a blanket around my shoulders and urged me to my feet. "Come now. Come along, Aeric. You can't stay here like this. We need to tell your parents."

Hair still wet, I moved through the hall that led to the wing where my parents lived. Gustave trailed along behind me, but other than him, I was alone, and the heels of my shoes sounded loud and hollow on the marble floor, each *thud* ringing out like a death knell.

The very thought made me flinch, and I paused.

Behind me, Gustave waited, so close I would have called it hovering had it been anyone else in the world.

He said nothing, and after a deep breath, I forced myself forward. At the double doors, I knocked and closed my eyes.

The faint *click* had indicated the doors were opening, and I looked just in time to see Solange, my mother's *Dame d' Honeur,* her primary personal aide, peer at me through the door.

Surprise flickered across her face, but when she saw me, her lips started to curve. Something on my face had her smile fading almost as quickly as it formed.

Even without me saying a word, she knew something was wrong.

I offered a polite nod. "Madame Laurent."

She stepped aside and waved me in. None of us said anything else until she'd shut the door behind me. Clearing her throat, she said, "We were sitting in the solar, Your Highness."

"Thank you." I hesitated a moment, then said, "Wait here with Gustave, please."

Her light brown eyes held mine a moment, then she closed them tightly before nodding. Gustave moved to her and offered a hand. I knew he'd wait several moments before telling her, saving my mother—and me—that awful task.

While I'd dressed, Gustave had filled me in on the precious few details he had, but German authorities hadn't shared much. I'd have to go there. I needed to be doing that already.

But my parents—

Anne—

My thoughts splintered and came to a stop as I entered the solar and found my parents sitting together at the table, laughing quietly as they paged through a large book. My mother, her dark hair with threads of silver showing through, gestured to something in the book and lifted her head to say something, a smile blooming on her face as she looked at my father.

The Sovereign Prince of Monaco, Fortinbras Nicolai, had a rare grin on his face, the one he allowed out only in private and most often for *Maman* and Anne.

Maman caught sight of me and shifted to face me, her brows arching. Her smile didn't fade, but there was a faint hint of bemusement in her voice as she said, "Aeric."

I rarely came to their quarters unless requested, so the puzzled expression on her face was understandable.

Papa looked at me as well, his expression settling back into a more remote set, although not entirely distant. He gave a faint smile and nodded, gesturing for me to join them.

My feet felt glued to the floor.

She was the first to realize something was wrong and rose slowly from her chair. "Aeric, what is wrong?"

"I have news, *Maman*," I said, my voice raw and harsh, as if I'd already cried a thousand tears for my sister. I crossed the distance and took the hands she'd lifted toward me, squeezing them. They felt delicate, like always. But for the first time, her hands also felt frail. My heart wrenched at what I had to do. "A lieutenant from the National Police left a few moments ago. *Maman, Papa...*"

My father was now on his feet, too, that severe expression locked in place. But it cracked and fell away in the next moment, leaving him looking vulnerable, tired, and broken.

"It's Anne." My voice cracked. "She's...Germany authorities found her and Karl. They're dead."

A broken noise escaped *Maman*, and she sagged, slumping into me.

My father caught her, holding her against him. "What is this? What happened?"

"I don't know." The huge, growing ache that had been rising inside me from the moment the lieutenant broke this horrible news was so large now, it felt like it might tear me into shreds. "Our national police had very little information. There were only two victims. That is all I know."

"The babies?" *Maman* whispered.

"I don't know." I met her tear-drenched eyes. "The plane is being prepared as we speak. I'm flying to Germany as soon as you give me leave, so I can find out what happened."

"Go," the prince ordered, his voice harsh and ragged. Then he turned toward my mother and folded her more fully into his embrace.

As I left, her sobs rent through the silence, and I felt each one, like a lash on my heart.

THREE

KITT

THE POLICE HAD LEFT.

It was a crazy way to think, but part of me had wanted to beg them to stay because I couldn't stand the thought of being alone in the house right then with just those two babies after what I'd just learned.

What do I do?

Pacing the mellow wooden planks of the living room floor, polished to a high shine, I wrapped my arms around my middle and fought to control the tears that kept trying to push in.

If I cried, Karol would notice.

Besides, if I *started* crying, I might not be able to stop, and even though Josef lived with his head in the clouds, even he would notice if I was crying.

Swiping my hands over my face, I shoved the heels of my hands against my eyes.

"Get it together," I whispered. "They'll be waking up soon…"

As if summoned by my thoughts alone, the sound of footsteps rang out overhead, and I swore.

"What the fuck?"

Immediately, I bit my lip, guilt-ridden for breaking the rule Anne had established—*please don't swear in the house. I don't want to risk the children overhearing.* Karl had teased her and pointed out that *he* cussed. She'd retorted, *Exactly. It's hard enough dealing with your bad habits.*

Tears edged closer, and a bubble of hysterical laughter burst out. "Don't you think it's a little stupid to be worrying about that right now?"

I had no doubt Anne would understand an F-bomb.

Would have.

She was gone.

"Frau Kitt. I want to make cookies now."

The imperious little voice behind me was a salvation, and I turned, plastering a smile on my face. It felt far too fake, but it must have been convincing enough for Karol because she only smiled back, a sweet smile that held hints of angel and imp. "Josef is still sleeping. We could make them now, and they'd be ready when he got up. Wouldn't he like that?"

"You're tricky," I said, wagging my finger at her. "He would love to have cookies when he woke up, but he'd also miss out on making them, and you know he loves that part too."

"Fine." She pushed her lip out, but the pout didn't last long, so I knew she hadn't expected her ploy to work.

Still, even knowing that, I couldn't stand it. "Tell you what. We'll look at recipes and see if we have ingredients for something new and fun. How does that sound?"

"Yes!" She rushed at me and hugged me around the hips, and I bent forward, hugging her tightly, taking comfort in her warm, sweet-smelling little self. How was I supposed to tell them? *Should* I tell them? The cops hadn't told me what to do. They hadn't said what was going to happen other than that the immediate family would be notified by local authorities.

Family. Anne's parents, and a brother. Anne's brother. I knew she was close to him, and her parents doted on the children. Anne and Karl visited her family once or so each year and her parents had traveled to Germany once. I recalled meeting them. Karol had been two.

I hadn't met the children's uncle, but Anne talked about her brother often.

That was it, though. Karl's family was gone. He'd been an only child, and his parents had passed away, first his father, then his mother.

It was just him.

Had, I reminded myself. It *had* just been him. Now he was gone, too.

ONE THING about kids as young as Karol and Josef was that they were still relatively easy to distract.

I had no idea how I would have handled direct questions, but fortunately, they didn't ask any. Their mother usually called around five on evenings when they took a holiday away from the children. That time had come and gone, and I still didn't know what to say.

It wasn't until a little after five-thirty that Karol asked about it as we sat down to eat a dinner of spaghetti.

As I fumbled for an answer, Josef's elbow clipped his glass of milk, and the flurry gave me a distraction to just mumble out a vague answer.

That was good enough for her at the moment, but I dreaded the seconds until bedtime.

If she or Josef asked again, I wouldn't know what to say.

After dinner, we dealt with the clean-up, and I hurried Karol into her bath.

Despite the nap they'd taken, both children showed signs of being tired at their normal bedtime. By eight, I had them tucked into bed.

"When will Mama be home?" Karol asked sleepily as I drew the blanket up over her shoulders. "Papa?"

"We'll check on that tomorrow," I said, my voice husky.

She wrinkled her nose. "Are you catching a cold? You sound funny."

"Maybe so. I'll drink some tea in a bit. Your mama always says that helps, doesn't she?"

"I like tea with honey."

"Me too." I kissed her forehead and rose, my breathing unsteady.

Outside Josef's room, I paused and waited until I regained my composure. Usually, the smart little guy was so involved in his art projects and reading his way through books several years above his age level that he didn't notice the world around him, but once he had his feet in the here and now, he saw quite well, and he was older than Karol. That could add up to trouble if he caught any hint that something was wrong.

A few more minutes, I told myself.

In a few more minutes, I could have some privacy and cry.

In his room, Josef sat on his bed, looking up through the skylight at the stars. "Do you think Mama and Papa can see the stars better in Dresden?"

"I think they can see them beautifully," I said, crossing to sit on the edge of the bed.

He looked at me then, his sandy brown hair and blue eyes, his facial features a younger mirror of his father. "Those cookies were excellent, *Frau* Kitt. We'll have to make them for Mama and Papa because we ate so many."

"*You* ate so many, you little sneak." I ruffled his hair, then nodded at the bed. "Lay on down, sweetheart. You need some sleep."

He obeyed, eyes still on the skylight and the stars beyond.

"I think I might want to be an astronaut."

"That sounds fascinating." Last week, he'd wanted to paint masterpieces on the sides of old buildings. And before that...a doctor who cured diseases. He'd do great no matter what he chose, with that sharp mind of his.

My heart twisted as I thought of how much his parents would never have a chance to see, but I banished the thoughts just as quickly, turning off the light over his bed so he couldn't see the tears that sprang to my eyes. I was losing the battle trying to control them. "You get some rest, honey. I love you. Good night."

"Good night."

He rolled onto his side with a yawn, and I rushed out of the room, lips pressed together.

I made it to the library in the back of the house and flung myself into the chair by the window, drawing my knees up and pressing my face against them. I tucked myself into the smallest ball possible and gave into the tears I'd been fighting from the moment the police had told me about the deaths of Karl and Anne.

What would happen now?

The children...they'd go to Anne's brother or grandparents, wouldn't they?

Would I ever get to see them again?

Even as I thought it, I felt selfish and small, because what mattered most was their needs, but the very idea of no longer being part of their lives cut deep.

Anne had been talking about hiring me on full-time as a nanny. My initial contract as an au pair was only supposed to last a year, but she'd made a few phone calls. In her position, she had more than a few powerful friends. Karl, too. She'd once mentioned that Karl had ties to old Germanic nobility. Between the two of them, extending my contract had been easy and it had come as no real surprise when my request for a permanent residence permit was granted.

Now my future was uncertain, and it terrified me. I'd been here for nearly two years, but my entire life had revolved around the children. Most of the people I knew outside the Weiss family, I'd met *because* of the family. I knew a few people vaguely from the bookstore I liked to haunt on my scheduled off days, but those were acquaintances, and I doubted any of them would be able to help me.

"Does any of that *matter* right now?" I whispered.

The logical part of me insisted it did, even as logic warred with ache and hurt, fear turning into a soul-sucking vortex inside me.

Germany and the Weiss family were more home to me than America at this point, and now all of that was slipping away.

And the kids. How was I supposed to handle it in the morning when Karol asked me again about when her mom would be home? And how did I handle it when Josef realized he'd never have the chance to make those cookies for his parents?

Another sob ripped out of me.

The storm, like the rain that had pounded the city for much of the day, eventually faded, first to a steady rain then away to a trickle. Head pounding, I sat there, feeling too emotionally drained to do anything more than huddle there.

If I moved, I felt like I'd shatter. But the pounding in my head grew steadily worse, and I knew if I didn't take something for the headache, it would get worse.

Dragging myself upright, I made my way to my room, the guest bedroom that had been customized just for me when I'd arrived, and I'd slowly made it more *mine* in the months since.

I found the prescription bottle for the migraine medicine the doctor had prescribed and popped one in my mouth, letting it dissolve on my tongue. My throat felt raw now, so after washing my face, I went to the kitchen and made tea, liberally lacing it with honey.

The house was too quiet around me, as if it too had been affected by the news delivered by the police. After several sips of the tea, the rawness in my throat eased. The pain in my head began to subside.

Logic told me I should start making some sort of plan, at least do some research and figure out what might happen next. There were several companies that specialized in connecting families with au pairs. Anne had reached out to me after a friend of hers from America had connected us, but surely somebody at one of the connection companies could at least point me in the right direction.

But my thoughts were clouded with grief, fatigue, and what

I could only assume was shock. That shock that followed after hearing about the death of somebody important in your life.

I thought of my grandfather. "Fuck. Not now."

Pushing back from the table, I eyed the tea and made a decision. Tea wasn't going to do it. Both Karl and Anne had told me I was more than welcome to have some wine from their cellar or have a drink from the well-stocked liquor cabinet, but I had never been much of a drinker.

One glass of wine made me so sleepy, I might as well drink it *in* bed.

And that was exactly what I was going to do.

Ten minutes later, I took a sip of the Riesling as I walked through the house, lingering in front of the wall of pictures in the living room. Anne with the children out by a lake. The same lake, Josef this time, spinning in circles while Karl hefted a smaller Karol into the air.

Another picture, taken when they'd last visited Anne's family in Monaco.

Anne was laughing at her brother while he, Josef, and Karol sprawled in lush green grass. I'd looked at the picture a hundred times, drawn in by the man's pale gray eyes, set in a face that was almost painfully handsome. There was another picture of him, standing with Anne, posing for what was clearly a formal event. Anne had a faint curl to her lips and a look in her eyes that made me think she was viewing the events around her with a fair amount of cynical amusement.

But he had no smile. He looked like he didn't know how to smile, or if he did, he didn't consider it worth his time.

If it wasn't for the photo of him playing with the kids, I would have been terrified at the idea of him being the one who might become the guardian for Karol and Josef.

Aching inside, I reached up, letting my fingers hover above the glass protecting the picture, Anne's bright, happy smile tearing me apart.

"Anne, I'll do my best to make sure they're taken care of, I promise," I whispered.

There was no answer, of course, just the silence of the house around me.

I sighed and turned toward the stairs.

A thunderous noise tore through the house before I took more than two steps, cacophonous and out of place. I jolted and almost dropped the glass of wine, recovering just in time, although I did splash it on the front of my *Doga* shirt.

The knock came again, and somehow, it was even *louder*.

Terrified the kids would hear it, I hurried into the foyer. Putting the wine on the antique Queen Anne table there, I went to the door and peered through the peephole to find a tall man standing just outside, his face tight and hard. Panic skipped through me, and I went to speak through the door, but he started to lift his fist again.

Instinctively, I unlocked and opened the door, one-handedly disarming the system as I did so.

"Yes?" I asked, staring up at him. I'd never felt so aware of my lack of height as I did in that moment, staring up at him.

His face was shadowed with a heavy growth of stubble, damp hair falling into his eyes. The rain had started back up, his shoulders damp and there were droplets on his lashes. As I waited for a response, a drop fell from his hair, hit his nose and rolled down to the tip.

"Who the hell are you?" he demanded. Without waiting for a response, he shoved past me. "Karol! Josef!"

His German was flawless but accented with French.

He started for the stairs, and I lunged after him, grabbing his arm.

"No!" I hissed, my shock and general reticence around people evaporating in my worry for the children. "Would you be quiet? They're *sleeping!*"

He slowed, then stopped, although judging by his size, it had been my words that made him pause, not me grabbing his arm. He swung his head around and gaped at me, his light gray eyes widening. "Their parents are *dead,* and the children are sleeping away unaffected?"

FOUR

AERIC

SLEEPING?

I couldn't believe what she'd just said.

The woman stood in front of me, obviously unsettled, and as I glared at her, she darted a look up the stairs. My nerves, already on edge, grew even more ragged.

"You never did tell me who you are," I said, narrowing my eyes.

"You didn't give me a chance," she pointed out, her voice trembling a bit at first, then firming. "I'm the au pair."

"The au pair."

She frowned, her rosy, full lips pursing in a scowl, and I hated that I even noticed. My sister was fucking dead, lying in a morgue and waiting for me to identify her. My primary aide, Guillermo, had offered to handle the matter, but that was a family responsibility. He had insisted on taking care of other details and contacting law enforcement to get more information, taking a car from the airport while I went to see about the children.

He was taking care of important matters, and instead of

taking care of my niece and nephew, I had to deal with this impertinent American. And she was American, no matter how flawlessly she spoke German.

"Yes." She crossed her arms over her chest and squeezed, a shiver going through her. I doubted she even noticed. "A caregiver for the children. That's what an au pair is. I—"

"I know what an au pair is." Voice growing louder with every word, I demanded, "How are those two children sleeping snug in their beds when their parents are dead?"

Her jaw dropped. "Would you *please* keep your voice down? The kids *don't* know!" She shot a look up the stairs, then reached out and grabbed my arm and pulled at me, trying to get me to follow her.

My jaw almost dropped at that. Save for Anne and Stacia, *nobody* was so bold to...*tug* on me. Like a dog on a fucking leash.

It was shocking enough that I actually let her do it.

The moment we were in the next room, she let go as if the mere contact burned. Perhaps it did. I still felt the imprint of her small hand through the layers of my suit coat and shirt. I had the odd urge to reach up and cover it.

"I haven't told them, *Herr*..." She stopped and blinked, surprise flickering across her face as she eyed me. "Oh. You're Aeric, aren't you? Anne's brother?"

"It's *Prince* Aeric." I crossed my arms over my chest, giving her an arch look.

She blinked owlishly.

Not the reaction I'd been expecting.

"You're the au pair for the grandchildren of the Sovereign Prince of Monaco. Surely you're aware of that."

Her full mouth flattened into a frown. "I'm aware, sir."

Her tone made it clear she wasn't about to call me anything more than *sir*. Fucking Americans.

"Why haven't you told the children?" I demanded. "Don't you think they deserve to know their parents are—"

She surged forward and grabbed my arm. *Again.*

"Stop," she hissed. "Please. Do you want them to hear it like that? What if they wake up?"

The panic in her eyes, and her obvious concern, penetrated the wall of grief and anger when nothing else likely would have.

I had to get my head out of my ass. She was right. It would be cruel, and traumatizing, for them to hear the news like that. I gave a curt nod, but before I could ask again, she let go and moved away, her movements jerky and erratic.

"You're right, of course." I started to offer a polite apology for raising my voice.

And she cut me off.

I managed to mentally pick my jaw up and listen because she seemed to have something important to say. Still, she'd *interrupted* me. I'd never had anybody—other than Anne—interrupt me.

"I didn't tell them because I wasn't sure *what* to tell them, and it didn't seem to be my place," she said, blissfully unaware of my shock. "I wanted to call her family, but I couldn't find her phone book. It's usually in the kitchen drawer, but it wasn't there and..."

She sighed, finally turning to look at me from several feet away. Clearly nervous, she tugged at the hem of her shirt.

The pink material stretched tight over a full pair of breasts, drawing attention to both those delicious curves and the ridiculously silly dog that looked to be doing an imitation of yoga.

"I've been caring for them for two years, and I adore them. I know they love me too," she said, shoving a hand through hair that couldn't decide if it wanted to be brown or a deep, rich red. "But I'm not family, and they should have family here when they learn about this, so I didn't tell them. I'm sorry if you feel that was a wrong move, but I did the best I could."

The logic was flawless, and I couldn't fault her for not telling them. I went to apologize again, but before I could, she tugged at her shirt again, then sucked in a breath—an erratic one, followed by a sniff.

Dread gripped me as she blew the breath back out. In the silence, I heard it catch in her throat, and I wanted to back away.

Not this. I was having a hard enough time just maintaining as I processed Anne's death. I couldn't handle it if this woman started to cry.

She blinked rapidly, and I saw her reddened eyes. A further look revealed wan features, and I couldn't mistake the shock or grief, either. Not now that I was looking.

Bracing myself, I reached inside my pocket for a handkerchief, even as I debated on texting Guillermo. I hadn't been able to leave Monaco without my aide, although I had evaded the routine security detail. I had no doubt they were already en route. For now, I was alone, but Guillermo wouldn't be far. I could contact him, and he could get here and pat and stroke and soothe. It didn't seem right to leave the woman who'd provided for my sister's children alone as she wept, but I had no desire to comfort anybody.

The pink material of her shirt rose and fell once more, her breasts catching my eye again.

Other things, maybe. But not comfort.

"I'm so sorry."

Jerking my head up, I scowled. "What?"

FIVE

KITT

The man glowering at me made me wish we'd stayed in the foyer, close to the alarm system where all I had to do was punch the panic button, and the well-trained, very extensive security service that monitored the home would arrive within minutes.

When I'd first come to work at the manor house where Anne lived with her husband and young family, there had been several guards who lived on the premises at all times, but one by one, they'd each left while Karl added more to the security system.

Even though I knew the man in front of me to be Anne's brother—and the next ruler of Monaco—the predatory way he watched me was unsettling, to say the least, and I found myself wishing there were still security men under the Weiss's employment.

The scowl was unsettling, but there was more than his obvious anger, and my heart broke a little for him even as his very presence left me unsettled.

"I'm so sorry about your sister, and Karl."

His brows shot up, but I ignored it. It was already hard enough to talk to strangers and one as confident—*arrogant*—as Prince Aeric of Monaco made it even more difficult. Every word I said, every move I made felt like the wrong one.

What could be the right ones at a time like this?

"Your sister...I adored her. She's...she was a beautiful person, so kind and funny. I'm very sorry for your loss." I licked my lips and tugged at my shirt once more. "The police told me that authorities in Monaco would notify Anne's family and I..." Lifting a hand to grasp at the insubstantial explanation that still eluded me, I tried to continue holding his gaze. I managed, but it was hard. "I just felt it wasn't my place to handle such a painful matter."

He blew out a breath and turned away, pacing a few feet before coming to a stop. He was in the same place I'd been when he knocked, and I wondered if he was staring at the picture of him with his sister and the children. As I watched, he reached up, making jerking motions.

I realized why in a moment when he looked back at me, still loosening his tie. He all but ripped it off, then his suit coat, draping them over the couch. "What happened?" he asked flatly. "You said the police were here. What did they tell you?"

He'd loosened the top few buttons of his dress shirt. I found myself hypnotized by the act and had to tear my eyes away. Cheeks hot, I looked around for my wine. Remembering I'd left it on the table in the foyer, I went to get it, lingering long enough to reset the system. Karl had always been emphatic about keeping the alarm set.

Blinking back the tears, I took a sip of wine before answering. "Not much, I'm afraid. They were on holiday in Dresden, and police there received a call. They were found dead. That's all I know." I took another sip, feeling guilty but needing it at the same time. I met his eyes squarely and lifted my chin as I held the glass. "It's been a horrible day. I was hoping a half glass would help me sleep."

He didn't even look at the wine.

"You know nothing else?"

"I'm sorry, no."

He closed his eyes and rubbed his face, a hard breath escaping him.

In that moment, the arrogance and confidence faded away, and all I saw was a man suffering.

Putting my wine down, I moved closer, hesitant to say anything, but unable to stay quiet. I hated seeing people hurt. "I'm really sorry, Aeric."

His name slipped out without any conscious thought —again.

But he didn't look up, didn't move.

"I'll be there for the children as long as you need me to be, as long as they need me. If there's..." I hesitated, wondering if he even heard me.

He looked up, and I found myself the focus of those pale gray eyes.

My heart stuttered a beat, and I had to swallow the knot in my throat before I could finish. "If there's anything I can do... any way I can help..."

His lids drooped. "Anything?"

Something about the timbre of his voice was different, and my heart shuddered, then sped up to a gallop, leaving me momentarily breathless. "Ah...if it will help with this. With the loss..." I gave a slight shake of my head. "Of course. How can I help? Are you hungry? Would you like—"

"Not for food."

He moved, and I had no idea what was coming until he cupped my face in his hands and kissed me.

Stunned, I stood there, unable to move, hardly able to breathe.

His tongue stroked over my lower lip, and I gasped. He took advantage, dipping into my mouth while pushing his fist into my hair. It tightened almost to the point of pain, but I realized I didn't mind—at all.

Using that grip, he tugged my head back.

A weird noise filled the air.

I heard it again a few seconds later, then again. It wasn't until he broke the kiss to run his mouth down my jaw that I realized the noises were coming from me, broken little whimpers.

He came back to my mouth, and I reached up, curling my fingers into the front of his shirt, sinking into him.

Wow...

It had been a long time since I'd had a man even try to kiss me, and I hadn't much liked it. Now, not only was a man kissing me, I was loving it, and it was—

Reality slammed back into place.

SIX

AERIC

I FELT LIKE I WAS SUFFOCATING.

Although I didn't know this woman with her big, sky blue eyes and tumbled hair of red and brown, I couldn't stand the feel of the tie around my neck another second. Rarely did I find it suffocating to dress in attire I'd been taught was appropriate for my station, but in that moment, I thought I might choke.

Turning away from her insightful gaze, I tore at the precise Windsor knot, swearing silently, cursing my sister for not being here, the fucking lieutenant from the national police who'd shattered a perfectly lovely day, *everything.*

Finally, I had the tie loosened, and I jerked it off, then shrugged out of the suit coat. Turning back to the au pair, I tossed the coat and tie on the nearby arm of the couch and flicked open the top buttons of my shirt.

The vise around my neck eased, and my muscles relaxed.

Then I realized she was watching me, a mesmerized look on her face as she eyed my hand.

A new sort of tension filled me, tempting me to undo far more than just the top two buttons of my shirt.

What would she do if I did?

You stupid fuck. Are you crazy?

It was possible. And if I thought she wouldn't take off running, I might have given in. The need to get out of my head was overwhelming. But she blinked abruptly, moving in a way that made me think she hadn't even realized she was staring.

With a slight shake, she averted her head, leaving me to brood and hurt and curse myself for being so selfish as to think about my dick at a time like this.

And still, the heat started to gather in my gut, low and familiar. Fuck me, it was more than welcome, because the last thing I wanted to do was think about the entire fuckery of the day.

"Not much, I'm afraid," she said, talking over her shoulder as she moved toward the foyer. "They were on holiday in Dresden, and police there received a call. They were found dead. That's all I know."

It took a moment to realize what she was talking about, but once I figured it out, the heat in my veins turned to ice. By the time she turned back to me, her wineglass in hand, the desire I'd felt to grab her and tumble her down onto the couch had faded. It hadn't disappeared, but I was once more thinking of all the things I didn't *want* to think about.

Even as I fumbled for words to ask the questions I had to ask, she met my eyes in challenge, lifting the glass. "It's been a horrible day. I was hoping a half glass would help me sleep."

I'd need more than wine, and the idea of *sleeping* was unthinkable.

Anne. Karl. Found dead. "You know nothing else?"

"I'm sorry, no."

Closing my eyes, I dragged a hand down my face. Nothing

else? How was that possible? Guillermo would know more, I told myself. He'd have to know more.

He certainly couldn't know *less*.

Anne...images of her started to swim through my mind once more, and the storm of grief pushed ever closer.

"I'm really sorry, Aeric."

The sound of my name on her lips penetrated the fog of grief, and I was able to push it back again.

"I'll be there for the children as long as you need me to be, as long as they need me. If there's..."

Her words trailed off, and I looked at her, focused on her blue eyes like a drowning man had been tossed a life preserver.

"If there's anything I can do...any way I can help..." Her words trailed off, and she swallowed, her throat working with the action.

At the base of her neck, I thought I could just barely make out the mad flutter of her pulse. Or maybe I'd lost my mind. It would explain why I had such a strong urge to press my lips to her skin, seek out her scent, discover her taste.

Tell her thank you. Go to your room and go to bed.

That was what I should do, because it was absolutely wrong for me to consider going to her, kissing her. But the harder I tried not to think about it, the harder it was *not* to do just that.

It was either think of her...or the horror of reality, and in that moment, reality wasn't welcome.

"Anything?" I took a step toward her as the heat began to slide through my veins once more.

"Ah...if it will help with this. With the loss Her cheeks flushed, then she frowned, a confused look in her eyes. She gave a slight shake of her head. "Of course. How can I help? Are you hungry? Would you like—"

"Not for food." I closed the distance between us and caught her face in my hands. Her skin was warm and smooth and soft, like her lips, I discovered a moment later as I took her mouth, sliding my tongue over the full curve, then dipping inside to discover the sweet depths.

She made a startled noise, then sagged.

I pulled her closer, enjoying the sweet taste of wine on her lips, her soft, ripe curves...and the noises she made.

Sexy little sounds, broken moans, and needy mewls urged me on. How would she sound when I had her wrapped around my dick, naked and begging for more?

Already desperate to know, I tore my mouth from hers and kissed a line across her cheek, down to her jawline, then her neck. I found the pulse in the hollow, rabbiting away just as I'd thought it would be. Kissing her there, I breathed in her scent, then started back up, ready to swallow her down in quick, desperate bites.

She grabbed the front of my shirt and arched closer, her belly cuddling against my cock. I caught one hip and rocked forward, and the feel of her was as every bit as perfect as her taste, as her scent.

She moaned again, the kittenish little sound driving me insane.

If she kept it up...

I slid my hand from her hip up to toy with the hem of that silly pink t-shirt. Under that shirt, I'd discover if she was as smooth, as soft, as warm...

She stiffened.

In the space between heartbeats, she went from soft and sexy female to stumbling away from me, her cheeks flushed, eyes unfocused and wide.

My first instinct was to reach for her, haul her back.

For a few short seconds, I hadn't thought about anything but her. Her mouth, her taste, the press of her breasts against my chest.

That was all that had mattered.

But then she shoved her hair back from her face, and I saw her hands, how her fingers trembled.

My brain snapped back on, and I stiffened, appalled with myself.

"I am so sorry," I said, having to force the words out. What in the hell had come over me? "That was completely out of line. Forgive me, please."

She licked her lips, and my thoughts stuttered to a halt as the desire to kiss her all over again slammed into me.

Maybe I *had* lost my mind.

It was possible, very possible.

She cleared her throat and went to speak, then stopped, looking like she struggled to find the words.

"I truly am sorry," I said again, locking down with an iron control. I'd handle matters with her professionally, properly, if it killed me.

"Of course." Her eyes darted up to meet mine before she focused on something on the wall behind me. "it's been a dreadful day for everybody. I don't think any of us are acting as we should."

Was that why you kissed me back?

I didn't let myself ask, though. I'd already crossed enough lines tonight.

Her cheeks remained a soft pink, and despite her calm, matter-of-fact handling of the out-of-line kiss, I had a feeling that even if we'd met under the best of circumstances and not the worst, I would have wanted to kiss her.

There was something about her wide mouth with its full top lip, how she watched me with nervous eyes, but so easily glared at me every time I did something she felt would be an offense to the children—even if it was just raising my voice.

The protectiveness she felt toward them was very appealing.

"You've had a long, difficult day. We all have." She turned away as she spoke, smoothing her shirt down in what I'd decided was a nervous gesture. Her hands went to her sides almost immediately after, then moved up, brushing at her hair, constantly in motion. Soon, she turned away, focusing her attention on the coffee table, and she fluttered around, straightening the few items there, the remote of the TV, a bowl that held a few odds and ends, including a racecar, a book, and a small toy horse, evidence of the family that lived in these walls. "Are you staying in Germany? Going back to Monaco?"

She bent over the table, and I grimaced, glad she wasn't looking at me. The round, perfect curve of her ass, plump and full, made it impossible to banish thoughts like how good she'd tasted and what it would be like to bend her over the couch and fuck her from behind, my hand in her hair, listening to those kitten-like moans as I filled her, having her wet and soft around my dick.

The look she shot my way was questioning, uneasy, and I reminded myself she'd asked a question.

It took a moment to remember what it had been, but then I found myself scowling all over again. "What? Of course not. No. The children shouldn't be left alone tonight, and they must be told about their mother and father."

"Well...of course. I understand that." She stammered, shifting from one foot to the other while a frown creased her forehead. It faded in a blink, and her nervous fidgeting did as well as she leveled a direct look at me. "However, they aren't alone. *I* am here. They have me."

SEVEN

KITT

Lack of oxygen to the brain, brought on by being kissed out of the blue, was the cause for my sudden recklessness. It couldn't be anything else.

Aeric gave me a cool, dismissive look, that arrogance returning to his eyes. He crossed his arms over his chest, clearly about ready to say something—tear into me again, no doubt.

No, I thought. He wasn't sending me away.

"You can't be planning to send me away. Not right now. It would be too traumatic for Josef and Karol," I said, folding my arms over my chest. I immediately regretted it because my breasts ached, the nipples tight and sensitive in ways they hadn't ever been before. Those few moments had a stronger effect on me than anything I'd ever experienced. And I couldn't let that kiss distract me either.

"I can't," he said slowly, almost as if he wasn't even familiar with the concept of *can't*. After a moment, he said it again, but it was more clearly phrased as a question. "I *can't?*"

I blushed furiously but held his gaze.

"I've been providing care for those children for nearly two

years. I love them dearly. They love me. In a few short hours, their entire world will be upended. They need something constant in their lives, now more than ever."

This, at least, was something I knew for a fact, something I understood. I might not understand adults and all the messy interactions that came with them, and I might not deal with other people if kids weren't in the mix, but I *knew* kids, and more, I knew Karol and Josef. I knew what was best for them, better than anybody else in the world now that their parents were gone.

"Are you implying that I, their uncle, don't love them? That I'm not constant enough for them?"

"Oh, I imagine you do love them." I gestured to the picture of them on the wall.

He glanced back with a frown, confused. I could tell when he saw it, and the emotion on his face left an ache in my chest, but I pushed on. "But they don't just need *love* right now. They need much more. They need attention and somebody who will be able to be there for them, take care of them and grieve with them. On *their* schedule. Nobody else's, regardless of how busy or how important that person may be."

"You're quite out of line," he said, his voice cold.

"When it comes to the children, I'll step out of line every time. The only time you've even been here to visit since Karol's birth was the summer they hired me, just a few weeks before I moved in, if I recall correctly. They see you a couple of times a year if that. That's not *constant,* and they need constant." I lifted my chin and stared at him in challenge. "They *need* it. They deserve it. Wouldn't Anne *want* that?"

He opened his mouth, then closed it, and I was surprised to see a dull red wash over his face. After a moment, he said, "Perhaps you're right. I don't have the...easiest of schedules. Traveling to Germany at the drop of a hat isn't something I'm able to do often." He grew defensive as he added, "And as you said, we have visited. They come to Monaco. I talk to them on the phone. I talk to Anne—"

He stopped, closing his eyes.

Guilt washed over me. "I'm sorry," I said quietly. "I don't doubt your love for her, or them. But surely you realize they should have somebody who doesn't have to work them in around a...schedule."

Aeric didn't answer, turning away instead to pace. Rubbing the back of his neck, he came to a stop in front of the wall of pictures.

"You've yet to give me your name. You don't just go by *the* au pair, I assume."

Flushing, I said, "It's Kitt. Kitt Bocho."

"A pleasure, Ms. Bocho," he murmured.

Hysterical laughter rose inside, but I didn't let it break out. I was making the biggest gamble of my life, and I absolutely sucked at poker. But if I didn't do something, he'd send me away. If that happened, I'd likely never see the children again. Karl had no immediate family, and Josef and Karol would go to Monaco. If I couldn't convince this man to keep me on as their caregiver, I'd be pushed out of their life, and that was it.

"I think we can both agree it's best I stay with the children for the time being," I said, forcing all the fake confidence I could muster into each word. "There is quite enough uncertainty in their lives already, don't you think?"

"But, of course." He looked back at me, cynical amusement lighting his eyes.

I didn't know if he was agreeing with me or just humoring me. But he hadn't told me to leave. Yet.

"You said you were told Anne and Karl were found dead in Dresden. You have no other information? The police told you nothing?" He came to sit on the couch and gestured at the nearby chair.

The crisis averted for now, I acquiesced, tucking my hands between my knees to keep from fidgeting.

"They wouldn't tell me much," I said softly. "I'm not family. But as I said, they were at their home in Dresden. The younger officer..." Frowning, I pinched the bridge of my nose, trying to remember his name. "Ah, Simeon Liberman. I can't remember if he's a detective...investigator." I pressed my fingertips to my temple, trying to soothe the ache beginning there. "I'm either having a language barrier here, or I'm just too tired. But he told me that the security system's panic alarm went off and nobody answered the phone when the company tried to call, so they sent officers out. Karl is...he *was* very..." I hesitated, uncertain how to phrase it.

"Intense?" Aeric offered.

I nodded. "Yes. Karl was intense about the security systems. Here, at the vacation home. Anne and I both have GPS tracking in our cell phones in case something ever happens, and key fobs enabled with GPS tracking chips and a beacon...thingie." I waved a hand in the air. "If something happens, you push the button, and the police are immediately notified. He was..." I almost said fanatical, but decided that might not be the best word, considering Karl had been married to a princess. And... they were both dead. "Anyway, by the time police arrived at the home, Karl and Anne were dead. They don't know if it was a random burglary or..."

I darted a look at him for the first time in several seconds, and the expression on his face left me frozen to the core.

Predatory fury blazed in his eyes.

"Ah...they wouldn't tell me anything else," I said, forcing the rest out. "I don't know if there is anything more to tell, and they can't say because I'm not family or if there's just nothing else as yet to tell."

He continued to watch me, unblinking, while that rage burned in his eyes.

EIGHT

AERIC

"You're telling me they were murdered."

Kitt flinched at the sound of my voice, but she nodded, not looking away.

Rising, I moved over to the window and stared outside into the darkness.

This, none of this, made sense. Of course, how could one make sense of losing their sister?

Anne had been twenty-five, far too young to die.

But to be *murdered*?

And the police had been alerted by a *panic alarm*?

I looked around the house, unsettled by something I couldn't put my finger on. Of course, it could just be that Anne wasn't here. That she'd never be here again.

Murdered.

I'd deliberately avoided thinking about the *how* as I raced to get to Germany, then here. I'd had to see the children, to make sure they were alright. But to learn this...

My phone rang. Irrationally furious at the interruption, I

jerked it from my pocket but stopped, stricken at the name on the screen.

"I..." Pausing, I took a breath and looked at Kitt. "I have to take this. Excuse me."

Ducking in the foyer, I swiped my thumb across the screen and entered my code, then used my thumbprint to unlock the device, frustrated at the extra layer of security I was now forced to complete.

"*Maman.*"

"Aeric."

The fragile, shattered sound of her voice hit like a one-two punch. "I should have called you sooner. I'm sorry. I just got to the house."

"The babies?" she asked, a tremor in her voice.

"They're fine." I darted a look up the stairs. "Sleeping. The au pair is here with them."

"Oh." A faint rush of air expelled from my mother, audible over the line. With the miles separating us, I felt even more helpless, unable to be there and do anything to offer comfort.

A deep voice, soft and low, murmured in the background.

"Anne adored Kitt," my mother said quietly. "She had nothing but praise for her."

"I..." I paused, bothered to realize my sister had never so much as mentioned the caregiver to me, but my mother had known. I'd always thought the two of us had a closer bond to each other than with our parents. "She seems quite devoted."

"She is, from everything I can tell. The children adore her as well. She's good for them. We'll have to keep her on. Offer her anything she wants. The children will need her." A watery sigh escaped my mother. "Have you learned anything?"

Random burglary...they were dead.

I looked around the house again, trying to figure out what it was that seemed so off about the place, but I still couldn't isolate it. I was too distracted, too unfocused.

Anne. Murdered.

I couldn't tell my mother that. Not now. Not when I had no answers or anything else.

"I'm afraid not. The police told Kitt very little as she isn't family and they knew one of us would arrive in Germany shortly. Guillermo is looking into it, but my first thoughts were of the children."

"As they should be." She cleared her throat. "Get some rest for now, Aeric. It is late, and there is nothing that can be accomplished tonight. Let us know what you learn."

"Of course, *Maman*."

I disconnected and moved back into the room, clutching my phone like a lifeline.

Murdered. My sister had been murdered, and I couldn't yet tell my parents because I knew nothing else.

My skin was hot and itchy, too tight, like it no longer fit and I'd split apart at any second.

I didn't want to do it here. "You were right about how this has been a difficult day. I think I need a few minutes to process everything, and I definitely need some rest. Anne always kept a bedroom for me, the one close to the entertainment room. I realize I'm unexpected, but is it ready?"

"I...yes. Anne always kept it ready for you."

I didn't need help finding it, but Kitt stepped in front of me to lead the way regardless, and I trailed behind her. As we passed by the entertainment room, I paused, eying the minibar. "I think I'm going to follow your lead and have a drink. Whisky, though. Wine won't cut it."

Kitt glanced at me, then paused, wrapping her arms around herself. "Of course. If ever there was a day for a drink, this is it."

I spied a box at the top of the bar, Macallan 25. Anne had a love for it, and I bought her a bottle every year for Christmas, which we'd share together the next we saw each other.

A knot settled in my chest as I went over and reached up to take the box.

I opened it carefully and pulled the bottle out, thinking of the last time we'd shared this kind of scotch.

Last year, at the Princely Palace in Monaco, Christmas Eve. If I'd known it would be the last time...

The children had been in bed. Karl had declined, claiming scotch gave him a headache, settling on beer instead.

We played cards well into the night, Anne giggling as she took Karl for everything he was worth.

He was a terrible gambler, but he'd laughed and smiled and played, clearly enjoying the game and her.

It had been a good night.

"I gave her this for Christmas," I said softly.

"I know."

The sound of Kitt's voice behind me caught me off guard, and I looked over to see that she'd moved into the entertainment room and watched with sad, compassionate eyes.

She looked at the bottle, then at me.

"They were..." She stopped and swallowed, her voice thicker. "They were so kind. They wanted me to feel like this was my home and told me I was welcome to anything in the house. But Karl did point out that bottle and said it was something Anne always saved to share with you, that you bought her a bottle every year and she always kept it to save for the next Christmas so you could enjoy it together."

"Yes." Impulsively, I grabbed two crystal highballs and left the room, carrying the bottle with me.

I didn't want to be alone after all.

Processing this horror alone...who the fuck wanted to do that?

The next door opened to the large suite Anne had always kept aside for me. The bottle tucked under my arm, I went through the door and looked back at Kitt.

She hesitated, looking uncertain. "You...I didn't see you bring any luggage. There are toiletries, of course, but—"

"My aide will be here in the morning. He has everything I need." I told myself to stay quiet. It was for the best if I did. But I sucked at making wise decisions. "Come inside?"

She blinked, sucking in a slow breath.

"To talk. Or even just sit with me and share a drink. I can't stand the idea of being alone with myself right now. It's just too much." I tried to smile and managed a halfway weak one. "I'll behave myself."

I wasn't entirely sure if I would, but I knew I couldn't handle being alone.

NINE

KITT

I saw him grab the two pretty, elegant glasses from the entertainment room, and I knew.

As I led him the few feet to the guestroom where he stayed, I felt him watching me, and I knew.

If I was smart, I would have just said good night there and bolted for the stairs.

But instead of bolting, I glanced from the open door to him and mentioned *toiletries*.

My face was hot because I knew what sort of toiletries Anne had in the well-stocked bathroom. Whether it was because she'd known something about her brother or because she'd just been thorough, I had no idea. The very fact that I was even *thinking* of such...toiletries should have been enough to make me run for the stairs, to hide in my room.

Karol and Josef were sleeping soundly and wouldn't wake until morning, and when they did, I'd have to sit there as this man shattered their world, and I needed to be ready to handle it. That meant I should rest. But instead, I watched him linger in the doorway, eyeing me, a bottle of scotch under his arm, two crystal glasses dangling loosely from one hand.

He hadn't even spoken, and I knew it was coming.

Tell him goodnight and go upstairs.

"Come inside?"

Say no. I looked at him, heart racing.

"To talk. Or even just sit with me and share a drink. I can't stand the idea of being alone with myself right now. It's just too much." He gave me a half-hearted smile, one he clearly didn't feel, before continuing. "I'll behave myself."

I looked past him into the room and thought of the kids upstairs, thought of my own bed upstairs, cold and empty. I thought of the ache deep inside my chest and of the tears I still trapped.

"I'm not very good at sitting and drinking," I said. "A couple of sips make me either sleepy or stupid. But I don't know if I want to be alone with myself either."

I edged a step closer.

"We'll make sure you only have a sip or two then. I won't let you be stupid."

His eyes drifted to my mouth.

I found myself looking at his. *What if I want to be stupid?*

I hurried past him, not trusting myself. I might blurt those words out, and judging by the way he'd acted earlier, I couldn't exactly trust him to help me...*not* be stupid.

You shouldn't trust him anyway.

Normally, I wouldn't.

But normally, he wouldn't pay attention to me.

Normally, he'd be in Monaco, and I'd be sleeping, waiting for morning and cleaning the house as I waited for Anne and Karl to arrive.

That wouldn't happen.

Normal had gone out the window.

He closed the door behind me. I drew in a deep breath at the sound of the faint click and wrapped my arms around myself, squeezing slightly in an attempt to center myself.

All it did was make me aware of my nipples, aching and tight, and I swallowed back a whimper.

"Here."

I turned to face Aeric and saw him holding out one of the glasses, with barely an inch of whisky in it. "You know, I was being facetious when I said one or two sips. I can handle a *bit* more."

"Try it before you say that," he advised. "If you're not much of a drinker, you should ease your way into it when it comes to scotch."

I rolled my eyes but took the glass and lifted it to my lips.

"Slow down."

Arching my brows, I looked at him.

"Like this."

He swirled the glass.

"Is this like a wine tasting thing?" I asked, echoing his motions.

"Sort of." He didn't try to hide his amusement. "A good scotch should be appreciated. It's not just about the taste, but the scent, the sight. There's no reason to rush it. People are always determined to rush the good things in life, and there's no need."

His voice had deepened, roughened.

And damn it, now my nipples were even harder than they'd already been.

"Okay, Prince Aeric," I said with forced levity, trying to

think about anything but the fact that I was getting turned on simply by the way he talked about scotch. "How do I appreciate scotch?"

"If you're going to choose to be proper now, it should be *Your Highness*." A faint smile curled his lips. "And watch, Madame Kitt, the Au pair...I'll show you."

He moved in closer and swirled the glass before lifting it, but not to drink.

"Breathe it in. The scent is almost as important as the taste."

I followed his lead, eyes on his. My knees felt a little weak, but I told myself it was because of the whisky's fumes. Nothing else.

Absolutely nothing else.

"Now, take a sip. Roll it around on your tongue. Just a small sip, though."

I did, and the rich, potent taste went straight to my head, the fire of it straight to my blood—and somehow right to my belly. The scotch. Just the scotch.

"Now you drink it, Madame Kitt. But slow."

"No rushing the finer things, right?" I said. Whoa. That husky voice. Was it mine?

His lids drooped and his gaze settled on my mouth.

Nervous, I backed away and took a sip of the whisky, aware of his watchful eyes. My nipples stabbed into my bra, the cotton rubbing against them torturously.

He took a sip of his own whisky then lowered it. "What do you think?"

"I think it's dangerous," I said without considering my answer.

His brows rose a fraction. He took another drink, then put the glass down, prowling closer. "The whisky?"

"No." I put my own glass down and looked toward the door. Was I going to be smart and leave?

He noticed. "I told you I'd behave."

Heart hammering against my ribs, I finally admitted to myself that I didn't want him to behave, that I didn't want to leave.

"If I said I didn't want you to behave, what would you do?" I asked, my voice trembling.

His lashes flickered, then his face went tight, features harsh. A low noise escaped his throat as he prowled closer. "First, I'd ask you if you know what you're asking for, Kitt Bocha."

"I think I do, yes."

"Are you certain? You better be, because while I'm normally a gentleman, I'm on a razor's edge tonight and I only feel it's fair to warn you." He sipped the scotch, eyes burning into mine over the glass.

"I'm not feeling very...level myself tonight. Maybe this is stupid, but for now..." I sucked in a breath and nodded. "Yes. I know what I'm asking for."

"Is that so." His tongue slid out, trailed along his lower lip. "Let's see how serious you are. If you told me you didn't want me to behave, the first thing I'd do is tell you to take that silly shirt off so I can see your tits."

Heat exploded inside, from embarrassment, yes. But something else.

"I..."

Swallowing, I looked down at my chest, then up at him.

He stood waiting.

"This is how it will be, Kitt. If you don't want me to behave, then you need to prove it with a bit of misbehaving yourself.

Show me those delicious tits. I've wanted to see them ever since you pushed up against me earlier."

My face went hot. My knees went weak. And between my thighs, I melted.

I wasn't sure if I had the courage for this, but recklessness and a desperate need to think of something but the pain of the day, to feel something but that pain, it all pushed me on, and after putting the scotch down, I reached for the hem of my shirt. Not giving myself a chance to think, I whipped it off and tossed it onto the nearby chair.

"Yes..." Aeric murmured. He gestured. "The bra."

That one was harder, but I managed. Dipping my head, I stared at my feet, painfully aware of his eyes on me as I fumbled with the clasp at my back. The shiny toes of his shoes came into my line of sight just as I worked it free, and I looked up, startled, to find him just a foot away.

Clutching the simple white cotton to my chest, I held his gaze, nerves clanging.

"Drop it, Kitt," he said, his voice a rough growl.

My fingers had frozen though. He either didn't notice or care, because he reached out and caught me by the upper arms. The feel of his fingers, naked against my skin, was a stark surprise and had the effect of unfreezing my fingers...and everything else. I dropped the bra and sagged, leaning into him, and had the delight of feeling my breasts crush into his chest.

I whimpered, my nipples beading up into tight little buds. The smooth material of his shirt rasped against them, and that was both delightful and awful.

"The look on your face..." He tugged me up onto my toes. "Look at me, Kitt."

I forced myself to obey, swallowing to loosen my throat.

The pale gray of his eyes had darkened. He looked me over, running his tongue across the inside of his lower lip as he studied me. "Are you ready to misbehave even more, Madame Kitt?"

I gave a jerky nod, the hot, sexy promises in his words sending a molten river of want running through me.

He caught my hip, his fingers spread wide to curve over my ass as he tugged me against him more fully. "Good." He skimmed his lips over the curve of my neck, nipped at my earlobe. "Get undressed and lay on the bed...and not under the sheets, either. I want to look at you. All of you."

Face hot, I moved slowly toward the bed. I heard him move behind me and darted a look to see him ducking into the bathroom.

"You're taking a very long time with those blue jeans," he said from behind me.

The sound of his voice from just a few inches behind me startled me, and I spun to face him. Swallowing, I tried to think of a response, but there wasn't one. What did a person say in this sort of situation? I had no idea. I'd never *been* in this situation, half-naked and alone with a guy, about to be completely naked...

Should I tell him that?

Immediately, I knew if I did, he'd stop.

I didn't want that.

"Have you changed your mind?" He tossed something onto the bed before tracing a finger along my jaw.

"No. I'm just..." I licked my lips. "Maybe I want you to take them off."

The look in his eyes told me he didn't believe me, but the slow-heated smile he gave me made it clear he had no problem indulging me anyway. He hooked his fingers in the front of my jeans and tugged me closer. I crashed into his chest with an *oomph*, breath exploding out. "Tell you what, *cher*...I want to feel those perfect tits against my chest. So, you unbutton my shirt, then I'll deal with the rest of your clothes."

It was almost easy, I realized, unbuttoning the small buttons that marched down the front of his shirt, one at a time. There was an undershirt beneath it, and without asking, once I'd finished with the buttons, I pushed the shirt off his shoulders before reaching for the hem of the undershirt.

He had to duck his head so I could pull the shirt off, and I dropped it on the floor as well, my breath coming in rough, ragged pants.

He was lean and perfectly built, muscled and taut, his pecs carved and dusted with a light smattering of hair. I'd never been one to give in to impulse, but the need to do so then was so strong, I couldn't have fought it if my life depended on it. Placing my hands flat on his chest, I curled my fingers and tugged.

He grunted and caught my hips, tugging me against him.

I felt the heavy weight of his cock push against my belly. Lower, a hot, wet rush gathered between my thighs.

He swore under his breath, the French raw and rough—I knew it was dirty—and I wanted to ask what he'd said, but I lacked the ability to think coherently.

Then he spoke in German. "I'm going to fuck you hard, Kitt. I won't stop until you're screaming...tell me you want that."

"I...please. Yes. Aeric."

"Good." He reached between us and yanked at the button of my jeans and dealt with the zipper, then jerked both denim and panties to my knees. He spun me around so my back was tucked against his front and banded an arm around my waist. "Look up, Kitt. Look at yourself."

He slid a hand down my hip as I worked to comply.

Feeling drugged, I lifted my head and rested it against his shoulder.

"Look," he said again, voice cajoling. Then he bit my earlobe, his fingers sliding over the curve of my belly...then lower.

I opened my eyes as he cupped me in his hand, two fingers slipping between my folds with practiced knowledge.

I jolted in surprise, then in delight as he sought out my clit and began to stroke, circling around and around.

"Do you see?"

There was a mirror on the large dresser across the room. It was impossible *not* to see. Nuzzling my hair, he said, "Lift your arms up and reach behind you...wrap your arms around my neck. It will lift those pretty tits even more...yes, that's it. Now ride my hand. Fuck yourself on it."

Shock washed through me at his words, but I was already doing it, rocking back and forth on his hand, desperate for more of what he was giving, desperate for what he *hadn't* given me.

He parted my folds and pushed one finger, then two inside. "That's it, *cher*...fuck yourself... take what you need. Do you want more?"

"Yes," I begged. "Please, more."

But instead of giving me *more*, he stopped. I cried out in anguish, pain all but cramping my belly. He pressed me forward, a hand between my shoulder blade, urging me down until I bent over the bed, my hands braced on the mattress. Bewildered and still aching, I went to look back at him.

I felt his hands grip my hips, then his mouth brushed over my butt. I tensed.

I had no idea what was coming next, and when he suddenly pressed his face against my pussy, I was stunned into silence, even as embarrassment turned my face red and a scream of pleasure locked inside my throat.

He licked, swirled his tongue over my folds, dipped lower to circle over my clit, then started all over again.

He stabbed his tongue repeatedly inside me, and each time, he lashed against nerve endings like a velvet whip, sending more pleasure than I thought I could handle.

Clenching up, I went to pull away.

He slapped the right cheek of my ass and said in a hard voice, "I don't think so, *cher*."

I barely processed the words, though.

An orgasm exploded, and I broke under the intensity of it, the strength in my arms giving way until I was face first against the mattress, shuddering and moaning and writhing.

"Fuck it...look at you," he said, his voice raw. He spoke in French now, and every word was one more stroke against my senses.

I whimpered and instinctively thrust back against him, needing more despite the climax still gripping me.

He thrust two fingers inside me. "It's not enough, is it? Here...I'll help."

Moaning, I clamped down around him, my hands fisting in the comforter beneath me as I rode the climax out.

It had barely ended when he urged me upright, then pushed me down onto the bed, staring at me, watching me hungrily as he caught the jeans and panties still tangled at my knees and began to drag them down. That task done, he straightened and pressed the flat of his hand to his boxers, stroking.

Eyes bold and hot, he kept that up for long moments before he finally freed himself and revealed the erect, proud thrust of his cock, letting me stare for several seconds before he closed his hand around his penis and began to stroke again.

"You're slacking on your part of the deal, but watching you come was so perfect, I'll let it go. I want to see you break like that when you're stretched tight around my cock, Kitt. Are you going to scream and whimper again?"

I shuddered, unable to breathe.

He lifted his fingers to his mouth and licked them clean, then fisted his cock again, stroking harder, rougher for a few more seconds. "I imagine you will. And I can't wait to find out."

Moaning, I sagged back onto the bed and closed my eyes.

He laughed, the sound low, full of arrogance but not cruelty.

"Open your eyes, Kitt. I want to see you."

It took too much effort, but I did so anyway, my face flaming.

He'd shoved his pants off and stood naked before me. If he had any modesty, I couldn't tell. My face was hotly red, but I couldn't look away as he tore open a condom. He cupped his balls in his hand, a wicked gleam in his eyes as he watched me watch him roll it on.

"You look so prim and proper, Madame Kitt, but I think you've got a dirty streak in you."

I had no idea how to respond to that, but fortunately, I didn't have to. He came down over me, pushing one thigh between mine to spread them.

He settled his hips in the cradle of mine, and I felt him intimately for the first time. Reflexively, I caught his biceps and stared at him, startled at the sensations, at everything.

He caught my lower lip between his teeth and tugged, eyes locked on mine.

"Last chance," he whispered after letting go.

"I think we're past that."

"Yes." He pressed against me, and I gasped.

The sound was lost as he took my mouth.

At the same time, he took me, hard and fast, thrusting in, deep, hard, fast. The impact was stunning, stark. His tongue lashed over mine, his mouth swallowing down any noise I might have made, although, at that moment, I didn't know what sound I *could* have made—was there a sound that simply translated as *shock?*

He withdrew and thrust again, then again.

I couldn't move.

Something penetrated, and Aeric slowed, lifting his head, although he kept his brow pressed to mine.

His expression, severe and intense, softened. "I'm being too rough...you're so small..."

He shifted then, readjusting our position, before reaching down between us.

His fingers strummed over my clitoris, and this time, when he moved, a noise did erupt from me—one of pure, dismayed pleasure. He did it again, and I tried to follow, but his weight wouldn't let me.

"Shhh...be still..." he whispered against my mouth.

I didn't *want* to be still. I wanted to move and chase down more of what he made me feel—

Then he thrust against me again, high and hard, moving so

he slid directly across my clitoris, and I clamped down around him reflexively.

Aeric groaned. "Fuck...that's good. You're so tight, *cher*..."

"Please don't stop," I begged.

"Oh, sweet Kitt...that isn't going to happen." He kissed me, taking me deeper and harder, each thrust knocking more oxygen out of me until there was none, until there was nothing but his body and mine, moving and straining—

I came, shuddering and moaning his name.

His hand clamped down on my hip with bruising force, locking me against him as his cock jerked, and I instinctively knew he'd started to climax too. He tore his mouth from mine, breathing hard and fast, a low noise in his throat.

But...he didn't say my name.

It didn't matter.

Not really.

At least that was what I told myself.

I almost even believed it.

TEN

AERIC

AN HOUR AFTER I'D FIRST HAD HER, I WOKE TO DARKNESS, curled up with her butt pressed snug against my cock and my face buried in her hair. My dick was already hard, and I skimmed my hand up her side to cup her breast.

She didn't wake at first, but her nipple went tight in my hand, and she moaned as I slid my hand between her thighs, finding her already—or still—wet from earlier.

Soon, though, she did wake, and she responded with the same shy but frenetic passion as before.

"You're so fucking hot," I muttered into her ear as she pushed herself demandingly back against my dick, all but begging me to impale her and take her right there.

If I could have been any other man in the world, a man without my responsibilities, I would have, and I would have relished every second of it.

Dragging my fingers through the slick evidence of her desire, I worked it backward, along her crevice until I found her darker entrance, and there I toyed with her, wondering if she was as untried. I suspected she was, and I wanted to explore her deeper, watch her blush and stammer as I asked if she'd ever had a man fuck her anally, then watch that dismayed, startled pleasure wash over her features as I introduced her to such a raw, base carnality.

She was inexperienced in general. If she'd had more than a couple of lovers, I'd be surprised, although the sheer sensuality she possessed was enough to lay me low.

And I wanted *more*.

I wanted to lose myself in her for as long as I could, just so I didn't have to think.

It was tempting, too tempting, the thought of preparing her and taking her like this, sliding my cock into the naked glove of her ass. There'd be no chance of pregnancy then, and I had a raw, nearly over-powering need to get as close to somebody—to her—as possible.

But I couldn't let grief drive me to recklessness. Still, when she didn't pull away, I drove us both a little crazy, teasing her and stroking until she was rocking back against me, her breath ragged, her every move a plea for more.

"If we had the time," I muttered against her ear. "If I'd found you at some other time, Madame Kitt...I'd do so many dark and wicked things to you. I'd prepare you to take cock here, get you ready so I could fuck your ass as surely as I fucked your hot, sweet cunt..." I pushed my finger against the tight entrance. She tensed, and I whispered, "Relax...push down on me and relax...don't fight it."

She whimpered but obeyed, and a broken moan of desire escaped her.

"You like it," I whispered against her hair. "You're so full of passion...so sexy and hot...you'd love this. If we had the time."

"Aeric..."

I heard the plea in her voice and steeled myself. "You're too little...and I was right. You're untried. It's a learning process, and I don't have the patience right now to teach you. You'd have to learn to take me, a bit at a time. I'm not a small man, and my cock is equally proportioned."

"But..."

I bit her shoulder. "No." Withdrawing my hand, I shifted and reached out, seeking the box of condoms. After tearing one open, I sheathed myself and rolled to my knees. "But I am going to fuck you again, Madame Kitt. And when I'm done, I'm taking you to the shower and washing you...then I might have you go to your knees and see how good you are at sucking cock."

I jerked her up to her knees, and without giving her a chance to respond, thrust deep. She tensed and cried out, the sound a mix of pain and pleasure.

I held back, staring at her pale, arched back. "Kitt?"

"Don't stop. Please."

So, I didn't.

SHE KNELT in front of me, eyes big and nervous.

"You've never done this."

She didn't answer, reaching up to curl her fist around me while the water pounded down around us. It had turned her hair nearly black, and drops clung to her lashes.

I kept her from her goal by simply pushing a hand into her hair and tangling my fingers in the strands, arching her head back until she met my eyes.

The beautiful blues were wide with want but sharp with temper at the same time. I enjoyed the picture she presented, water dripping down her face, her neck, droplets rolling along the slopes of her breasts before beading on her nipples.

Stroking my thumb over her lower lip, I said it again. "You've never done this."

"So?"

"Just stating a fact." I pressed down on her mouth, and she opened for me. "I like the thought of being the one to strip that particular virginity from you...to be the first man to feed you cock and watch you swallow me down."

Her cheeks went red, but it wasn't embarrassment. The flush spread down her neck, to the top curves of her breasts. Her nipples tightened, her chest heaved as she breathed harder, faster...sheer arousal darkening her eyes.

I reached down and flicked her right nipple, watching as she shuddered.

"Do it, Kitt. Suck my cock and show me how you enjoy it."

She swayed forward, as if I'd dared her, and she was one who couldn't turn down a dare.

The first caress of her lips was pure bliss and each one after even better. With my hand in her hair, I guided her until we both fell into a rhythm. Soon, I had her head clutched between my hands while she fisted my dick in one hand and the other...

"Are you playing with yourself, Kitt?"

She rolled her eyes up to glance at me, then her lashes fluttered down.

No real answer, so I pulled her off and looked down just in time to see her fingers slip inside her cunt. She stopped when she realized she'd been caught.

I fisted my dick and began to pump, watching her slim fingers stroke. "Do it again. Make yourself come."

"I'd rather you do it," she whispered.

"You're sore. I've been rough, and I'm big. I want to watch you bring yourself pleasure...right here while I finish myself, thinking about how hot it was, watching you suck my dick and thinking how you were masturbating. Were you doing it the whole time?"

She gave a nervous nod.

"Good. Do what I said, Kitt."

She did, stroking herself as she knelt in front of me, her gaze dropping to watch as I jerked off in front of her.

Her sensuality, raw and naked, was a beautiful thing and some part of me was angry—for a million little things and a million big things—and Kitt was right in the mix. Why was she here, now? Somebody who wasn't afraid of the sort of passion I needed, right here, at the worst place and time.

I caught my balls and squeezed hard. Her eyes widened.

"Sometimes you need a bit of pain...or I do. You loved it when I bit those pretty, perfect nipples, didn't you, Kit?"

She whimpered.

A warning shiver raced down my spine.

Her lids drooped, mouth falling open.

And just as a heavy burst of semen exploded, striking her in the chest, she came with a sob.

―――――

WE FELL asleep in the bed not long after tumbling into it. Her hair was mostly dry, but only because I'd insisted, rubbing at the silken, soft strands with a towel until I'd absorbed as much moisture as I could. She was nodding off by the time I decided it was done well enough.

She blinked at me owlishly as I gave my own hair a few

cursory rubs with the towel before urging her to her feet, then back to the bed.

The last clear memory I had was pulling her up against me and burying my face against her neck, glad she was there if for no other reason than because I couldn't stand the thought of sleeping alone.

Of being alone.

If I was, I'd never sleep.

I did sleep. But not for long.

Kitt stirred in the bed, and the movement, the awareness that I wasn't alone had me opening my eyes, watching from under my lashes as she sat up, then looked around.

Immediately, thoughts of the past day snapped into focus, including the memories of the past few hours, taking her twice before hustling her into the shower and watching her take my cock in her mouth.

The thought stirred that part of my anatomy, but I ignored it this time, watching as she rose and moved around the room, apparently unfazed by the lack of light.

She picked something up from the floor, and I wasn't surprised it was her shirt.

That silly shirt with the silly dog.

When she pulled it on over her braless breasts, I had to fight the urge to give up the pretense of sleep just so I could roll over and hit the light, see her nipples pressing against the fabric, her curvy legs sticking out from under the hem.

But I stayed as I was, watching as she gathered her clothes and slipped out.

Once I was alone, I rolled onto my back and closed my eyes.

It had been more than two years since I'd been here, in this house. More than two years since I'd seen my sister for more than a couple of days around Christmas, or for a few when she'd come to visit the summer before last.

And now I'd never see her again.

"Damn it."

The words broke, and a vicious pain struck me in the chest, stealing my breath. Jackknifing upright, I swiveled around and sat on the side of the bed.

She was gone.

I couldn't pretend anymore. I couldn't lose myself in the distraction of a woman, and I couldn't busy myself in the worry for my niece and nephew.

Tears burned my eyes and slipped free. Clenching my hands in the sheets beneath me, I bit back the furious shouts of denial that wanted to come free. Raging at the injustice would do nothing but wake the children, frighten the woman providing care for them.

No, I wouldn't give in to that rage here.

I'd use it.

But I couldn't fight the grief anymore. Bending forward, I buried my face in my hands.

All those memories that had haunted me during the day came flying back, and this time, I didn't push them aside.

The two of us, learning to swim, and Anne crowing when she realized she was better at it.

The two of us, along with *Papa*, riding in the Alps on a summer holiday. She might have been the better swimmer, but I was the better equestrian, and she never did give up on trying to beat me in a race. She never quite succeeded, and we had so much fun, just in the trying of it.

Anne, crying and clinging to my neck when I left the country to attend Yale University in the United States. "If you'd wait another two years, I could come with you. You need some-body to keep you in line."

"And who would keep you in line, darling?" I'd asked her, hugging her close. I'd miss her more than anything, I'd known at the time. I'd been right.

We'd talked to each other almost every day.

Even when she left Monaco for Germany not long after her marriage to Karl, we'd still stayed in near constant contact. She'd been nagging me the past few months to come for a visit. I kept putting it off, because of the responsibilities I kept having thrust on me.

I'd regret it every day now, not making time to come up, even for just a day or two. An afternoon.

Anne.

I shoved the heels of my hands against my eyes, the tears running freely now.

"Anne...fuck. Why?"

ELEVEN

KITT

My doga shirt smelled like him.

Part of me wanted to curl up in the bed and breathe that scent in, but instead, I tucked the shirt in the back corner of an almost empty drawer and pulled on a pair of loose cotton pants and a tank top before moving down the hall and up the stairs to check on the children.

It wasn't necessary. They slept through the night and had from the time I'd arrived to work for the Weiss family, but the news I'd received made it impossible for me to settle without seeing them at least once more. For all I knew, it could be the *last* time.

Tears blurred my eyes as I looked in on Josef, thinking about how he'd just told me he wanted to be an astronaut, looking away from the stars only long enough to give me a quick grin, like he couldn't stand to not have his eyes on the skies for more than a few seconds.

And while he had his head forever up in the clouds, little Karol seemed to have her feet planted firmly on the ground.

Inexplicably drawn toward her now, I eased Josef's door

closed, then walked down the hallway until I reached Karol's doorway. While Josef wanted the door shut so nothing interfered with whatever world he imagined while he slept, Karol couldn't stand to have hers closed. I didn't know if it was because she had some hidden fear she wouldn't voice or because she didn't want to miss anything that might happen while she slept.

Peering around the doorframe, I spied Karol curled up into a tight little ball in the middle of her bed, a ragdoll with a tattered crown clutched under her right arm. The only time in her life she was ever remotely quiet or not trying to pick a fight with the world—or climb her way to the top—was when she was sleeping.

But even in sleep, she controlled things. Scrunched up in a little ball, she guarded her space and kept her ragged little princess close.

I had the craziest urge to go in and cuddle her. Karol had the bad habit of sneaking down into my room and climbing into bed with me in the quiet hours right before dawn.

That had never been Josef, and I knew the time was coming when Karol wouldn't be so quick to cuddle either. Josef was already showing signs of it, and Anne had despaired, playfully, about how quick her young man was growing up.

I wanted to promise my lost friend that I'd be there for both children, but I had no way of knowing if I'd be able to keep that promise. That was up to Aeric, to his mother and father.

Would they even let me *see* the children anymore?

I had no idea.

What if Aeric took them back to Monaco in the morning, and I was left here—

"I won't be left here," I said softly, rubbing the ache that had settled in my chest. My permanent residence permit wasn't in immediate jeopardy, but the very idea of trying to find another family to work with just then filled me with a vicious, seizing sort of terror. It was so deep and intense, I couldn't even breathe.

While the trapped air in my lungs fought and clawed to escape, I backed away from Karol's bedroom, covering my mouth with my hand to still the muffled sob that tried to break loose.

I made it inside my room, barely. Smacking my hand against the door to close it, I stumbled to the bed and dropped down. Grabbing my pillow, I buried my face against it and started to cry.

The sobs all but choked me, stealing my breath, but I couldn't stop. Burrowing deeper into the pillow, I clung to it and wished *it* was *somebody*.

AT SOME POINT, I dozed off.

The silence lay heavy on the house, and that stirred me out of an uneasy slumber. Head aching and my face itchy from the tears, I rose and went to the bathroom, stripping out of my clothes and shoving them into the laundry hamper. Everything from the past day drifted through my mind in a surreal haze, like something that had happened in a dream or to somebody else.

But I couldn't take comfort in that or even hope for it. I knew all too well that this was *my* life, and it was only going to get worse.

And I wasn't the one dealing with the worst of it. I'd lost a friend, but the kids had lost their mother. Aeric had lost a sister.

Washing my face and dabbing on some moisturizer, I lingered long enough to take something for my headache before leaving the bathroom. There was a white noise machine on the bedside table, and I turned it on as I lay down, letting it wash away that echoing silence.

It didn't do anything to dull the roar of thoughts in my head, but I hadn't expected that.

I had practice when it came to blanking my mind, a skill born out of necessity in the years after my grandfather died. Rolling onto my side, I focused on the window that stared out over the backyard and found a focus—the pretty fountain in the center of the garden just beyond my window. Landscape lights turned the water silver in the darkness, and I focused on the liquid play. Every time my thoughts started to drift, I pulled them back.

Eventually, I slept again.

The next time I woke, I could feel somebody watching me.

I took a deep breath and smelled soap, shampoo, and apple juice. Without opening my eyes, I said, "Somebody got into the refrigerator without asking again."

"How can you tell?" Karol demanded.

Popping open one eye, I stared at her through my hair for a long moment. "I can see through walls."

"But you were asleep!"

"I can see when I'm asleep."

"No, you can't." She giggled. "That's just silly."

"Then how do I know you had juice?" Sitting up, I peered at her, my eyes adjusting to the lights she'd turned on when she slid into my room. Able to piece together a couple more details, I fixed a sober frown on my face. "And how do I know you spilled the juice if I can't see through walls while I'm sleeping?"

Her jaw dropped, and her mouth hung wide open.

"How did you know that?"

"I already told you." Reaching out, I tapped her nose.

She crossed her arms over her chest and stared at me, clearly not buying into my story. I took care not to look at her sleeves, wet and fragrant with juice, as I met her gaze.

"I'm going to be an au pair when I grow up," she announced. "Then I'll see through walls when I sleep."

She gestured imperiously for me to get up.

Biting back a smile, I let her pull me to my feet, and we headed down the hall, but my amusement was gone by the time we reached the kitchen. Josef was already in there, and he had pulled the little stepping stool over to the counter and was peering into the toaster.

Judging by the open plastic sleeve of bread, I had to assume the toaster wasn't empty.

"Aren't you supposed to wait for me before doing that, Josef?"

"I saw that Karol was getting you," he responded. "How do toasters work?"

I went to correct him about the kitchen rule and stopped, too tired just then that he'd done a bit more than bend the rules this time. "That sounds like a good question for you to research when you have some of your free time on the computer."

He slid me a look, frowning.

Laughing, I crossed over to him and ruffled his hair.

"I know you hate to be reminded that internet isn't just for fun and games, but you can learn all sorts of things online."

"If we can learn all sorts of things online," he said in a matter of fact voice, "then why do I have to ask to look things up and why am I only allowed to have thirty minutes a day?"

"I only get twenty-five!" Karol huffed.

"All right, that's enough." Holding up my hands, I caught their attention. "You know the rules. Your..." I hesitated, the words catching in my throat. "You know the rules. Kids should do more than spend half their day online like zombies." I winked at them, striving for a lightness I didn't feel. "You'll have your entire adult life to do that if you want. Now...what are we doing for breakfast...besides toast?"

THE SUN HAD BARELY BEGUN to peek up over the horizon by the time I'd finished breakfast. Slices of ham, eggs, and of course, toast prepared by Josef filled the plates I put on the table that Karol had sat with a care that would have made me laugh if I hadn't been so distracted.

Turning back to the counter to get the plate of toast, I caught sight of a reflection in the window over the sink, and I went still. One of my distractions had decided to make his presence known. My heart hammered in my chest, and I forced a deep, steady breath into my lungs before turning to nod at him.

Karol saw and turned to follow my gaze, her eyes widening. "Who are you?"

Josef, carefully spooning eggs onto his plate, hadn't noticed his uncle. "Who is who?"

"Him, silly." Karol pointed at the tall man filling the doorway, staring in at the three of us. Well, mostly at the kids.

For a brief moment, our eyes had locked, and my heart skipped a beat, but that was over now, and he only had eyes for his niece and nephew.

"Uncle Aeric!" Josef launched himself from the chair and flung himself at the man.

Aeric caught the boy mid-leap and hefted him.

I could see the emotion on his face, watched as he closed his eyes and regained control before speaking. "I think you went and grew up on me since I've seen you. How old are you now, Josef? Fifteen? Eighteen?"

"No! I'm *five*, Uncle Aeric." He drew back.

Aeric clearly didn't want to let him, but then the man's arms eased, and the two males stared at each other appraisingly. "You never come to visit us," Josef said finally.

"I know. I'm sorry about that." Guilt flickered across Aeric's face, and he shifted his attention to the girl who was now standing by the table, worrying the cuff of her pajama top. "Hello, Karol. Do you remember me?"

"No."

Her bluntness made me wince, but Aeric was unfazed. He just nodded. "It's been months since I saw you. I think it was at your birthday. Grandmama and Grandpapa threw a party, and you had pony rides. Do you remember the ponies?"

"Maybe." She slid me a nervous look before adding, "I've got pictures in my room of the ponies. I like looking at them, but I don't remember them very well. Did you ride the ponies?"

Aeric lowered Josef to the floor and gave Karol a serious look. "I don't think there's a pony out there big enough for me. I'd break the poor thing's back."

Silently, I agreed. He was rather large.

"You are very big," Karol said after considering him for a moment. "Your feet would probably drag the ground, and that would be no fun at all."

"Exactly so."

"We have pictures of you." She edged a little closer. "Mama says you are very good with horses."

"Does she?" Aeric's voice was husky. His eyes flashed to mine for a second, then moved back to Karol's.

"Yes. I like horses. Much more than ponies." She gave him a smile, revealing the charming dimples in her cheeks. "Mama and Papa say I'm not old enough for a horse, but maybe you can let me have one of yours."

"Karol!" Torn between amusement and horror, I moved to her. "You don't go asking somebody to give you one of their *horses*. It's—"

"I don't see why not. I have thirteen horses. I don't ride all of them." Aeric came closer and hunkered down in front of Karol. There was a sheen of wetness in his eyes, and he blinked it away as he smiled at the girl. "You look so much like your mother, Karol. I bet you hear that a lot, don't you?"

"Yes." Fully aware she'd enraptured yet another adult, she leaned against me. "Thirteen horses. That's a lot."

Before Aeric could respond, I nudged her toward the table. "Go on and sit down, honey. You have eggs, and you hate it when they get cold."

She sighed but trotted back to her seat as I gave Aeric an arch look. "Will you help me in the pantry?"

I half-expected him to refuse, but he followed along, probably curious.

"You can't tell her you'll give her a horse just because she asks!" I glared at him.

"Why not?" He folded his arms over his chest. "She'll be coming to Monaco, and both her mother and I had horses of our own when we weren't much older than her."

"That's not the point." I almost jabbed him in the chest but refrained. "Her mother and father have been...they *were* trying to teach both of them about responsibility and privilege and..."

The cool look he gave me left me feeling out of sorts and foolish, but I stood my ground, glaring at him. "Would you go and offer her a horse out of the blue if Anne had been standing there?"

"That's hardly—"

I cut him off. "Don't tell me that's not the point or that it isn't the same. Very soon, their lives will be turned upside down, and I *know* children. Not just those children, but yes, I know them very well. Children need consistency and limits, and you can't start off by promising her a horse because you're grieving inside."

Hurting, for him and Karol, I softened my voice as I added, "It won't help. Maybe it seems like it will, but in the long run, it won't. What she needs is you, her grandparents...love, attention, and time."

"I..." He stopped, brows coming together over pale gray eyes. Finally, he looked out the door, head cocked as he listened to the two children out in the kitchen laughing. "I don't care for the fact that you may well have a point. Very well."

He said nothing else and turned on his heel, striding out and leaving me there.

Blowing out a breath, I rubbed the back of my neck. The muscles were already tense, and it was only going to get worse as the day went on.

TWELVE

AERIC

KITT LOWERED THE PHONE, LOOKING SOMEWHAT DAZED.

Already on edge, I moved to her, hand outstretched.

She just frowned at me and lifted the phone back to her ear.

"Can you hold a moment, Sarah?" Then she lowered the handset again and pressed it to her chest.

I tried not to think about that chest, although it was harder when she'd just drawn my attention back to it.

"What?" she said, clearly irritated.

"I'll speak to them." I snapped my fingers impatiently.

"Why?"

"Because it's my *sister*."

She shook her head. "I don't think that's relevant. It's Sarah, a friend..." She cleared her throat. "She lives a few minutes away and wants to know if I can take her son to school when I drive Josef in. Her baby is sick, and she hasn't slept..." A confused look passed over her face. "School. Should we even send them?"

I made a snap judgment because there were things we needed to discuss and calls I needed to make. I couldn't risk the children overhearing, and surely, they deserved at least one more day before I shattered their world.

"Yes. Send them."

Kitt blinked at the finality of my voice but swallowed and nodded. Still, she hesitated. "What if somebody heard and says something?"

"Nobody could have heard." I frowned and shook my head, thinking back to the brief conversation I'd had with my aide, Guillermo, as well as Solange, my mother's. They'd been in close conversation with various heads of state in the German government—*no* news was to be leaked about my sister's death, or her husband's, until my family had time to address the people of Monaco. That was scheduled to be done at a press conference this afternoon. "When does school let out?"

"Josef's kindergarten ends at twelve-thirty, and I pick Karol up after I get him. But—"

"Then there's nothing to worry about." I breathed a sigh of relief. I had a bit of time. "My aide and people from my country's government have been in contact with the chancellor's office and the head of the Federal Foreign Office. My father spoke with the chancellor himself. Nobody will breathe a word of this until after the press conference this afternoon when our country is informed."

"Oh." She blew out a breath, and some of the tension left her. "So, you think I should take them."

"Yes. You said yourself, consistency was important."

With a wan smile, she lifted the phone to her ear. "Sarah, I'm sorry to keep you waiting...yes, I can take him to school. I'll probably be a few minutes late. We're having a hectic morning here, but I'll be there as soon as I can."

Hectic.

It was an interesting way to phrase it, and as she lowered the phone, I thought once more of last night. But before I could say anything, she darted a look at me, then cut around.

"I have to get them moving. Karol is probably already dressed, but Josef always needs prodding. He's prone to picking up a book and forgetting where he is or what he's doing if people don't remind him to stay on task."

She didn't even look at me as I spoke, and I was left staring at her back until she disappeared around the corner.

JUST OVER AN HOUR after I hugged both Karol and Josef, promising to see them once they were done with school, Kitt let herself back into the house. Standing in the big parlor immediately off the front hall, I had a moment to quietly observe her without her noticing, and I watched as she lifted her hands to her face, shoulders rising and falling on a heavy sigh. When she finally looked up, she had a defeated, lost air about her that pricked at me and...

She spotted me and jumped, a startled, strangled noise escaping her throat.

"I frightened you."

She offered a weak smile. "A bit. I'm jumpy."

"Understandable." Gesturing for her to come into the parlor, I said, "Why don't you sit? We should...talk."

Wariness flickered across her face, but she hid it quickly and gave me a polite smile. It was a mask, I decided. I didn't like it. But it was probably for the best.

"Of course." She came in and sat, smoothing down the trim black pants she'd dressed in.

I looked her over, taking in the blouse and pants, the neat flats on her feet. "No silly t-shirts today?"

"Ah..." Her cheeks flushed. "I usually go for a bit more of the casual dress look during the week when I'll be out of the house for the job. The silly t-shirts are for when I'm staying home all day or my off days."

"So, you have a collection of them."

Her chin went up. "Yes. Anne and the children bought five for me on my birthday, as a matter of fact. Karol actually picked out the doga shirt herself and bought it with her allowance."

"Really." The idea of my sister paying her children an allowance was bemusing, but I'd never been a parent. Perhaps it was that responsibility matter Kitt had mentioned earlier. "What did Josef pick?"

"One that read, *Doesth Mother Know Thou Weareth Her Drapes?*"

She said it in English, and I shook my head.

"Ah...do you speak English?" she asked, her cheeks going pink. "Anne does...she did. I just assumed..."

"I speak English perfectly well," I said, scowling as I replied in the language. "But I'm not following."

She blinked at me. "*The Avengers.*"

I was still confused.

"The movie? What Iron Man says to Thor when they faced off for the first time? It's one of Josef's favorite lines."

Vague recollections of watching the movie with Anne flickered through my mind, and I turned away. "Oh, that."

Kitt said nothing and the awkwardness returned. Awkwardness, and on my part, some level of bitterness. For the past ten years of my life, I've been focusing more and more on the duties that came with being next in line to rule, and it had left less time in my life for...well, a life.

I didn't resent *Anne* for having that time. But there was some small, petty part inside that resented the fact that Kitt and Anne had bonded over things like movies and whatever in the hell else there was out there to bond over while I'd been busy being Prince Aeric. I took time out for my love of cars and Formula One racing.

That was it.

Once more, that crushing, suffocating weight returned, and I needed a few minutes away, a few minutes to breathe and think.

But first...I had to clear up the matter of last night. "We should discuss last night."

"There's nothing to discuss." The words spilled out of her so fast, I had the feeling she'd just been waiting for this to happen, for the chance to discuss this.

Turning to face her, I crossed my arms over my chest. "There is something to discuss. Sex. We had it. Or are you pretending you didn't climax and moan under me?"

"I..." Her face went a hot pink.

Instantly, I wished I'd found another way to phrase it because damn if I didn't want to do it all over again. Make her climax, make her moan...and watch her cheeks turn the same pink they were now as she did so, like she had with those climaxes, so sudden and unexpected.

But it was too late to take the words back.

A wicked part of me that I'd always been forced to keep leashed was determined to see how she responded. "Well?"

I'd deliberately put an arrogant edge into my voice, suspecting it would provoke her. It did. Her chin went up, and as small as she was, she somehow managed to look down her nose at me. "No, sir. I'm not *pretending* it didn't happen. I'm simply telling you that it was one of those...things."

"One of those...things." I made a gesture with my hand, inviting her to continue. "Explain it to me. What sort of *thing* was it?"

She set her jaw, and although the glint in her eye bordered on the edge of mutinous, it wasn't quite there. I wasn't entirely sure how she managed this strange mix, shyness and hesitancy, mixed with determined pride.

It was intriguing—

No, I told myself. It wasn't. I couldn't be intrigued by her.

She was the caretaker for my niece and nephew, nothing more.

But I didn't cut her off when she started to speak, either.

"We're both grieving," she said, her voice halting, again showing that shyness I'd sensed from the beginning. "Anne's your sister, but she was my friend too. One of the best I ever had. One of the *only* I had."

A haunted look passed through her eyes, and she looked away.

Those words caused something unsettling to rise within me, an ache that I didn't particularly care for. I smashed it down and kept my focus on the here and now.

I spent all day yesterday trying to act as though there was nothing wrong for the sake of the children, and once they were safely in bed, I thought I'd have a few minutes...but you showed up...and...well. I didn't think. I should have been more responsible, but I wasn't. I'm sorry for that and—"

"Wait a minute," I said, holding up a hand. "Are *you* claiming responsibility for what happened?"

She finally looked at me again, her summery eyes widening slightly as I took a step closer.

"I...well, no. There were two of us involved, after all."

"Yes," I said firmly. "There were."

It was a good thing she acknowledged it too. Otherwise, I might have felt the need to remind her.

I almost kicked myself for even thinking that and jerked my thoughts back on track.

"But that's not the point. None of this is the point." I paused, gathering my thoughts. "It was one of those things. You're right on that. But it won't happen again. I'm sure you understand, but I have specific responsibilities."

I hesitated, not certain how to proceed from there.

Her cheeks were once more bright pink, but she said in a measured tone, "If you think I've gone and planned out some sort of childish fairytale fantasy after last night, then you're even more arrogant than I thought."

At first, I wasn't sure I understood.

Then, once I knew I *had* understood, I gaped at her for several seconds, more stunned than I could recall feeling in quite some time.

I didn't think I'd ever been more thoroughly put in my place.

I didn't care for it. A sharp retort bubbled up, but I bit it back. Really, was she wrong? I took a few more seconds to think it through before replying coolly, "It isn't a matter of thinking you've developed some...childish, fairytale fantasy, although thank you for properly putting me in my place, Ms. Bocho. Realistically, I've always known I wasn't a fairytale prince, but it's good to be reminded of one's place."

Her lids flickered, but if I'd been hoping to make her feel

chastised, I was going to be disappointed. I wasn't looking for that, though. Not really. I wasn't sure what I wanted—maybe to see that cute chin of hers go up again.

"But back to the matter at hand, I do have specific responsibilities, and I rarely indulge in...relationships, even merely physical ones, without establishing rules first. We didn't do that. I don't want there to be confusion."

"There is no confusion." Her face was pale now, save for two splotches of color on her cheeks. Her eyes had gone darker, too. "We had sex. I don't recall hearing a declaration of undying love, or offering one."

I didn't care for the expression on her face, but I didn't know what to do about it, and I had no idea what specifically had caused it, and this had to be said, so I continued.

"Good." I wanted to tell her, emphatically, it wasn't going to happen again, but I already wanted to see her naked in the light of day, and damn it, I'd never been very good at lying—particularly when it came to lying to myself.

Although I had no real intention of sleeping with her again, I couldn't deny that if the circumstance presented itself, I'd probably throw my good intentions to the wind.

She continued to watch me, and the tension between us took on a weight so uncomfortable, I found myself looking for a reason to walk away.

But it was Kitt who found a reason—or was given one.

A knock on the door startled both of us, and she blushed, smoothing her hair back from her face as she turned away. "I should get that."

I turned toward the fireplace, brooding. The hearth held a pretty display of candles, and I stared at them, trying to blank my mind and calm my thoughts. Whoever in the hell was at the door, I hoped Kitt got rid of them quickly because there were too many things we needed to do, needed to discuss—

"Sir." Kitt's voice, polite and proper, came from behind me.

I closed my eyes, resisting the urge to start cursing in half a dozen languages. It wouldn't do any good. I didn't know much about Kitt, but she seemed terribly proficient. If she was talking to me, then whoever the hell was at the door was there to speak to me, and that could only mean the person knew I was here.

I bought myself another second or two, staring at the pretty display of candles in the hearth. "Yes, Ms. Bocho?"

"The police are here."

Turning, I watched as two men in suits moved to join her. One of the men was older, likely in his fifties. His suit was poorly fitted, although well-made. The other was younger, likely close to my age. His suit was definitely on the cheaper side, but it was obviously tailored to fit his tall, muscled form.

I'd had enough dealings with law enforcement in my own country that I recognized these men for what they were, even without Kitt's introduction.

I nodded at them, folding my hands behind me as I looked them over. "Gentlemen."

"Your Highness." The older man nodded at me and introduced himself as Basil Feidelberg before gesturing to his younger counterpart. "This is Investigator Simeon Lieberman, my partner."

"A pleasure." Out of habit, I looked around, thinking only to send somebody to bring coffee and tea.

But there wasn't anybody.

That was odd, wasn't it?

Kitt cleared her throat. "I'll bring coffee if anybody wants it."

Feidelberg glanced at her and offered a short nod. "Thank you, Ms. Bocho."

Once she was gone, I took a seat and gestured for them to do the same.

"Your Highness, we're terribly sorry for your loss." Lieberman glanced toward the doorway before continuing. "Might I ask what you've been told?"

"Nothing," I said curtly. "Only that my sister, the Princess of Monaco, and her husband are dead, leaving my niece and nephew orphans. The authorities in Monaco could only tell me that they'd passed. But when I arrived here last night, Ms. Bocho, the family au pair, told me that they'd been found dead in their home in Dresden. Murdered." I paused a moment before adding, "I do hope you're here to tell me more."

"We're still very early in the investigation," Feidelberg said, drawing my attention toward him. He glanced toward the door, eyes following the pathway Kitt had taken. "Might I ask what you know about the au pair, Ms. Bocho?"

"Only what my sister has told me, and a small bit of information from my mother. I can tell you that the children adore her. My family would have had her investigated quite thoroughly, though. I assure you of that." Hooking my ankle over my knee, I studied the older man. I saw nothing in his eyes but a deep, driving intellect. Still, there was something about his question that left me unsettled.

"How long—"

I lifted a hand and shook my head. "I'll apologize, officers, but I won't be answering any questions until I get some answers myself."

Feidelberg stiffened, broad shoulders going back even as he squared his jaw.

Lieberman almost looked amused.

I stood and stared them down. "A member of the royal family of Monaco was murdered in your country, gentlemen. As it stands, this is already on the edge of becoming an international crisis, and you're caught in the middle of it. Do you want to make matters worse by withholding information from Princess Anne's only brother, the Hereditary Prince of Monaco?"

They shared glances but remained quiet.

"I assure you, if you need further encouragement, I can have the chancellor on the phone within two minutes."

Feidelberg cleared his throat. "Your Highness...that won't be necessary."

THIRTEEN

KITT

"WE'D HOPED TO HAVE MORE INFORMATION TO GIVE YOU, Prince Aeric."

At the sound of Feidelberg's voice, I hesitated, not certain if I should enter the room. There was something about his voice, his tone that made me think I wasn't supposed to hear the discussion.

I darted a look backward and immediately felt silly. What was I doing? Looking for permission?

"Just tell me what you know."

I shivered at the chill of Aeric's response, so icy and flat. Borderline emotionless, but that, in and of itself, was a lie. He had *so* much emotion trapped inside, a well of it, pain and anger and grief.

Yet the man speaking could have been discussing a stranger. The weather. A damn traffic accident.

The chill in his tone didn't throw me the way it would have a day or two earlier, but it was still unsettling.

The quiet lingered, and Aeric, clearly pissed, shattered it

when he barked, "And might I remind you just who it was slain within the borders of your country, gentlemen."

I closed my eyes. I didn't *need* reminders. Somehow, I doubted the officers needed them either, although the reasons were completely different.

"I understand, Prince Aeric." It was Feidelberg again, and he sighed, sounding weary. "There is no easy way to put this, sir, but your sister and brother-in-law appear to have been targeted. From our preliminary investigation, there is no sign that this was a botched home invasion or random attack, but rather a planned and deliberate attack."

Sucking in a breath, I sagged against the wall and closed my eyes.

I couldn't be hearing this correctly.

How was it possible?

Who would *want* to kill Anne and Karl?

The pain already ripping at me magnified, and I closed my eyes, forced myself to block it all out. I had to because, if I didn't, I'd lose my mind.

Karl had been shot while he was still in bed, sitting but getting ready to rise. Anne had been shot in the back, hiding on the floor with her phone in hand next to the bed.

Calling for help, I thought in horrified bewilderment. How close had help seemed, only for her to die within seconds of reaching out?

On the verge of being sick, I focused on the tray in my hands, breathing in slowly through my nose before blowing each breath out with equal deliberation.

Breathe, I told myself. *Breathe and focus and think about the kids.*

Get a grip, I told myself only seconds later. *The worst of it has to be over, right?* How *much worse can it be?*

But that was a dangerous question.

Things could *always* get worse.

"At present, that really is all we can tell you, Prince Aeric. Now...if you would, we do have questions that need answering. Particularly regarding Ms. Bocho, the au pair for your niece and nephew."

Tendrils of dread curled down my spine, and I pressed my lips together, muffling any sound that might escape.

"Why are you asking?" Aeric asked.

"Routine questioning, Your Highness," the younger cop said. Lieberman, I thought. It was Lieberman. "We have to look at everybody connected to your sister."

"Everybody." Aeric's reply sounded droll, but there wasn't any real humor in his tone. "Very well. I don't know much about Kitt at all, but I can tell you she's devoted to the children, and it's obvious she's distraught over what has happened. Oh, and she would have passed any sort of background check needed to work for the royal family."

"Background check?"

"Of course." Aeric made a low, amused noise. "You didn't think the royal family of Monaco would allow somebody to care for the children of the Princess of Monaco without first making certain that person was both qualified and safe? She underwent more of a thorough background check than either of you."

There wasn't an answer from either of the cops, and I breathed easier, although the band around my chest only relaxed an inch or so. It hadn't released completely. I didn't know if it ever would.

"There's nothing specific you're looking to know, is there?" Aeric asked, his question pointed.

"No," Feidelberg responded. "Quite frankly, it's just an avenue we're pursuing. One we have to pursue. We have to eliminate all possibilities until we come to the one we can't. It's how we work cases."

"Sounds tedious. And I believe you're wasting time on this particular avenue. Don't you have anything more worthy of chasing?"

"It's early yet," Feidelberg said, his tone mildly defensive, "but we do have a number of possible suspects. Did you know any of Weiss's business associates? Friends he might have hung out with at a pub after a day's work and had a drink with?"

Grateful they'd moved on from me, I pushed off the wall and headed into the living room. "Sorry I took so long," I said, forcing a smile. It was just one more hard thing to pull off in a series of them.

Lieberman rose and met me halfway across the room, taking the tray. "Thank you."

He gave me a charming smile and retreated to his seat, placing the tray in the middle of the table. I was left with the option of hovering or sitting on the couch. I chose the couch and began pouring for everybody without being asked.

"Thank you." Feidelberg took the coffee from me and took a sip, watching as I passed cups out, but his gaze followed me. "How long have you worked for the family, *Frau* Bocho?"

Even though I'd known there would be questions for me, it was still unsettling to have the brawny cop focus his eyes on me. His tone stayed neutral, but I couldn't help but feel like both of the cops glowered at me in accusation.

"Almost two years." I forced a smile as I took the last cup

and laced it heavily with cream and sugar. My hand was steady as I picked it up and sipped. "I was hired when Anne decided to go back to work. Karol had just turned a year old."

I felt Aeric's consternation and darted a look at him. "She volunteered at a non-profit that focused on poverty and hunger across the world." I folded my hands around the cup to keep from fidgeting. "She was very devoted to it."

"You called her *Anne*," Lieberman said. "That seems rather...informal, considering she was the daughter of the reigning monarch of Monaco. Was your relationship that close?"

"I...well, yes." Blood rushed to my cheeks. "I'm sure you've noticed, but I'm American. When I arrived in Germany, I didn't even know Anne had a title. She introduced herself as Anne Weiss, and when I called her Mrs. Weiss, she laughed and told me to call her Anne. She...well...it was several weeks before I even knew she was part of Monaco's royal family. Josef was the one who told me. We were sitting down to dinner, and he pipes up and says, 'Mama is a princess. A real princess. She has a tiara, and everything and her brother is a prince. I'm a prince, too, and that means Karol is a princess.'"

"I imagine that was surprising."

I laughed. "Surprising? Yes. Anne told me I looked like I'd just swallowed a live frog, then she waved a hand and said she was the same woman who'd been in the kitchen with me, scrubbing vegetables for a salad while the cook prepared the dinner."

Aeric watched us all with an unreadable look, and I couldn't tell if he was bothered by everything he was learning or perplexed. I didn't know what to say.

"It...well...we don't have royalty in America. She acted so

normally, and she clearly wanted me not to treat her any different, so I didn't."

"You were friendly. Would you say you were friends?"

Looking at Feidelberg, I nodded cautiously. "Yes. I'd say we were friends."

"How was the marriage?"

"I..." The shift away from Anne and me to Anne and Karl was almost enough to give me whiplash. "It was fine. They were happy."

"No fights? No sign that either of them were having an affair?"

"What? No!" My face heated, and I squirmed, uncomfortable in so many ways. "Why would you ask such a thing?"

"It's part of the job, Frau Bocho. It's completely routine." Lieberman leaned forward, catching my eyes. "How was Mr. Weiss's relationship with you? With the children?"

Putting the coffee down, I pressed my fingertips to my temple. I wanted to ask them to slow down. It was like they wanted me off pace and uncomfortable. "Mr. Weiss and I were friendly enough. He wasn't home as often as Anne was. His job. Sometimes he was out late. Probably once or twice a week, sometimes more. But he always spent Saturday afternoons with the children. Sunday evenings too. Even if he was traveling, he'd come back home for the weekends. He had a standing breakfast date with the children and all of them attended mass as a family."

"So, she was *Anne*, but he was Mr. Weiss?"

"I...yes." Squaring my shoulders, I looked from one officer to the other. "Anne and I spent more time together. I *knew* her. Mr. Weiss was kind to me, and he loved his children, but it wasn't like we sat up and laughed about books or anything."

"And you did that with Princess Anne."

Put like that, it sounded crazy, but I still managed a nervous nod. "Yes."

"Tell us about the children. About their routine and what a typical day was like."

I picked up my coffee once more and took a sip, trying to gather my wits. I also wished for more than a little composure.

For the first time, I wished it was something much, much stronger. Pure moonshine, maybe.

As I started to talk, Aeric got up and slipped from the room.

FOURTEEN

AERIC

How much was there about my sister that I didn't know?

I knew she had a passion for trying to help those in need. A couple of years before she'd married, the two of us had gone on a trip to Africa, and through her eyes, I'd seen many of the reasons why she felt so drawn to her cause.

But I hadn't known she'd made it such a focal point of her life.

Circling around the house, I came to a stop in front of the arched doorways that opened into the formal dining room.

One time. I'd been here and shared one meal with her and her husband in the formal dining room one time.

It had been two years ago, and it had been just before they hired Kitt. I'd cuddled little Karol while Anne chased the playful and inquisitive toddler Josef had been through his bath and into his pajamas.

She'd been exasperated when she came into the room and took the baby from me. *Thank goodness the* au pair *will be here soon.*

Kitt had mentioned standing in the kitchen with Anne, scrubbing vegetables while the cook prepared a meal. With a scowl, I moved into the kitchen and looked around.

There was no cook.

Not only was there no cook, there weren't any servants on hand at all, save for Kitt.

She'd taken the children to school herself. She'd answered the door herself. She'd answered the phone herself.

When I'd visited last, there'd been a butler on hand, a cook, a driver. People who filled the small household, hired by Karl because he'd insisted he be the one to provide for the small family, according to my father.

But I'd yet to see one of them during this visit. Thinking back to the few times I'd visited, I pulled up images of the house as I remembered it. My father had wanted details. I remembered that. I'd taken it upon myself to get a self-guided tour of the entire home.

The lower level housed the entertainment room in the main wing, and the east wing had been for the household employees.

So, I'd go there and speak to them.

Ten minutes later, I stood in the middle of the hall, rubbing the back of my neck and feeling more confused. There clearly *were* no household employees. At least none who lived on the premises. Not even a bodyguard, which left me feeling more than a little unsettled.

Maybe the bodyguard went with them on the trip?

Had there been a victim I was unaware of?

But that made no sense. Either the bodyguard had failed at his job, and if so, why hadn't we been told? If he'd died along with Anne and Karl, wouldn't we have been told?

Something didn't add up.

Frustrated and wanting answers, I started back upstairs.

The voices of the officers made it clear I couldn't storm into the room where they sat with Kitt unless I wanted to air all of this in front of them—and I sure as hell didn't want that.

Left with no choice but to wait, I went back into the kitchen and started to check the cabinets and refrigerator.

I could put together a fucking lunch by myself. Angry for no discernible reason but satisfied that I had a plan of action, I started pulling items from the fridge. Perhaps I couldn't follow a recipe, and I had no idea the purpose of scrubbing vegetables, but even I could prepare a meal. I wasn't helpless.

TWENTY MINUTES LATER, there was a mess on the counter, alongside two massive sandwiches.

"The cops are...wow. What did you do, blow up a sandwich factory?"

Turning, I found Kitt in the doorway, staring into the room, her eyes wide.

"I made lunch." Grabbing the plates from the middle of the disaster, I lifted them into her line of sight and brandished them. "I thought you might be hungry."

"Oh, I'm starving. Nothing like being interrogated," she said with a humorless smile.

I had the urge to apologize, but before I could, she went to a cabinet and opened it, taking down two glasses. "What would you like to drink?"

I told her, and as she went about getting two glasses ready, I took the plates over to the table and sat, waiting until she joined me to do the same. I mechanically ate my sandwich, not tasting the spicy mustard, the cheese, or any of the toppings.

Kitt finished before I did, lowering half of the food back to her plate. "I think that sandwich is enough to feed me for a week."

"Then you don't eat enough." But a look at her showed she had more color to her face, which pleased me. I took one more bite before putting my own sandwich down. "I need to ask you something."

"All right."

She reached for her water, her eyes resting on my face.

"Where is the staff?"

She paused, then took a drink before lowering the glass to the table. Her brow was puckered, lips pursed in a thoughtful frown. "What staff?"

I gestured to the house, then the kitchen. "The *staff*. My sister might well be happy volunteering, and perhaps she was content with learning to drive and even cooking, but I don't see her giddy with the idea of shopping for groceries or cleaning this large house or doing the laundry or any number of things that are required to keep a house like this. And where was her bodyguard? And the two men who watch the children?"

My voice had been climbing, but I couldn't stop it. There were so many things going on that I didn't understand, that I couldn't understand, and I needed answers.

"I..." Kitt swallowed and looked away. "There were people who worked here at one point, sir—"

"Aeric," I bit out, my temper flaring even more. "If you can call my sister *Anne*, you can damn well call me Aeric and look at me when you speak."

Her eyes shot to mine, and something akin to annoyance flickered there. "And you could *not* shout at me. I'm just as confused and lost as you are, *Aeric*."

I blew out a breath that felt like had been burning in my lungs. "You're correct. Now...answer the questions, *Kitt*."

Her full mouth thinned out to a sexy scowl, but she nodded curtly. "The cook stayed on for about a month after I arrived. But then Anne told me Alice had found a better offer with another family. I didn't even see her leave. She was just gone. The driver had been on staff when I started, but a few days later, Anne asked if I'd be comfortable getting my license here, and I told her as long as I had a few days to practice, I would. Thomas gave me a couple of lessons, then took me to apply for the license. After I passed, he left within a few days." She shrugged and picked at the crust on her sandwich. "One by one, they all left."

"And who cares for the house?"

"Well, mostly Anne and I do." She shifted, tugging at her shirt, and I found myself missing the silly pink t-shirt with its silly dog from yesterday. "A cleaning service comes in several times a week, but Anne and I handle the small things. She works with the children to make sure they each understand how to pick up after themselves, and they have chores after dinner."

A cleaning service. And my sister handling things?

Something about this wasn't right. No, not *something*. Many things.

But I couldn't even begin to explain all the ways or even figure out the right way to start. Brooding, I finished my sandwich in silence, then rose, mind already elsewhere.

Something Kitt had said poked at me, and I paused long enough to collect the plate and the glass of water, carrying them to the sink to rinse off. But I didn't know what to do with them next.

Wasn't that a thing? I'd been given the finest education in

the world, and I had no idea what to do with the dishes I'd used for lunch.

Kitt joined me at the counter, and I watched as she wrapped up half of her uneaten sandwich, then put it aside, rinsing off her dishes. She stepped back and tugged at something on the counter, and I realized it wasn't just one of the cabinets. The dishwasher. Of course, I knew what one was. She put her dishes inside and beckoned for mine.

Turning them over, I started to clean up the mess I'd made when I put the sandwiches together, rinsing off the knives, closing containers. In under five minutes, the kitchen was set to rights, and I turned to look at Kitt.

"I want to go to Dresden," I said, holding her eyes.

She licked her lips, her expression troubled.

"I need to know more," I told her. "This sitting here and waiting isn't working for me. I need answers, and I don't know where to find them here. So, I'm going to Dresden."

"Of course." She moved away from the counter, pacing a few steps before coming back to stand just steps away. "What about the children?"

Confused, I stared at her. "What about them?"

"What are you going to do with them?" she asked. She stood with her hands clenched into fists at her sides, her gaze locking with mine. She looked nervous and scared and uncertain and determined, an oddly endearing mix.

When she started to nibble her lower lip, I had that odd urge to cup her face and do some nibbling of my own. She squared her jaw and demanded, "Well?"

And my attention jerked back to the matter at hand.

The children.

What about the children?

FIFTEEN

KITT

"What about the children?"

With a lost expression, he sagged back against the counter, and for once, that proud expression was gone, and those wide shoulders slumped. "What about them?"

"What are you going to do with them?"

I half-expected him to parrot the question back to me. *Do with them?*

But he didn't. He pushed a hand through his hair while a frown creased his forehead. "I don't know, Kitt," he said, looking back at me after what felt like a lifetime. "This is nothing we ever talked about."

He swallowed and looked down, but before he did, a naked expression of pain flickered across his features. "We never talked about this. About anything like this. I have no idea what she wanted, or what she had in mind."

"Do your parents know? I mean, did Anne ever talk to them?"

"I don't know." Uneasy, he pushed his hands into his pockets and stared at me. "I'll have to talk to my parents. They must know something or have some sort of idea in mind. My mother, at the very least. She's so very practical."

I wondered if there was a will. Surely there was. Anne had seemed too logical, too down to earth to leave such things to chance. But Aeric had a far-off look to his face, and without warning, he said, "If you'd excuse me, I should call my parents. They want to be updated and this...well, perhaps they have answers."

I watched as he left, then leaned against the counter. That hadn't gone as I'd hoped. We needed to figure out how to handle telling the children—and it needed to be done *today*.

Aggravated at myself, with him, with the police, frustrated with Anne for not preparing me for this—although who could prepare for their own death in an adequate fashion? I had no idea. I was just aggravated.

It's worse for him, I thought. *So much worse.*

Sympathy stirred, and I pushed away from the counter. I should go see him, offer to help, assuming there was anything I could do. Even if he was talking with his parents, I could simply just sit and be there, couldn't I?

I drew even with the kitchen doorway, and the phone rang. Checking the caller ID, I frowned. It was Josef's school.

Immediately, I answered. "Hello?"

"*Frau* Bocho?"

I recognized the stern voice of the man charged with running with the small private school where Josef attended. "Yes, *Herr* Bach. What can I do for you?"

"I need you to come to the school, *Frau*. Right away. It's urgent."

I'D BEEN FORCED to leave a note for Aeric. He'd already been on the phone with his father, in the middle of a very emotional discussion, and I couldn't interrupt, so I jotted down a note and left it by the phone in the front hall, hoping he'd see it.

Mind already racing with a million things, I wondered just what had upset Samuel Bach, the firm headmaster of Josef's private primary school.

My mind managed to concoct a thousand scenarios in the time it took me to drive the fifteen kilometers from the house to the school, and none of them settled my mind easily. I'd left my phone in my purse and couldn't even do a quick search to make sure there was nothing on the news about the school. It was too early for the flu and Josef was ridiculously healthy.

So, what was it, then?

I played that question over and over in my mind during the drive, never once finding the answer.

Finally arriving at the school, I hopped out, grabbing my purse. As I strode toward the front doors, I couldn't keep from looking around. Everything *seemed* normal from out here. That was a good sign, right?

My heart banged inside my chest, and I felt far too uneasy as I passed through the doors. It was a warm, open environment, and I'd volunteered here more than once, loving the environment and how the teachers and students were treated.

I'd never find a school like this in the US, and sooner or later, I'd have to return home. Nothing, nobody would compare to what it had been like to work for the Weiss family.

Despondent, I tried not to think about it as I made my way into the office to sign in. More than a few of office personnel stared at me, and I tried not to notice as I greeted the administrative assistant. She stood by her desk, the phone in her hand. She nodded at me, but her normal smile was missing.

I didn't have time to sit before Mr. Bach appeared in the doorway of his office, imperiously waving me into the room. Eyes drilled into me as I made my way over to him, sending my anxiety level skyrocketing up into the stratosphere.

"Close the door, if you would," Bach said, his tone curt.

I did so and looked around, half-expecting to see Josef, but there was nobody in the room except us.

"Please sit."

I did so, feeling like I was facing *my* principal rather than Josef's headmaster, and not caring for the feeling one bit. He sat behind his desk and gave me a hard look.

Slowly, I sank into the hard, ladder-backed chair, clutching my purse in my hands.

"Why was Josef sent to school today?"

I blinked, shaking my head. "I'm sorry?"

A muscle pulsed in his cheek. "Josef's parents are dead, and you sent him to school *without* telling him."

"I..." My mind raced. "Wait a minute. How do you know about his parents? That wasn't supposed to be made public until later today."

His eyes narrowed. "It's quite public."

"It's not supposed to be!" Shooting to my feet, I looked around the small office, feeling sick. "Their uncle assured me it wouldn't be made public because Anne's father wanted to make sure they had time to address the nation. Their uncle, Prince Aeric, is in Berlin now. We'll tell them this afternoon, but he wanted them to have one more day to..." My voice broke. "He wanted them to have one more day. We were going to tell them this afternoon after his father told the people of Monaco. You... well, you know who she is..."

The hard set of Bach's features softened slightly, and he sighed, pinching the bridge of his nose. "Of course, we're aware." He frowned, then waved at the seat. "Please, *Frau*. Sit. This is...upsetting for many of us."

"Tell me Josef doesn't know," I said, slowly sinking back into the hard chair, but I could tell by the troubled look on his face that I was asking for the impossible.

"One of the older children said something to him. He...he didn't understand, of course, and he went to class very upset. The teacher hadn't expected to see him, and when she witnessed him so upset, she tried to comfort him and brought him to the office as another teacher watched her class. We realized he didn't know and called a counselor in. We were in the process of calling you when he started screaming and crying. He'd..." Bach looked away then, uncomfortable. "Two staff members in the office were discussing it. He overheard."

I was going to be sick. I was going to—

No, I told myself. I didn't have that luxury. Josef needed me.

"Where is he?" I demanded, rising once more. "I need to see him. I can't imagine how heartbroken he is."

"He is very distraught. But..." Bach was on his feet as well, one hand outstretched, "*Frau*, you cannot see him."

I went stiff. "What?"

"We had to call the authorities." He looked away. "I'm terribly sorry. I...I'm very sorry. We handled this poorly from the beginning, I can see that, and of course, the princess's people deserved to hear it from Prince Fortinbras." Pausing, he swallowed, and his face went pale before slowly going several shades of red. "This will become quite an unpleasant ordeal, I'm afraid.

If it was to be kept quiet until Monaco's people could be informed..."

"Yes." Numb now, I paced a few feet from the chair, still clutching my purse, holding it like a talisman now. "None of this was supposed to be made public. And Josef...I don't understand. Why can't I see him?"

"Well." He cleared his throat and squirmed, his discomfort increasing by several degrees. Judging by the glint in his eye, he was also angry once more, but I didn't think I was the source of his ire now. "*Frau* Bocho, I'm very sorry. We handled this badly, and I wish we could undo the past hour. You're another innocent party in this and one who has no control over matters. But..." He cleared his throat and tugged at the sleeves of his sport coat, aligning them precisely. "My priority is now the children. You're not family. You're not even a citizen of Germany. Your employers are dead, and that could put your very residency in this country in jeopardy."

"I have a permanent residence permit," I said stiffly, my face heating. "We obtained it just a few months ago. They were planning to hire me on as permanent nanny for the children. My legal residence is *here* now. It has been for more than two months."

He shifted uncomfortably. "You still are not family."

"Their uncle..." I felt helpless. I couldn't just sit here, knowing that Josef was alone and hurting. "Their uncle is here. He's the...he will be the next Prince of Monaco. *He* is family."

"Maybe if he was here, this discussion could go a different way. But he isn't." Bach looked away. "As it is, we have somebody coming who'll take temporary custody of Josef—"

"What? You *can't*!" I lunged forward, slamming my hands on the desk and gaping at him. "First, because of the carelessness of your staff, Josef learned that his parents are gone, with nobody who loves him there to comfort him, and now, some stranger is going to take *custody* of him? How much do you want to traumatize that boy?"

Shamefaced, he looked back at me. "*Frau*, I assure you, the staff members will be dealt with—"

"And that does *nothing* to undo the harm already caused. How can you put that sweet boy with a social worker? I've been taking care of him for two years!"

"But you're not his guardian." Bach adjusted his tie. "There's nothing more I can do. If you'd just kept him at home, then—"

"Don't you dare try to blame this on me." I jabbed at the air with my index finger. "If any of you had sense, you would have thought that there was a reason he was sent on to school. Did it occur to you to call and simply *ask* instead of accusing me? Instead of snarling at me over the phone?"

He drew his head back.

"And you can damn well imagine how furious their uncle and grandparents will be over this. If you hadn't been so careless in your handling of this tragic situation, I'd almost pity you." The anger and fear fueling me gave me more courage, but it was draining fast, and the nausea was returning.

It looked like Bach felt the same, and I didn't feel the least bit of regret for causing it. "Can I at least see him?"

He flicked a look past me but shook his head. "I've been advised not to allow it."

"Advised." Snorting, I grabbed my purse and fished out my phone. "I'm calling the house and advising the prince of what's happening with his nephew. He can go collect his niece—"

"The authorities have already arranged to pick up little Karol too." He looked green now.

I wanted to explode. Setting my jaw, I said, "Please tell me the children will be kept together."

"Of course. I was assured—"

I turned on my heel, the contacts on my phone already pulled up. In the main part of the office, everybody was quiet, and the accusatory looks I'd received earlier had faded. Well, we had been rather loud. Two women, both younger than me, stood on the far side of the room, trying hard to be invisible. One was a tall blonde, the other a slender redhead not much taller than me. Both were red-faced, and the blonde was crying despite clear attempts to stop.

"I assume you two are the ones Josef overheard," I bit off, my voice icy. The blonde looked away, but the redhead gave a short, stiff nod. "Perhaps in the future, you'll learn to discuss sensitive matters someplace where a *child* won't overhear you."

The redhead squared her shoulders, opening her mouth, but before she could say anything, a calm, hard voice spoke up. "Everybody will be much more careful in the future, *Frau* Bocho."

I looked back to the headmaster standing in the doorway, jaw tight.

"Good. I'd hate to think of another child in this school being scarred because of the carelessness of the staff."

The redhead, again, looked like she was going to speak, but her friend grabbed her arm and squeezed tightly.

Unwilling to spend another second there, I turned away and strode through the door. As much as I wanted to tear through the building and find Josef, I knew that wasn't the answer.

They wouldn't allow me to see him, and the way my luck

was going, they had police officers standing on hand, and I'd be tackled from behind right in front of the boy, which would only make everything that much worse.

No, I'd have to walk away right now. Walk away and call Aeric. He needed to know that people knew, somehow. And he needed to know what was happening with his niece and nephew.

I wasn't looking forward to the conversation.

My heart broke for Josef and Karol as I hurried to my car. *We'll take care of this, sweethearts. I promise.*

SIXTEEN

AERIC

Sitting on the side of the perfectly made bed in Anne's bedroom, I stared at the picture I'd picked up from the bureau.

It showed her with the children, all of them smiling. It was a recent picture, taken within the past few months. The children smiled with carefree abandon, but the smile didn't reach Anne's eyes.

This wasn't the first picture I'd seen where she seemed to just be wearing a smile rather than truly feeling it. All the recent pictures were like this.

I'd been able to access the computer using the password on the computer for the children, which allowed very little *real* access, but I could look at the pictures.

There was strain in her eyes. It was easier to see in the awkward, sometimes blurry pictures taken by Karol or Josef, but even the ones marked as being uploaded by Kitt, it was easy to see signs that Anne wasn't as happy as she should be, as happy as she appeared.

"What was going on?" I asked the pretty brunette in the portrait.

There wasn't an answer, of course.

The ringing of the phone shattered the quiet, and I rose to answer, hoping it was some sort of news.

"Aeric!"

Instantly, I recognized Kitt's voice.

"What's wrong?"

"The children know," she said in a ragged voice. "At least Josef does. I'm looking at the headlines for one of the papers in Berlin. The news is all over the place. Josef heard somebody talking and...he knows!"

Fury blistered inside. I put the picture down before I gave in to the urge to fling it. Heads would roll.

"Bring him home," I said. "Get Karol and bring them home—"

"I can't." This time, a half-sob broke out of her as she spoke. "The headmaster at the school contacted the authorities when he learned the news. Since I'm not family, they—"

"I'm family. Where is this school?" I demanded.

"It won't matter." She was crying now, the tears in her voice obvious, but she kept speaking. "Somebody with the state just picked Josef up. I sat in my car and watched. Aeric, he was crying and—"

"Why did somebody from the state pick him up?"

"Because I'm not family. I'm not a German citizen."

Shoving the heel of my hand against my right eye socket, trying to shove back the headache that had erupted out of nowhere, I bit back the growl growing in my throat. "We'll take care of this, Kitt. Just calm down."

"Yes. Of course. I'm going to the police station. I...well, you need to know how to get custody of them. They can't just place the children with strangers when you're here, right?" With each word, she sounded steadier.

"No. We'll take care of it. I'm calling my family, then I'll meet you at the police station. Can you text me the information?"

I STRODE through the doorways of the police station.

Lieberman paced, apparently waiting for me.

"Where are Ms. Bocho and my niece and nephew?" I demanded before he could get even a word out.

"Frau Bocho is here, speaking with Lieutenant Feidelberg and our superior. I've got a call into the local division of family services to see who has been assigned to work with the children so you can speak to—"

"I don't want to *speak* to them," I said shortly. "I want to have them brought here so I can take them back to their home."

Lieberman cleared his throat. "Yes, well. Let's join the captain and *Frau* Bocho."

I didn't like the way he wouldn't look at me.

As we rode the elevator up to the fifth floor, I checked my phone and saw from a text that Guillermo was already in contact with the authorities and my father's aide was at work, finding a lawyer.

"None of this was supposed to leak to the press until my family had a chance to inform our people," I said rigidly. "I want to know how it leaked to the journalist of that website."

"We're working on it, but I believe somebody at the coroner's office was involved." Lieberman cleared his throat.

"I want a name. Whoever helped participate in my nephew being traumatized. I won't tolerate it."

"We're working on it, Your Highness."

He'd better work faster. The elevator doors opened, and I strode with him, kept the pace quick enough that he had to stretch to keep up with me.

"Through the double doors there," he said, gesturing ahead.

I pushed through and scanned the room, still moving.

He went to point, but I'd already seen Kitt, sitting in a glass-walled office, her shoulders back, cheeks pale.

I pushed inside, and the man behind the desk broke off, mid-sentence.

Feidelberg shot to his feet. "Your Highness. I'd like to—"

"Where are Josef and Karol?" I demanded.

"I...sir, they're being placed with a family for a few days, no longer, while we try to straighten a few things out." Feidelberg shot the man behind the desk a quick look, but the other man didn't so much as blink.

I focused on him after reading the nameplate on the desk. "Schneider. My niece and nephew *have* a family. I am family. I want them brought to me."

He shifted, studying me with an unreadable gaze. "Prince Aeric, I assume?"

"I'm not in the mood for niceties and introductions. When will my niece and nephew be brought to me?"

"Lieutenant Feidelberg has already explained it will only take a few days. He is working personally with family services to make sure they're with a good family, somebody who is good with children and can help young Josef through this."

"He needs his *family*," I snapped.

Schneider cocked a brow. "Perhaps you should have kept him home and told him there."

I narrowed my eyes. "You should proceed with a great deal of caution, sir. My father is already in the process of hiring a lawyer to deal with this mess caused by the school. You don't want to step into the middle of it, do you?"

"I'm just trying to do my job." He shrugged, looking unconcerned. "You've already been made aware that there is evidence pointing to suggest that your sister and her husband were targeted. We want to make sure the children are safe. That should be a concern of yours as well."

Caught off guard, I stared at him for a long moment, then shifted my attention to Lieberman and Feidelberg. "Do you have reason to believe they *aren't* safe?"

"It's too early to say," Feidelberg said. "This is likely just a precaution, but we want to clear all avenues first. This will only take a short time, Your Highness. I understand it's traumatic and not ideal—"

"Not ideal?" Kitt interjected, her voice hoarse. "Josef found out his mother and father were dead because he heard two women talking in the front office of his school! And rather than let somebody who loves him talk to him and explain, you sent him off to stay with strangers! *Not ideal* doesn't even cover it."

Her words laid me open.

I shouldn't have sent them to school.

I was the one who made that call.

"Had you informed your charges, *Frau* Bocho," Schneider said, "this could have been avoided."

"You're out of line," I said, stepping forward and blocking his view of her. "*I* was the one who decided to hold off on telling them. She hadn't said anything to them, yes, but she's their au pair, an employee, as you apparently have made her aware, repeatedly. It wasn't her place to tell them. When I arrived in Germany, it was late. The following morning, I still hadn't figured out the right way, and my father had already assured me no news would leak about their deaths until that afternoon, once the children were home. *None* of this should have been an issue, and regardless, it was *my* decision." Staring down at him, I asked, "Are you going to call me to task, Schneider?"

His face turned a dull red, and he looked away. "It's all very unfortunate, Your Highness. I'm not calling anybody to task. I'm just speculating how things could have gone differently."

"Perhaps you could speculate on your own time, then." Tucking my hands behind my back, I gave him a hard look. "We've got enough on our minds and enough to deal with without a bystander who knows little about the family interfering."

Schneider's face reddened, and he went rigid. "I'm supervising this investigation," he said, voice stiff. "I'm an officer of the law. That's *hardly* a bystander."

"You know nothing about this family, and you seemed to have assumed that the au pair was making decisions when I was the one behind those decisions. I believe *uninformed bystander* is quite fitting, Schneider." I stared down my nose at him, daring him to respond.

He wanted to. His jaw worked as he held my gaze. He stood so rigid when a knock came at the door, he jolted, although he didn't look to see who it was.

"Marie, I said I wasn't to be interrupted," he said, not taking his eyes from my face.

"Sir, the chancellor's office is on the phone. They're...quite adamant."

"Perhaps you should take that call," I suggested with a thin smile.

Without speaking, Schneider stormed out of the office.

I indulged in a few petty moments of thinking about how easy it would be to have his job. One phone call would do it, and he'd be out of this office within the hour.

But I had more important matters to deal with, and he wasn't worth my time.

"I apologize for my supervisor," Feidelberg said, moving to stand behind the man's desk.

"I'll take the apology directly from him when I'm ready, Feidelberg," I said shortly. "For now, you can help resolve this by bringing my niece and nephew to me."

He looked away for a brief moment, face tight. When he looked back at me, it was clear there wouldn't be any quick resolution. "I'm very sorry, Your Highness." Feidelberg slanted a look at Kitt and nodded at her. "*Frau* Bocho. Truly I am. But we have little say in this matter. We received a phone call from a contact within the Ministry of Family Affairs, Senior Citizens, Women, and Youth. After we answered some of their questions about the investigation, they decided it was best that the children be taken into federal custody until their guardianship and safety can be ascertained."

"The *Ministry* decided." I all but spat the words, so furious I couldn't see straight.

But before I could continue, Kitt pushed in front of me—quite literally pushed in front of me—wedging herself between me and the desk where Feidelberg stood with his hands folded in front of him, watching both of us closely.

"The Ministry?" she demanded. "You mean the same

Ministry that allowed certain atrocities to carry out within Brandenburg up until just recently?"

"Now, that's hardly—"

"Don't!" she snapped, her voice edging on shrill.

I had no idea what she was talking about, but when I moved to her side, there was an expression in her eyes that had my gut clenching.

"Don't tell me that's hardly anything we should concern ourselves with or any other platitude," she said, gesticulating angrily. "It's damn clear to me that, at some point in the very recent past, the Ministry had some serious issues in judgment. Why should we trust those children will be safe with anybody you place them with? For even a day or two?"

"The Ministry took those matters very seriously, *frau*," Lieberman said, clearing his throat.

Both of us looked at him, but after just a moment's appraisal, I shifted my attention to Kitt. "What matters?"

"Abuse." Her mouth went tight. "Brandenburg's Ministry of Youth had a huge scandal several years ago where the abuse of foster children was so endemic, there were suicides. Children were hospitalized, overmedicated, medicated unnecessarily. It was awful."

Blood roared in my ears as that information spun through my mind.

"*Everyone* took those issues seriously, *Frau* Bocho," Feidelberg said stiffly. "And the boy and girl aren't going into the foster system. The Ministry has simply taken custody of them for a few days as we work to solve the case and make certain there is no threat to the children."

"As I have no children at present, that boy is in the line of succession," I bit off. "There are any number of threats *to* him, and I hardly think the typical foster family is equipped to handle that. He should have a bodyguard at the very least."

Feidelberg tugged at his tie and blew out a breath.

Standing off to the side, Lieberman cleared his throat. "I'll make some calls, but this matter isn't under our control."

Turning to him, I said, "Then you'd best make sure those calls you make are to very, very important people. I've already notified my parents, and when I leave, I'm making another call. If the chancellor's office wasn't calling about this issue, they will be. Very shortly."

SEVENTEEN

KITT

WE'D NO SOONER LEFT THE OFFICE THAN AERIC STARTED making those calls.

Numbly, I walked along at his side and likely would have gone right past the elevator, but he caught my arm and stopped me. I was too numb to feel embarrassed as he guided me to the door. I was too numb to feel *anything*.

The children had been put in temporary custody.

How had this happened?

Anne, Karl...I'm so sorry.

A small noise escaped me, and I pressed my fingers to my mouth to keep any other noises from slipping out.

Aeric spoke into his phone in rapid-fire French, and my tired brain simply couldn't keep up. As the floors blurred by, he rubbed my back, and when the doors opened, he guided me out with his palm resting at the dip in my spine.

The skies had clouded up, and as we stepped through the doors, a slow drizzle started, picking up with intensity as we walked down the street. I followed along with Aeric numbly, although my car was parked on the next block.

He finished his phone call and nudged me into a quicker pace. "We'll both be soaked if we don't move. Come on, Kitt. My father's aide already has a lawyer at work on this here in Berlin. Where's your car?"

Vaguely, I waved a hand in the other direction.

Aeric cupped my chin in his hand and guided my face up so he could look into my eyes.

"Give me your keys," he said after a moment.

"I...what?"

"You're in no state to drive. Give me the keys."

He was probably right, and I didn't think to argue, just fishing the keys from my purse and placing them in his open palm. He guided me to the gleaming black Mercedes Benz waiting at the curb and opened the door. "In you go."

I sat down, mind still chasing itself in circles. He slid into the seat next to me a moment later and started the car. He pulled out his phone and made another call. Although I couldn't have slept, I closed my eyes and turned my head in a weak attempt to offer privacy.

Josef and Karol must be so afraid right now, so scared and lost. *I'm sorry, guys. I'll do my best to fix this...*

I jumped at the sound of a fist rapping on the door and looked over just in time to see Aeric roll the window down and pass the keys over to a tall, powerfully built man wearing a light raincoat. He gave me a quick nod but kept his attention on Aeric, their conversation low save for when Aeric asked for more detail about the car.

"Um...it's parked by a small deli." I gave a description of the car and wrapped my arms around myself, chilled despite the mild temperatures.

Aeric saw me shivering and frowned.

"Sorry," I said. "I think it's nerves."

"You don't need to apologize for being cold." He nodded at the other man, then put the window up before slipping out of his suit jacket.

"No, that's not necessary—"

"I already have it off," he said simply. "Take it, please."

Since there was no point in resisting, I accepted the expensive material and draped it over me like a blanket. The heat from his body instantly surrounded me, and as silly as it was, I immediately felt somewhat calmer.

As he pulled away from the curb, he spoke out loud, activating the car's Bluetooth system to make a call.

I squirmed uncomfortably as I realized just who he was calling.

The freaking *chancellor.*

She wasn't the one to answer, of course, but once he gave his name, she was on the phone in moments, and I closed my eyes, wondering how in the world I'd fallen into a place where I'd be sitting in a car with a man who could command the attention of a world leader in mere moments.

"Your Highness, I want you to know I'm already at work on this. I'm terribly sorry..."

I listened for a few moments, hopeful, but as the conversation shifted focus to *police procedural matters* and *safety of the children,* I squeezed my eyes closed and resigned myself to accepting the fact that Josef and Karol might not be coming home today as I'd hoped.

"Those children are *not* to be placed in some random home," Aeric said, drawing my attention back to him.

"They won't be. I already have a solution in mind. I need some time to make sure it will work."

I let their words roll over me once more, staring out the window as the rain started to come down harder. What if it began to storm? Karol hated storms. She tried to pretend otherwise, but they scared her. What if—

"Kitt."

"Hmm?" I continued to stare bleakly outside, distantly aware that the car was no longer moving.

"We're here. Come on. Let's get inside." Aeric rubbed my shoulder several times. "Come on."

Finally, the words penetrated, and I looked around. He'd parked at the side door, near the broad overhang with the passenger door closest to the entrance. Fumbling out of his coat, I went to hand it to him, but he shook his head.

"Keep it for now. You're still shivering. Get a sweater or something once you're inside, then I'll take it." Climbing out before I could argue, he came around the car.

My stiff fingers didn't want to manipulate the door handle, but I managed and even climbed outside before he offered assistance. I already looked pathetic. I didn't need to make it worse.

I settled the coat on my shoulders like a cloak, breathing in his scent and letting it calm my frazzled nerves. The scents of bergamot and something foreign and exotic and delicious filled my head, a welcome distraction from the nerves jangling so loudly inside.

Once inside the kitchen, though, it didn't work as well. Clutching the lapels of the coat around me, I went to stand in front of the refrigerator. Each child had a work of art displayed. They chose a new one each week, and when the old one came down, it was placed with care inside keepsake boxes Anne lovingly tended to.

I'd have to replace the pictures soon and tuck these away.

Behind me, I heard Aeric's phone ring, then his voice, low and quiet as he answered the phone. Blocking the sound out, I kept my attention on the pictures and told myself that the children would be back here—*soon*—happily drawing away.

Everything will be okay, Kitt. Everything will be okay.

I had no idea how much time passed as I repeated that lie to myself, over and over, trying to calm myself. Vaguely, I realized I could no longer hear Aeric speaking. Had he left the room?

Inexplicably, the thought of being alone terrified me.

My mouth started to tremble, and I pressed my lips together to stop the telltale movement.

"Kitt."

The sound of his voice filled me with intense relief, and a sigh shuddered free. I saw him move out of the corner of my eye, standing closer. I tried to force a response out, too afraid to look at him because, if I did, he'd see the tears I couldn't hide.

He curved a hand around my neck and urged me to look at him.

"Are you all right?" he asked.

"I..." Swallowing, I stared at him. Then I broke away from him to pace. "How do I answer that? My employers and friends are dead. The children I love like my own have been taken from their home and will be spending the night with strangers. And I'm helpless to do anything! I feel like I'll soon come out of my skin, and I just..." Stopping in the middle of the floor, I shoved my hands through my hair and pulled. "I don't even want to think about this. That's awful and selfish and—"

"Human."

I jolted to hear him all but murmur the word in my ear. I spun around and found him standing behind me, just inches away. Needing air, I backed up, but he followed me, matching me step for step until I bumped into the waist-high kitchen island with its smooth marble surface.

"It's human," Aeric repeated, lifting a hand.

I shivered as he traced a fingertip along my lower lip. Instantly, my blood went hot. Maybe I'd just been waiting for another look from him, another touch, because my body was already clamoring for more. I had to lash it all down as I met his eyes.

This was the last thing I needed to be thinking about. The very last thing.

But then our gazes locked.

He slid his hand to my neck, then up into my hair, tugging and twisting, tangling in the curls as he pulled my head back. "I want to stop thinking for a little while myself, Kitt. I've got a brilliant idea on how we can manage that too."

His mouth covered mine just as a whimper slid free.

This was a bad, bad, bad idea.

And I didn't care.

He wasn't gentle—and I didn't care about that, either. As his tongue stole into my mouth, I wiggled and tried to press closer, but he was already leaning into me, and I felt the hard thrust of his penis against me. He ate at my mouth, like he was dying of hunger and I was starving myself.

When he pulled away, I groaned and tried to pull him back, but he didn't allow it, staring down at me with wide eyes that had gone stormy with want. He shoved his hands into my hair, holding me in place as he looked down at me. It was a hard, stark look, and I shuddered as his eyes raked me up and down.

"I want to fuck you so bad right now. Until you're moaning and shuddering and weak..."

Just hearing the words come from him made my insides clench and turn into so many hot, twisting knots. It should have hurt, and in a way, it did, but I knew relief was waiting...*right* there.

"Please," I said, staring at Aeric. "Please..."

He bent down and kissed me roughly, using his free hand to lift my chin, then stroking down until it curved over the front of my neck. I could feel my pulse rabbiting against his palm, and my nipples drew tighter, almost in envy, I thought, because I wanted to feel his hands on me there. I wanted to feel his hands cupping my breasts, his mouth closing over my nipples and sucking, biting...

"Look at me," he said, voice rough and raw.

"I am."

"I don't have any more condoms."

My breath froze in my chest, and a pained noise escaped me.

He pulled me up close against him. "Oh, don't worry...I'll take care of that ache, and you'll take care of mine." He slid a hand between us and cupped me, rubbing me with blatant, bold intent. "It wouldn't be a hardship to watch you go down on me again, let you suck me off until I come in your mouth. I'd enjoy spreading you out right here, licking you, tasting you, fucking you with my fingers... I might even roll you onto your hands and knees and teach you how to take my cock in your ass. It will be rough, but you've shown a taste for liking it that way."

"I..." Gulping, I stared at him.

He kissed me again, brutally.

"But I want that cunt wrapped around my dick. Are you on birth control?"

How could he even think rationally? The way he talked to

me had my brain on fire, and then he shifted and talked about logic and life and things that should matter more than having his cock inside me...I whimpered under the onslaught of desire that pulsed inside.

"Kitt!"

He cupped my face in his hands and arched my face up to meet his.

"Are you on birth control? The pill?"

"I...uh...I have an IUD." His eyes continued to bore into mine and nerves got the better of me. "Female stuff. I had to do something, and the pill didn't help, so the doctor recommended the IUD. I got it last year and..." A wheezing sort of breath escaped me as he rested a hand low on my belly, the burning desire in his eyes lightening momentarily, replaced by compassion.

"I haven't hurt you, have I?"

Blood rushed to my cheeks. "I...no." I tried to look away, afraid he'd see the truth in my eyes, but he wouldn't let me.

Still, he mistook the reason for my discomfort, passing his thumb over my lip as he smiled down at me, the inferno once more blazing in his gaze. "You're such an enigma, Kitt Bocho. You blush talking about birth control and even when I tell you that I want you on your knees, sucking me off, that I want to lay you down and eat your pussy, then have you bend over while I teach you how to take my cock up your ass, yet you start moaning and shaking, just thinking of it." He slid his hand inside the coat and palmed my breast through my clothing, pinching lightly. "Your nipples are hard, just like I thought they'd be. You want me to do all those things to you, Kitt?"

"Yes," I whispered, the word all but soundless. The air

trapped in my lungs was making my chest ache, and I forced myself to breathe out.

The pressure eased, but only for a few seconds because I was lost to the intensity in his eyes as he drew back, wolfish hunger in his eyes.

"Good. Because I may well do every last one to you before I'm done with you." His gaze scorched me. The heat, the want, the purpose...

Pinpricks broke out across my skin as he reached up and began to unbutton my blouse.

"Seeing you wearing my coat does something to me," he said, voice incredibly calm, especially compared to the super-nova blistering in his eyes. "I want to see you wearing nothing but that."

Our gazes locked and held as he continued unbuttoning my shirt. With the suit coat still hanging from my shoulders, he slid the shirt off, nudging it carefully away until it fell away and drifted to the floor. My bra soon followed, and then he guided my arms into the sleeves of his ridiculously large coat, taking the time to roll the sleeves up so my hands and forearms were free.

"I look like a kid playing dress-up," I said, my voice husky.

His response was to catch me around the waist and turn, spinning us in a one-eighty, then putting me down and turning me around until I faced the glass-fronted refrigerator. It went opaque when the doors hadn't been utilized, and right now, it cast a dark, smoky reflection of us. I drew a shuddering breath as he tugged the coat open, baring my breasts. Although the reflection was hardly clear, I could still make out enough to see his hands as he cupped me.

"Do you think I see anything remotely childlike about you?" He tugged on my nipples.

My knees went weak.

"I didn't hear an answer."

He slid one hand down the midline of my torso, popped the hidden button on my slacks and stole past the waistband of my panties. Two seconds later, he parted me and slid two fingers over the tight bud of my clitoris, then farther on down, hooking them inside.

"Does this help?"

I arched against his hand and cried out.

My pants fell to my ankles, and he turned me back around, nudging me up against the counter. I slapped my hands down for support, sucking in much needed air.

He licked his lips, backing away a couple of steps as he looked me over.

"I wanted to see you naked like this the first time. Now, I'm going to enjoy every second of it." He reached up and tugged at his tie, the movements slow and certain, as if he had all the time in the world.

And I was dying inside, one slow second at a time, my knees trembling, my thighs weak, my core hot and molten.

He *knew*. I could tell by the way he stared at me, watching from under the fringe of his lashes, gaze hooded, cheeks flushed.

"Your nipples are so tight. Do they hurt, Kitt?" he asked as he shucked his shirt, letting it fall to the floor.

"Yes." His chest was a work of art, like something you'd find in a museum. I couldn't think of another way to describe it. Itching to touch him, I curled my hands into fists, but I couldn't keep from licking my lips as I ran my eyes over each delineated muscle, every line, and ridge.

He noticed.

A faint smile, a little arrogant, a little proud, curled his lips. "Do you like what you see, Kitt?"

Meeting his eyes, I nodded.

"Would you like to touch me?"

"Yes."

"Then do it." He stood there so confidently, so comfortable in his nudity.

The silk lining of his suit coat rasped against my nipples as I took a step toward him, then another. Each rasp made my belly heat more, and I was already so hot, I wasn't certain if I could handle much more. But there was no way I was going to turn down the chance to touch him.

Smoothing a hand down his right pectoral, I sucked in a breath. The light dusting of hair on his chest added to the sheer masculinity of him, and I couldn't resist the urge to curl my fingers in, tug a little.

Aeric grunted.

I looked up at him. "Is that..."

"I like it. I don't think there's anything you'll do I won't like." A hard breath shuddered out of him, seeming to make his entire body vibrate. "But whatever you want to do, you need to do it, because the longer I look at you, the longer you stare at me like that...the more I want to bend you over the table and fuck you until you're screaming my name."

My knees wobbled, and it was just as much instinct that had me bracing my hand on his chest as the need to touch. Needing to balance myself, I looked at him and gulped. "If you keep saying things like that, I'm going to melt."

"You'll melt anyway. I can't wait. I want that pussy melting and soft against my mouth, around my dick. So, if you want to touch..." He took one of my hands and guided it lower. "Do it. I'd love to feel your touch here."

I whimpered as he guided my hand to his cock, folding my fingers around him.

Sensory memory hit hard, and I remembered being on my knees, licking and sucking and stroking with my tongue.

"I know what you're thinking about. Do you remember how I taste?"

"Yes." I couldn't quite keep the waver from my voice.

"Do you want to go down on me again?"

I nodded as an ache pulsed between my thighs.

He bent down, sweeping something up from the floor, then he came for me. I sucked in a breath as he did the same with me —sweeping me up. Gaping at him, I clung to his shoulders as he carried me through the house, down the hall to the guest wing where his bedroom was located.

Heart hammering in my chest, I closed my eyes.

Seconds passed. Just seconds. It felt like less than that and lifetimes, all at once. Before I'd so much as gathered myself, he lowered me to the ground, and I opened my eyes to look around.

We were in the sitting area of his room, sheer drapes drawn over the window overlooking the garden. Expression inscrutable, he lowered himself onto the wide, plush chair there, legs spread, body slumped in a negligent, sexy sprawl.

"Do it, then. Suck my cock, Kitt."

Mouth dry, I took one step closer, then another, bumping into the smooth material of the chair. Under the fabric of the coat, I felt overheated, sweat breaking out along my brow and neckline. "I want to take this off."

Aeric let his eyes roam over me with lazy abandon. "Why?"

"I'm hot."

A smile tugging at his lips, he nodded. "Go ahead."

I stripped out of it, telling myself not to be self-conscious. As I went to kneel, he stopped me, one hand lifted. "Wait."

Heart hammering, I stared at him.

Aeric's eyes met mine, and he lifted his other hand, opening it so that a length of crumpled red silk spilled out. His tie.

"I want to tie your hands behind your back."

"Tie my..." Apprehension curled inside me even as curiosity flickered. "Why?"

"Because." That burning gaze slid down leisurely, landing on the triangle of curls between my thighs. "You're a dirty girl, Kitt. The last time you sucked me off, you started playing with your pussy. I don't want you doing that this time. You're already on the verge of coming, and I want to decide when you come."

My knees threatened to buckle, so I locked them. "Who decides when you come?"

He smiled at me, a wide, wicked flash of his teeth. "I do."

"That's not fair."

"Neither is life."

Pursing my lips, I stared him down, aware he was letting me make the decision, although we both already knew I'd already decided. Still...

"Can I tie you up? I mean...if we ever do this again?"

"I've never let a woman tie me up." He cocked his head, a thoughtful look in his eyes.

"Have you let a man?"

The question escaped before I could stop it, and immediately, I wished the words back, but it was too late.

A laugh burst out of him, and he slid a hand down his torso, cupping his sac, squeezing and tugging. Hypnotized, I stared.

So intrigued by how his hand moved on his body, I barely even heard his response at first.

"No, *cher*. That's not my cuppa, as they say. Although I suspect you're entirely open to such experimentation. I think you'd enjoy having a woman join you and a lover. Have you ever played such games, Kitt?"

Cheeks flaming, I shook my head. I'd never even thought about it.

But under the weight of his gaze, I realized he wasn't wrong. And the faint curl to his lips told me he knew exactly what I was thinking. He stroked his tongue along his lower lip, then said, "I'll tell you what, Kitt. If we ever do this again, I will let you tie me up...provided you tell me a fantasy of yours."

"You're very good at guessing them."

"It's more enticing when you tell me." He lifted a hand and twirled his finger. "Turn around. I'm ready to feel that mouth on my cock."

I did so, and moments later, gave the tie a tug. It was snug but not tight, going from my wrists up several inches.

"If you pull on the loose ends with enough force, it will come loose," he said as I continued to stand there. "Turn around now, Kitt, before I lose patience and order you onto your knees."

Somehow, I knew he wasn't talking about having me go down on him, either.

I turned slowly, nervous, but the look in his eyes filled me with a weird, heady sort of elated power. His mouth parted as he raked me up and down with a look.

"Those tits are perfect," he rasped, fisting his cock as he stared. "Being bound just makes them even more beautiful. Kneel, Kit."

I did so, gingerly, the balance I'd learned through years of yoga coming in handy.

He pumped his penis harder, the dark-colored head disappearing inside his fist only to jut back out at me, rude and demanding.

I licked my lips.

His breath came harder, and he said, "Are you thinking about licking me?"

"Yes."

He stopped working his cock and shot out a hand, fisting it in my hair. "Show me, then." Urging me closer, he guided me in, using one hand to hold his dick steady, the other on my neck.

The ache between my thighs was so intense, I had to squeeze my legs together. I moaned as I opened and took him inside.

So did he, bringing his free hand up and then he had my head bracketed between his hands as he thrust up into my mouth.

I gagged at first.

"Just breathe, Kitt...breathe in through your nose...that's it. Relax your throat. That's it...fuck, you're good at this. Can you take more...*ah, fuck!*"

He moved then, pulling me off, and I glared at him, but all he did was stand and guide me back to him, a stark look to his features. "Open up for me, *cher*. Let me fuck that pretty mouth. I'm going to come down your throat. You've got me so hot, I can't think straight. I'll come, then I'll take care of you..."

He devolved into French as I obeyed him. I only randomly picked up a phrase here and there, including something along the lines of *I'm going to come so hard.*

Need was a scream inside me, and I jerked at the restraint

around my wrist, completely forgetting that he'd told me how to undo it. Yet the frustration of not being able to touch him the way I wanted added to the throbbing fire between my thighs.

"Kitt!"

He gripped my head and forced me to be still, rocking deeper, then deeper still until I felt the head of his cock at the very back of my throat. I couldn't breathe, but in that moment, I didn't care because he started to shudder, coming hard and fast.

Reflexively, I jerked, my nails biting into my palms while over me, he talked, a mix of English, German, and French that I could only partly understand. "That's it...a bit more...pretty little..."

Then he pulled away, and I swayed, panting for air and off balance.

He bent and caught me, hoisting me up, then turning.

Dots danced in front of my eyes as he put me on the chair, my hands still bound behind my back. Trying to focus on his face, I stared, but everything seemed to be moving.

I figured out why just in time to suck in a deep breath, the first I'd taken in several minutes.

Aeric had knelt behind me, taken my ass in his hands, and before I could make a sound, he shoved his face against my pussy, like he wanted to devour me.

And that was exactly what he did.

HOURS LATER, muscles loose and lax, my mind blissfully blank, I lay on my belly, half dozing.

When Aeric pressed his mouth to my spine, I didn't stir. Not at first.

But then he kept at it, and by the time he'd reached the dip just above my butt, I was awake and clutching at the sheets, my face already hot and heart pounding hard.

"Awake now?" he murmured, shifting on the bed behind me.

It was his bed.

We hadn't left it for anything more than get a bite to eat or grab a quick shower.

Well, *I* hadn't.

Casting a look back over my shoulder, I saw that Aeric was dressed. Partly, at least, in a pair of jeans with his erection straining at the denim. The fabric was soft and worn, rubbing against my thighs as he pulled me up onto my knees.

"I'm not done with you yet." He reached around and cupped my chin, bringing my face around to meet his as he brought his mouth down in a deep, drugging kiss, tongue thrusting past my lips demandingly.

He had me back on my knees moments later, several pillows from the couch wedged under me, their sturdier presence supporting me better than regular bed pillows would. He'd bound my hands together with the tie again, but in front of me this time, guiding them down until they were tucked into the notch of my thighs. Biting my lip, I shot him a look, but I wasn't quite so nervous as he guided me down until I was face down with my butt lifted for him.

He bent down and licked me, then pressed an open-mouthed kiss to my pussy that brought a warbling cry to my lips, muffled against the mattress. It ended in a shocked cry as he brought the flat of his hand down on my right butt cheek.

I jerked in surprise, my flesh burning and a deep, wanton craving for more twisted my belly into knots.

"More?" he muttered against my sensitive flesh.

"Please..." I rolled against him as best as I could, instinctively offering myself for just that—*more*.

He swatted the other cheek and stabbed his tongue inside me, then asked again. "Again?"

"Yes, damn it!"

He chuckled, then told me, "Let me know if you want to stop."

Stopping was the last thing on my mind, and he could likely tell as I thrust myself demandingly against him, seeking both his mouth and the flat of his hand, and he gave me both. Soon, my throat was raw from begging and crying out, and the skin of my buttocks was sensitive, and I needed to come so bad every other word out of my mouth was *please*.

But instead of letting me come, he stopped.

I moaned and rocked, not even able to form words now, the need was so strong.

Aeric pushed his hand into my hair and tugged, slowly drawing up. He'd moved so he could peer into my eyes, and the pale glitter of his gray eyes as he watched me would have left me shaken if I could have thought past my need to come.

"What are you willing to let me do to you?" he asked, trailing one hand down my neck, over the inner curve of my right breast, pausing to circle the nipple before continuing onward until he reached the wet folds between my thighs.

"I..." The band around my chest was so tight, it took a concentrated effort to breathe. "What exactly are you wanting to do? I don't think I'm up for exhibitionism or anything like that."

A deep, rumbling chuckle echoed from his chest, momentarily lightening the intense expression on his face. But it returned quickly, and he traced a lazy circle over my clitoris before dipping his fingers into my pussy. "I told you earlier what I wanted to do to you, Kitt. Bend you over and open your ass... teach you how to take me there."

His fingers slid farther back, and I gasped as they slicked over me, spreading the wetness of my pussy backward.

My mind went blank.

My body, though...well...

I whimpered and rocked into his touch.

He pressed against me with more intent this time. "What are you willing to let me do, Kitt? Fuck you here?"

The answer slid out with no conscious thought on my part, and my mind was still grappling with it as he urged me back down over the pillows, once more tucking my hands between my thighs. But this time, he pushed something into them. "I invaded your privacy earlier, Kitt. I imagine some people might be surprised to know you had a vibrating egg tucked away inside your nightstand. I wasn't. I was glad to find it."

I jolted when it clicked on, then moaned as he tucked the round, buzzing sex toy more firmly against my clit.

"Now..."

I caught my breath, nervous despite the rising hunger, but when he pressed against me, it was to fit his cock to my pussy. "We'll be taking this slow."

Then he thrust inside, filling me with one long, driving thrust that had my spine arching as he filled me completely.

"Fuck..." He rasped it out, long and low once he was fully seated. His balls slapped forward, striking my bound hands, and he withdrew just a bit before pushing back in. "You feel like perfection, Kitt."

He shuddered and withdrew, surging forward again and

again, his hands framing my hips. I felt every ridge of his cock, and he moved so slowly, then even slower still, pausing with just the head wedged inside before gliding back in an increment at a time.

I moaned and tried to move back on him, but his hold prevented it.

He let go of one hip and spanked me, harder than before, shifting his other hand and bracing it in the middle of my lower back. "Be still, Kitt...you're just going to take it. Take *me*..."

I sensed the movement behind me, then he was touching me again, pressing against the dark, tight opening of my ass, his fingers slick now. "Take *this*..."

Gasping, I froze as he pressed down. He didn't enter, though. Just the promise of it. Or the threat. The temptation. I couldn't decide.

"I found the lubricant you keep in your drawer too. I'd hope to find something else. A dildo, perhaps. I would have liked to spread your thighs wide and fuck you with that, perhaps with your hands tied over your head while you squirmed and whimpered...like that. Just like that. You want more?"

My skin felt tight and hot and small, and I didn't know if I could take much more sensation, and although his cock pulsed and throbbed inside me, he wasn't even *moving*.

No. His hips weren't. But other parts were. I shivered as he used one of his hands to push on my right butt cheek, exposing me...opening me.

He slicked his fingers over me again, then withdrew.

That brief pause let sanity return for a few brief seconds, but just a few and my body was already teetering on a precipice, craving the pleasure I knew he could give. When his fingers returned, I simply shivered. The egg pulsed and vibrated against my clit, and when his cock jerked inside me, I clamped down around him, my muscles clenching and milking instinctively.

The hand on my ass tightened. "Kitt..."

"Aeric..."

"Push down." He pressed against me, a blunt, thick finger probing at my ass.

Awash with sensation, I shivered and tightened around his cock, and he swatted my left butt cheek. "Push down, Kitt."

This time, I did.

I whimpered at the burning pain, and he flexed his hips, sending waves of sensation racing through me. He spanked me again, and he invaded me, pushing his finger inside my ass, then withdrawing before starting all over again, working lubricant deeper.

I shivered, caught between pain and pleasure, his cock pulsing, my pussy clenching, and everything in me waiting, wanting.

"Take more," he said throatily, twisting and screwing yet another finger deeper before retreating and starting all over again.

I felt another pinch of pain, but hovering so close to orgasm, I was more aware of the need to come than anything else.

He knew it too and began to thrust shallowly, only giving me half of his cock, while screwing his fingers into my anus, stretching me. It was too much, and not enough, and soon, I was pushing back on him, on both his cock and his penetrating fingers.

That pinch of pain deepened, but orgasm moved ever closer, and it was going to be glorious—

He stopped.

"No..."

"I'm not stopping, *cher*. Not unless you tell me. But you're on the edge, and that's the perfect time..."

I didn't have to ask what he meant.

He pressed the head of his cock against my anus.

I tensed.

"Easy...we'll do this slow...unless you want me to stop."

I had a chance to tell him right there. The thick, huge weight of him burned, pressing against me, but my throat wouldn't relax enough for me to say a single word. My entire body trembled, and the whisper of pain hovered, but just beyond that whisper lay a roaring storm, and I wanted to throw myself into it.

"Kitt?"

"Don't stop." Arching my spine, I pushed down like he'd instructed earlier.

He groaned and lapsed into French again, but the thrum of blood screaming in my ears was too loud for me to hear him, much less translate. He sank inside, and that whisper of pain became much, much more.

Just when I thought I couldn't take it, he eased away, settling into a coaxing, teasing rhythm. My fingers were slippery on the egg, and my clit was swollen, so engorged, so sensitive, the vibrations from the toy were almost too much, but I didn't dare stop.

He spanked my right cheek lightly, and I sobbed, convulsing under him as I started to come.

"Bad girl," he said, even as he smoothed his hand over my hip, then began to rock against me, working deeper, inch by slow inch.

Caught up in the climax, I moaned and rolled my hips, seeking more, and something inside unclenched. Then he was moving easier, hands gripping me to hold me in place as he impaled me on his cock.

"That's it...take more," he said. "As much as you can...sweet..."

He caught me by my shoulder and pulled me up. I cried out as the movement forced me more completely down on him, but before it became too much, he wrapped his arm around my waist to support me. Mind spinning, I sank back into his hard, muscled form, his chest and thighs aligned to me, molding me.

There was no time to acclimate to the new change because he cupped my right breast and tugged on my nipple, hard, twisting and teasing as I writhed, rocked, and bounced on him, desperate for a relief I didn't know how to find.

But he knew how to give it.

He slid his left hand down my torso, pulled the egg from my hands, and plunged two fingers inside me.

"You're so wet...Kitt, I think you'll burn me alive, you're so hot and wet... are you ready for more now?"

"Yes. Aeric...please."

His powerful thighs flexed. His arm tightened around my waist.

His toying fingers left me, and I moaned in dismay, but all he did was tug on the tie, freeing my wrists. "Play with that pretty pussy, Kitt. Fuck yourself with your fingers while I fuck this delightful ass."

He gripped me close, holding me in a way that let him lift me as he opened me—spreading the cheeks of my butt wider for his invasion. My head fell back against his shoulder.

"Do what I said, Kitt, before I bend you back over and spank you."

I did, thrusting my fingers inside. I gasped, shocked. "I...I feel you, Aeric."

He didn't respond, his breathing coming harder and faster. Mine was too.

I was going to dissolve. Or explode. Something. He moved faster and faster, and some part of me was aware that this was too much—it hurt, but the pleasure outweighed the pain, and I chased the knife-sharp edge with Aeric.

He moved suddenly, pushing me face down again, and I sobbed as he came into me, deeper, harder.

"Too much...sorry, *cher*...fuck, that's good...is that better?"

"Don't stop!" I begged, reaching back and desperately clinging to his wrist.

He twisted out of my grasp and caught mine instead, shoving it to the small of my back. "Hot, wild little thing...come for me, damn you, before you kill us both."

He spanked me, three times, hard and fast.

I came.

It was brutal and rough, and for a few seconds, everything went a little dark.

EIGHTEEN

AERIC

She was still sleeping when I climbed from bed just after seven the next morning.

The whole fucking day had been exhausting. We'd spent far longer at the police station than I'd realized, then I'd spent far longer wrapped up in her, losing myself in her.

Guilt tugged at me now.

It had been coming up on six when we'd gotten to the house, and after making all the calls I could think to make, logically, there had been nothing else we could do.

I'd wanted to *not think,* and after receiving one final call from the chancellor, I'd breathed a little easier. The Minister of Youth for the city-state of Berlin would keep the children with her. She had state-assigned security because of her job, and she'd take the next few days off.

The chancellor assured me that matters would be resolved within that time. She'd also told me that Mila Kelly, the woman who'd be caring for Josef and Karol had been close friends with Anne and Karl and knew the children. She had children of her own, and the families spent a fair amount of time together.

I'd gone to tell Kitt, knowing she'd be relieved, but she'd looked at me, wide-eyed, her mouth trembling as she told me she didn't want to think.

My own desire for the same had risen. Standing so close to her had played havoc on my nerves, driving me to insanity and stupidity.

But I had no regrets.

Guilt, perhaps, thinking of my sister, my niece, and nephew, and Karl.

But I didn't regret feeling Kitt's soft body submit and yield, nor did I regret feeling her curled against me as we slept.

It had been comfort, something we'd both needed.

Just as she now needed rest. Shadows lay like bruises under her eyes as I stood by the bed, pulling a shirt on and quickly buttoning it. Guillermo had texted a half hour ago with news.

One of the best lawyers in Germany had been hired by my parents—a total shark, he'd told me. Guillermo loved Americanisms.

I was fine with a shark if that was what we required to get my niece and nephew into my custody. Apparently, Anne and Karl *had* talked to my parents about custody of the children should something happen to them—they had wanted me to be their guardian. The discussion had taken place at a dinner, and both of my parents' aides had been present as well as several of my father's advisers. Guillermo assured me that would facilitate matters, and the lawyer was busy making phone calls and tying things up neatly, but I could expect to hear from him sometime this afternoon.

I wished he'd said this morning, because if he had, it would have given me an excuse to put off a duty I hadn't been able to attend to yesterday after everything went to hell.

I had to go to the morgue and see my sister and Karl.

It was the very last thing I wanted to do.

In her sleep, Kitt sighed and rolled over onto her belly, the sheets tangling lower on her spine. In the cool air-conditioned room, she shivered.

Catching the blankets we'd kicked off, I caught them and drew them over her shoulders.

I was glad she still slept. If she'd asked where I was going, I would have likely told her.

And she would have offered to come with me.

As foolish as I'd found myself being around her, I would have accepted...just as I would have accepted whatever comfort she'd offer, just as I would have offered her whatever comfort she needed.

She'd slid right under my skin, and I couldn't quite figure out how. The circumstances, surely. It had to be that. No woman had ever gotten to me like this.

"IT'S HER," I told Feidelberg without lifting my eyes from her face.

To his credit, the man didn't ask if I was sure. At my request, we'd taken care of Karl first, and I'd steeled myself to see my sister, fearing she'd look as destroyed as he had. They'd clearly cleaned him up, and I knew they'd work harder still on him, but the bullet had gone in above his right eyebrow, a surprisingly small, neat hole, but a hole nonetheless.

Thanks to the talk with the officers the day before, I knew Anne had been shot from behind, but I couldn't for the life of me remember if they'd said where.

But her lovely face was...untouched, and I'd breathed out a sigh of relief.

"Where was she shot?" I heard myself asking.

"In the back. The bullet entered her heart and killed her instantly." Feidelberg's gruff voice was surprisingly gentle. "She wouldn't have felt any pain. Neither of them did."

"Thank you."

"I'm sorry, Your Highness." Guillermo stood with me as we looked down at Anne.

She didn't look like she was sleeping.

That tired, trite line so easily passed out at funerals had never impressed me, and I hoped nobody tried to use it when we had her memorial, then laid her to rest.

My sweet, beautiful little sister looked dead, and it was so obscenely wrong, I couldn't wrap my mind around it.

Guillermo lingered a few steps away, and although I knew he wanted only to help, I needed privacy. Without looking at him or Feidelberg, I moved closer, so close that I brushed the edge of the metal table where she lay. "I need a few minutes alone, please."

Neither of them spoke as they left us alone.

After the door shut, I reached up and brushed my hand down Anne's dark, silken hair, as soft as ever. Our mother had always loved her hair. "This is going to break her heart, Anne. It's going to break all our hearts."

My eyes burned, but I blinked them clear. I hadn't shed a tear since I'd been a very young child. I'd cry for my sister. I knew I would. But not here. Not now.

"I'll take care of Josef and Karol, love. I'll make sure they're happy, and they'll always remember how you loved them. I'll even make sure they continue doing chores if that's such an important thing to you."

There must have been some part of the very young child I'd once been still left inside me because the urge to beg her to wake up came over me.

"I love you." Giving her hair one last stroke, I turned and walked out.

Out in the hall, Feidelberg and Lieberman waited. "Have you learned anything yet?"

Lieberman looked at his partner. He was the quieter of the two, although I'd seen the intelligence shining in his eyes.

Feidelberg cleared his throat. "It's still early yet, Your Highness. We're looking at all angles, though, I assure you. We will find who did this."

I leveled my eyes on him, the urge to demand he work faster, harder, boiling up my throat.

He inclined his head, as if he was already prepared for what I had to say.

I held back, though, giving each of them a nod and turning on my heel.

I wanted to get out of this place that smelled of sanitizer and death.

⸻

I WALKED into the house and found it smelling of sanitizer and life. The lemony smell was too close to whatever cleanser they used at the morgue, and immediately, I went to the nearest windows, wrenching each of them open, my chest tight, lungs starved for air.

"Aeric?"

The sound of my name on her lips was so strangely soothing, even if it was extremely inappropriate. The lemony scent still swirled in my head, and the memory of Anne on the table at the morgue clamped down on me like a vice.

As Kitt drew nearer, I wanted nothing more than to turn around and grab her, bury my face in her neck and cling tight, until the scents faded, the memory faded.

Because I was too tempted, because such thoughts were too dangerous for me, I shoved them aside, casting for something, anything to say that would put much needed distance between us.

"Do you have any idea how out of line it is for you to call me *Aeric* as you do?"

There was no response.

Annoyed by the silence, I turned away from the window, braving the lemony scent and glared at her. "No answer?"

"I'm not sure what you want me to say," she said finally. "I don't live in Monaco. I didn't grow up in a country that recognizes royalty. On top of that, it's kind of weird for me to think of you as *your highness* or *Prince Aeric* after last night."

Her cheeks went pink as she tossed that out, but her chin went up as well.

When I didn't respond, she mockingly said, "No answer?"

Irritated, I turned back to the window. "Why does it smell like a lemon factory exploded?"

"I told you that a cleaning crew came in a couple times a week." She cleared her throat. "Today was their scheduled day. I completely forgot, and once they were here, it seemed rude to cancel, but I told them to call before they come again since you might want to stop the service or at least spread it out more for the time being."

I waved a hand. "The cleaning service isn't an issue. They can continue at their regular schedule. But no more lemon cleansers. I hate the smell."

I hadn't until today. But I doubted I'd ever smell lemon again without seeing Anne on that table.

"I'll pass the message on. I...um...are you okay?"

I bit back the retort that rose instinctively. Yes, I needed distance, but now that Anne was in my head again, being the rude bastard didn't come as easy as it had just seconds ago.

Anne wouldn't think well of me for it, not if she was as close to Kitt as I believed she likely had been.

"Rough morning, Ms. Bocho. I just need—"

The doorbell rang.

I pushed up from the windowsill and closed my eyes as she said, "I'm sorry. Excuse me while I get that."

I didn't turn from the window and watch her go, nor did I turn when she reentered, even when she said, "There's a man here to see you, sir. Herr Gunther Haas. He says he's a lawyer hired by your family to help with the children. Shall I let him in?"

"He's here to help with Josef and Karol, isn't he?"

I heard her annoyed huff, but she said nothing. A moment later, she said, "Herr Haas, he's in here."

I turned, linking my hands behind my back as a tall, thin man, likely in his early forties came striding in, carrying a briefcase in one hand. He stopped a few feet away and gave a polite nod. "Your Highness. I'm Gunther Haas. I'm terribly sorry to be meeting you under such awful circumstances, but I'm going to do everything in my power to alleviate these current difficulties promptly."

"Thank you, Herr Haas." I gestured to the couch. "Will you sit?"

He hesitated and glanced at Kitt before looking back at me, his expression grave. "Is there someplace more private where we can talk?"

Kitt had already slipped into the room, but stopped at his words, her mouth tightening in unhappiness.

I was too concerned about the look I'd seen from him, though, and I couldn't keep dwelling on her, couldn't keep letting these thoughts of her dominate my mind.

It was all likely because of the emotional upheaval we were going through together. While it was understandable, certainly, it couldn't be healthy to keep indulging as we had been.

"Of course. My sister's library is just down the hall." I looked at Kitt. "Kitt, would you..." I'd been about to ask her to bring tea, but the way her brows shot up made me decide against it. "Excuse us? Please?"

"Of course, *Aeric*," she said with effusive sweetness. "I was in the middle of things earlier, and I need to get back to them."

I could feel the lawyer watching me, so I refused to stare after her as she left, despite the strong urge to do so. "This way, Herr Haas."

"Gunther, please," he insisted as we started down the hall in the opposite direction that Kitt had gone. "Am I correct in assuming that is Kitt Bocho, the children's nanny?"

"Au pair," I corrected. "She was brought in from America almost two years ago."

"That's a bit unusual," he commented as I gestured for him to enter the library. "Typical au pair contracts last a year."

The soft blues of Anne's study washed over me, along with the scent of lavender. She'd always loved lavender. Nothing in here smelled of lemon, and I breathed in, the chaos in my head easing a fraction.

Aware of Haas's close appraisal, I shifted my attention to him and gestured for him to have a seat. I took the armchair near the window and tried not to think about how often my sister must have sat here, on her laptop or phone, or simply reading a book.

Aware Haas seemed to want some sort of response, I thought back to what Kitt had said. "Ms. Bocho and my sister seemed rather close, and the children adore her. Anne made some calls and was able to get Kitt's contract extended another year. I believe they were going to hire her on as a full-time nanny."

"That is most definitely unusual," Haas said.

His tone had me narrowing my eyes. "Is it?"

"As I said, families tend to hire au pairs only for a year."

I waved the comment off. "My sister doesn't—" I closed my eyes for a moment. "She didn't care for what others *tended* to do. She wasn't one to buck the rules simply for the sake of doing so, but I've seen Ms. Bocho with the children. They are close. I've talked with my mother, and Anne did nothing but sing her praises and not just because of my niece and nephew, either. Anne truly loved her. It's no surprise to me that she pulled a few strings to keep Ms. Bocho on longer."

"Hmm." He tugged off the thin wire spectacles he wore and cleaned the lenses, looking at me with a decidedly near-sighted look, squinting slightly to focus on my face until he once more settled the glasses back on his nose. "And how was the relationship between Ms. Bocho and Mr. Weiss?"

"She got along well with him." Shrugging, I shifted in the chair, fighting the impatience rising inside me. "She—" I stopped abruptly and narrowed a closer look on him, apprehension rising. "Why do you ask?"

He flicked a look at the closed door before responding. "There's no discreet way to put this, Your Highness, so I'll simply be blunt. During the course of the investigation, it's come up that there is a possibility Mr. Weiss was engaged in an affair, and it's uncertain whether this matter might somehow connect to the murders of both him and your sister." He paused briefly before continuing. "The primary reason the children are being held in protective custody, for the time being, is because there are concerns that the woman he was involved with was Kitt Bocho."

The words didn't make sense. Staring at him, I waited for him to elaborate because there simply had to be more.

But he said nothing.

As the silence stretched out, becoming heavy and strained, I cleared my throat. "I'm sorry. Can you repeat that?"

"The cops believe your brother-in-law might have been sleeping with Ms. Bocho," he said, delivering the words in a matter-of-fact voice, as if this was a simple fact that everybody already knew. "It's quite common. She's young and attractive—"

Rising, I stared down my nose at him. "My sister is hardly an ugly old crone," I said coldly, cutting him off.

"I...Your Highness, of course. Forgive me, I never meant to imply otherwise." He stood as well, lowering his head and folding his hands meekly in front of him. "It's simply...well, these young women often come to foreign countries looking for all sorts of new experiences, and sometimes, they look for more than just a cultural exchange."

His bluntness from moments earlier had disappeared, and he no longer looked at me straight on, still staring at the floor.

It didn't matter. I was enraged, a deep well of fury rising within. It had already been there, lingering, barely banked, for hours upon hours, and I'd smothered it because I had other priorities.

Those simmering embers would no longer be smothered, having new life breathed into them. Still, I managed to keep a relatively flat tone as I demanded, "What proof is there of this...affair?"

"The police haven't shared that much of the investigation with me, Your Highness. They're being very quiet about everything, given the gravity of the murders, and their concern for the safety of your niece and nephew."

"Their safety." A hard laugh burst out. "They cannot possibly suspect Kitt if they believe the children are in danger. She'd open a vein before she harmed them."

He shifted uncomfortably and looked at me once more. "Perhaps that is the reason."

"Excuse me?"

"I'm merely speculating, but if your sister discovered the affair, she'd end Ms. Bocho's employment, and she'd have to return to America, leaving the children. She could have arranged this, thinking that she'd then stay on to care for the children."

"That's preposterous."

He didn't blink. "She's still here, isn't she?"

"It's a ridiculous idea." But I heard her voice.

I'll be there for the children as long as you need me to be, as long as they need me.

We can both agree it's best I stay with the children.

What about the children?

Logic suggested that her questions, her concern for the children was expected, desired even, and of course, it was. But now that Haas had put forth this dark suggestion, everything she'd said took on a more sinister aspect.

Aware I'd been quiet too long, I sat and blanked my features. "This entire idea is nonsense," I said even as images and ideas festered and bloomed in my mind like a poisonous mutant flower. "What are the plans to get the children back into my custody? My mother tells me it was made very clear to her, in front of witnesses, that Anne and Karl both wanted me to be their guardian should the need ever arise."

"Well..." His eyes drifted to the door.

"We're not discussing Ms. Bocho," I said icily. "We're discussing the children."

With a stiff nod, he began to speak.

And I did my damnedest to listen, although I already knew I'd have to have Guillermo speak with him and make certain I'd missed nothing important.

THE HOUSE WAS PRETERNATURALLY quiet as I closed the door behind Haas.

No music played.

No children laughed.

Several windows had been opened, and through them, I could hear the soft music of birds singing in the trees, the wind rustling the leaves, but that was it.

Thankfully, the scent of lemon cleanser had faded. It was still there, but it no longer overpowered. Swallowing the bile that rose inside my throat, I stood in the main hall, waiting for

Kitt to appear, but after several minutes passed and I remained alone, I blew out a slow breath.

It did nothing to calm my raging nerves.

Don't be a fool about this, I told myself. *Anne wasn't an idiot. She would have known if Karl was fucking around on her. Kitt hardly seems the seductress.*

Even as I thought it, images, memories—and lust—burned through me. There was no logical reason for the way I'd reacted to her. I could almost imagine she'd cast a spell on me if I was one to believe in such. But I'd been the one to move on her, each time. There was no denying that.

Not that she'd resisted.

A dull throbbing settled at the base of my skull, but I willed myself not to think about it.

I'd talk to Kitt, clear this up. Forcing my stiff legs into motion seemed harder than it should have been, all my muscles locked tight. Wherever I found her, maybe what I'd do first was fuck her, rid myself of this toxic anger. Just thinking of it made the muscles unclench while blood started to pool in my groin.

That was definitely the ideal plan, I decided. It was nonsense for somebody to think that Kitt had been involved with Karl. She didn't have what it took to carry on such a ruse under my sister's nose. I had a hard time believing Karl would do such a thing to Anne as well. He'd always seemed so besotted with her.

The anger started to ease as I searched the lower level of the house for her. I was unsuccessful and started up the main stairs to the second level where the family's bedrooms were located. I almost called out to her, but the odd hush of the house silenced me at the last moment as memories of Anne on the slab at the morgue swam back up.

That was all it took to put me back on edge.

What were they doing to find her killer?

Rambling about a woman my sister had clearly adored and implicating her as being connected somehow?

It was absurd.

Anger welled up again, muscles tightening as I found both Karol's and Josef's rooms empty.

Acid, bitter and sharp rose up to choke me, and I clenched my hands into fists.

Frowning, I moved on down the hall to where Karl and Anne had slept.

It, too, was empty, and the quiet gloom threatened to swallow me whole. Backing away quickly, I turned on my heel and strode down the hall to the only remaining room on this floor.

Karl's library. He had an office downstairs, and although the room on this floor did hold some books, Anne had confided in me once that this was more of a man-cave than a library. I'd smirked at the idea, but the pool table, mini-bar, top-flight gaming computer, big screen TV, low, wide couch, all of it was clearly designed for entertainment, and the décor was decidedly masculine. As I drew nearer, I saw light slanting through the door and heard rustling.

I stepped into the doorway, thinking I'd find her cleaning.

She had a fire safe open on the pool table.

"What in the hell are you doing?" I demanded.

She jerked her head up, her face going white as her eyes widened.

"I asked you what you were doing," I bit off. The guilty expression on her face tore into me, and I struggled to make sense of it. What was this?

"I..." She swallowed and looked around. Papers were strewn all over the pool table, and it was clear that whatever she had been doing, she'd been doing it for quite a while.

Striding over to her, I grabbed the pages she held and jerked them from her grasp. "Did my brother-in-law leave his safe unlocked, Kitt?"

"No," she said quietly.

"Where did you find the key?" I shoved my free hand out, glancing at the pages, but my gaze strayed back to hers.

"He keeps it in his sock drawer."

"Odd that you'd know that...unless you're doing the laundry?" I snapped my fingers, waiting for the key.

Her hand trembled as she reached up. I saw it then, in plain sight, jutting from the lock.

"Leave it," I bit off. "I have to go through this mess you made. What were you doing, digging through Karl's private papers?"

She backed away, her hands moving to her waist to twist nervously, and she still wouldn't look at me.

"I..." She stopped and swallowed.

The silence stretched out, and I swore, flinging the papers down as paranoia and anger pushed back in, taking hold. And now it wasn't just *anger*. It was something else, something obscene. *Had* Karl put his hands on her?

The idea of somebody else touching her enraged me on a level I couldn't understand, disturbing me in a way I didn't want to consider, and it infuriated me more.

"You're hiding something."

She flinched at the sound of my voice, her lips thinning out. "What?"

A sneer curled my lips at the look of guilt in her eyes. "I didn't want to believe it."

"I...what?"

"The lawyer just left. Do you know what he told me?" I demanded. Without giving her a chance to respond, I continued. "Apparently, the children can't come back home because of *you*."

"Me?" Her eyes flew wide, her mouth falling open. "What do you mean?"

"Don't give me the innocent look now. We both know what you're hiding. And to think I was so pissed off he'd had the nerve to suggest it to me. I was angry *for* you." Blood pumping furiously with both rage and that insatiable hunger for her, I slashed a hand through the air. "But then I find you in here *sneaking* around. What are you looking for? Money? Did Karl slip you extra on the side?"

"What are you talking about?" The color had drained from her cheeks once more.

"Answer me!"

"I'm trying to!" she shouted. "But I don't know what you're asking me!"

"You've been sleeping with my sister's husband!" I spat it out like the bitter, ugly truth it was.

Her face went blank, and she stared at me uncomprehendingly.

Finally, she licked her lips and shook her head. "No."

It was a faint whisper of sound, barely audible.

That, combined with the stunned shock on her face, made me almost consider that maybe I was misreading things. But I steeled myself. She was in here, snooping for some reason, and I hadn't missed that guilt in her eyes.

"No? But it explains so much. You're in here digging where you have no right. You're nervous and guilty about something." I looked around the library at the mess. "And this."

"No." Again, her voice was weak, catching this time.

Turning my back, I refused to look at her.

"That...I've been trying to find custody papers or a will, *something*," she said, her voice rising.

I snorted, still not looking at her. "Surely that's nothing to be so nervous about. You could have simply said that. Get out, Kitt. You're no longer welcome in this house."

Silence slammed into the room, a heavy weight.

Turning, I stared at her. "Did you not hear me?"

"This...Aeric—"

"Arrogant American you may be, but you do *not* have the right to use my given name," I snarled. "*Sir*, if you're too proud to address me properly, but you will *not* call me by my given name, not after you betrayed my sister, not after the harm you've brought to my niece and nephew."

Tears rushed to her eyes.

Clenching a hand at my side, I ignored them. "You have fifteen minutes to gather your things—*only* your things—and get out of this house, and I suggest you start making plans to return to America immediately or I'll have your visa canceled."

"You can't." She swallowed, but this time, her chin went up, and she met my eyes squarely despite the tears, despite the trembling of her lips. "I have a permanent resident permit, *sir*. I have every right to stay here."

"Do you really think I can't make that disappear?" I said coolly. "Your time is running out. But if you'd like to be thrown out of here with nothing more than the clothes on your back... please...continue."

NINETEEN

KITT

WALKING BY HIM WAS ONE OF THE HARDEST THINGS I'D
ever done in my life.

I could feel the press of sobs inside, the agony of humiliation. This was my *home,* and I was being thrown out. No, I
didn't own the beautiful house through which I now walked,
and I had no legal claim on anything but the things I'd bought or
been given, but for almost two years, I'd lived here, and both
Anne and Karl had urged me to treat this place as if it *was*
home.

Now the man I'd given my virginity to was throwing me out,
after accusing me of sleeping with my employer, while
betraying my other employer, who had been the best friend I'd
ever had.

I felt the weight of his gaze with every step, but I didn't take
the main staircase, didn't run down it just to get away from him
that much quicker. I kept my steps measured and walked to the
smaller set at the end of the hall that would take me almost
directly to my room. I had just over ten minutes, and I had to get

my things because I had no doubt he'd throw me out. Perhaps physically. Or maybe he'd call the cops.

Neither option boded well, and if the cops really did believe I had something to do with Anne and Karl's death...

A hard breath, almost like a sob, escaped me before I could stop it. Wrenching open the door to the stairs, I started down, moving faster with each step until I was almost running.

I slipped just a little over halfway down and caught the handrail, my arm wrenching hard at the impact of catching my weight.

Would it really matter if you fell?

I tried to ignore the insidious little voice, that doubt, that demon that had haunted me for much of my life. It had been silent for several years now, after finding a place for myself in college, working with children at a daycare, then here in Germany with the Weiss family.

But now...

What would it matter if you fell? Bust your head open on that lovely Italian marble, and he can call for a quick clean up. He has men waiting right outside the house. They'll come in, look at you, and just make a few calls and it will be dealt with. Your life here is over anyway, and you have nothing back in America.

"No," I said to myself, forcing more strength into the word than I really felt. The other part, the part of me that had forced me to go on, always, shoved the thought aside.

Don't think like that. Don't. You promised Anne, remember? You promised you'd take care of the children, and even if you can't see them, you owe it to her to do something.

I'd found several things that I'd planned to show Aeric. None of it was what I'd hoped to find, but every last piece, all of it shoved into a battered manila envelope and folded down, had filled me with a sense of unease so acute, I still couldn't shake it.

The small notebook, roughly the size of a cellphone, had initials and phone numbers jotted on several pages, sums of figures on another. It was tucked into my back pocket while the envelope itself was still awkwardly folded and half-jutting out of my front pocket. As I headed down the hall, I listened for him and dared to dart a look up the stairwell.

I saw his shadow, but he hadn't started down yet, so I hurried to my room and grabbed the envelope. Swinging my duffle bag from the floor, I put the envelope in the inner zipped pocket and dumped the bag on the bed.

Part of me knew I should just give him all the information, but I had an awful fear that anything I told him now would be tainted by the rage he had burning inside.

Also...I didn't want to be left with nothing, no way to find answers.

From my dresser, I grabbed t-shirts from the kids and shoved them into the duffle. A music box Anne had given me caught my eye, and I spent a precious minute carefully wrapping it in several of the silly shirts from the family, then used a couple pairs of shoes to help wedge it in place before shoving jeans and more shirts in around it to protect it. More shirts, a hoodie, panties, everything I could until the bag was so full, I struggled to zip it.

There were entire bookshelves lining one wall, and I eyed them, feeling my heart break even more before turning my back on them to grab my backpack. The most important books were on the small shelf by my nightstand, and I grabbed those, pushing them into the backpack, along my iPad and Bluetooth keyboard.

Spying a few drawings from the kids, I folded them and tucked them inside another book, then put the book in as well. What else?

Helpless, I looked around the room. There was so much. Pictures of us in small frames sat on the wide window sill, and I lunged for them, gathering up all the smaller ones and rushing back to dump them on the bed, grab another shirt, wrap them as best I could before stowing them into the backpack.

Permanent resident permit. Passport. ID. Money.

I spun to get my purse, and my spine pricked, alerting me to his presence.

Aeric stood in the hallway, eyes glittering as he watched me. Averting my gaze, I grabbed my purse, then opened the drawer where I kept my passport. My permit, ID, credit cards, money, all of that was already in my purse, but I checked again. As I shoved the passport in there, I felt the car keys. Grabbing them, I pulled them out and dropped them on the floor. Spotting my phone next, I stared at it for a long moment. It didn't belong to me either. With regret, I turned away from where it sat charging on the nightstand.

Blowing out a heavy breath, I then hefted the duffel bag and my backpack. I had to fumble to get everything into place, and the weight of my backpack tugged relentlessly at my shoulders. I squared them, gave the room one last look, acutely aware of Aeric still watching.

Without looking at him, I turned left and cut through the kitchen to the mudroom and the side door. My heart ripped right down the middle as I walked away from the house where I'd first found any real happiness.

I didn't let myself look back.

Tears had started to fall, and there was no way I'd let him see me crying.

LESSONS LEARNED from Karl drove me to the nearest train station where I paid for a week's long rental to stow the duffel. He'd scolded me the first time the family took me out to learn more about the place that would be my home for the time being. We'd been in Mitte, Berlin's city center, on our way to the Tiergarten when he saw that I'd left my purse hanging loosely at my side, unzipped for anybody to pick through while I gawked at the old city around me.

Aren't pickpockets a problem in the States, Kitt?

Anne had always laughed at him, but eventually, it had become second nature. It wasn't smart to walk around the city with everything I carried hanging from my back or in a duffel at my side.

It would also be exhausting.

A reusable, collapsible shopping bag, neatly stowed inside a zip-up pouch with a small clip, hung from the zipper on my backpack, and I took it off, opening it and carefully transferring the picture frames into the bag. I stowed it on the top shelf of the locker, then added the books.

A few more shirts went next. I kept one shirt out and grabbed a pair of jeans and underwear from the duffel, pausing long enough to check the envelope once more.

It was exactly where I'd left it, and I could feel the little notebook in my back pocket too. I'd forgotten socks and every single toiletry I owned. But it was too late to worry about that now.

Throwing the clothing into the now empty backpack, I zipped the duffle, then pushed most of my credit cards, my bank book, and passport into a side pocket and closed it. After locking everything up, I stood and looked around.

I had no idea what to do next.

Heart full of dread, I reached for that book and opened it, skimming the information, turning each page slowly.

Stopping at one in particular, I read it again, name by name, although some were harder to read thanks to the heavy, scrawled scratches that had been used to mark out the letters and figures.

A series of letters—initials, I thought, next to rows of numbers.

Eighteen rows, I counted, and all but one were crossed out, each line getting harsher and more erratic.

Crammed down at the bottom were the letters KB and the number 23,000.

It had jumped out at me, almost obscenely.

Just last week, Karl had asked me what all I planned to do with the money they paid me. He'd teasingly asked if I was saving up to buy a fancy car or go on an exotic vacation. I'd laughed it off and told him that aside from the portion I paid every month on my college loans, I banked almost all the money, but I was starting to look at investing the funds.

Later, he'd approached me and asked, kindly, how much I had, if I didn't mind him asking. He was curious because he knew a number of investors who might be willing to help me out, but in order to know which one to talk to, he needed to know what kind of figures he was looking at.

I'd told him.

Roughly 23000 Euro. That was how much I'd had set aside

in my bank account after working for them for almost two years. I had few expenses, and they paid me better than the typical au pair was paid.

Twenty-three thousand euro. The initials *KB*.

I didn't know how to make sense of any of the information I'd collected, what any of it could mean.

But this...

"You know how to find out, Kitt," I told myself.

Blowing out a breath, I adjusted the crossbody strap of my purse, then shoved the book into my front hip pocket. Tears threatened, but I refused to give into them now.

I had to figure out the truth. It was all I had left.

TWENTY

AERIC

Standing in the doorway of Kitt's room, I rubbed the heel of my hand over my chest. It had been three days since I'd watched her walk down the drive, a backpack pulling at her shoulders while she lugged a heavy duffel bag at her side.

I'd told myself I'd call and make sure she'd actually left the country, but I hadn't done it.

Part of me was afraid she wouldn't, and I'd feel compelled to follow up on my threat to have her forced out. I was going to have enough difficulty looking at my niece and nephew again once I brought them home to pack up before we left for Monaco. I'd seen them briefly the night before, visiting the home of Berlin's Minister of Youth, Mila Kelly. It had been nearly impossible to leave them, but I'd done so.

In truth, I likely could have taken them with me to the airport—I doubted Mila Kelly would have stopped me. We could have flown straight to Monaco, and I could have cuddled the children. Not that I knew much about cuddling, but my mother did, surely. We could wait for the German authorities to solve the murder of my sister and brother-in-law while we dealt with the grim and necessary task of laying them to rest.

But it hadn't felt right.

Both Josef and Karol had been content enough with Mila. Chancellor Ava Neumann had been quite right about that. Mila Kelly had four-year-old twin boys, and both Conrad and Darrick had clearly managed to keep my niece and nephew distracted. I'd been surprised at just how easily they'd done so. Surprised, and a little dismayed, something that Mila had clearly seen.

Mila was an attractive woman with smooth ebony skin. At nearly six feet tall, she cut a very commanding figure. As the children played, she'd spoken to me in a low, calm voice, explaining that my niece and nephew were too young to easily understand the finality of death. Josef's grasp of it was more concrete than Karol's—she seemed to have already forgotten—but even Josef didn't fully understand yet.

That was why they so easily played with the two twins and Mila's big, bear-like husband, a man easily my height, but with a broad barrel chest, a big laugh, and gingery red hair that curled madly around his wide, friendly face. He spoke German with an Irish accent, an interesting combination if ever I'd heard one, and even with my foul mood, he'd managed to make me smile a time or two.

And the children had laughed and shrieked and played like nothing was wrong—right up until it was time for me to leave. Then they'd begged me to stay, and Karol had started to cry when I said I couldn't.

Even now, hours later, I felt sick with guilt.

It was for the best, I told myself.

I had enough to handle and worrying about how the children were processing the loss of their parents while I still struggled to find answers was more pressure than I needed to take on.

You could just take them and go, I told myself again. None of Mila's guards would dare stop me. There was diplomatic immunity, and there was being a prince. With Monaco and Germany being on good terms, nobody would want to risk threatening me.

But brotherly instincts held me here. I hadn't been able to protect Anne when she needed me most.

This, however, I could do this. I could push for answers, find a resolution.

"You're not finding much of one standing here and staring at her bed," I told myself, rubbing my hand over my eyes, slumped in the doorway.

I'd gone to the police again, but neither Feidelberg nor Lieberman had been available. After sitting for more than two hours, I'd given up and gone to the lawyer's office, but Haas had little news to offer me. Paperwork was being finalized. I could expect to have the children transferred into my custody by the middle of the following week, if not sooner.

He'd offered to arrange a visit between us, and I'd risen from the chair, giving him a bored look. *I've already seen them. Last night.*

I'd left while he was still talking, annoyed with him for reasons I couldn't entirely explain. He was simply doing his job after all.

"A job," I muttered.

That was what I needed to do—find something to occupy my mind before I went mad.

Eying the clutter and disarray of Kitt's room, I took a few steps inside, but immediately stopped. The faint scent of lavender and verbena that had clung to her hair still lingered. Setting my jaw, I backed out.

No, I wouldn't attempt to occupy my mind in here.

I'd do it elsewhere.

If I had to surround myself in her scent, I'd find myself replaying those last few minutes over and over in my head until I truly did go stark-raving mad.

AS I PROWLED through the house, I made a call to Guillermo.

"Can you arrange to have packing boxes and supplies delivered?"

"Of course, Your Highness. Shall I hire a moving company?"

"No." I stopped in the doorway of Karl's library, shoulders tensing as I remembered seeing Kitt standing behind the pool table, head bent as she went through the safe.

The key was on the dresser down in my room, lying right in the middle, a glinting reminder every morning I awoke.

"I'm going to start packing myself," I told my aide.

"Sir?"

"If I don't find something to occupy my mind, I'll go insane," I told him. "There's nothing else to do but start going through their things so I might as well do it."

Guillermo knew me well enough not to offer false comfort or suggestions he knew I didn't want, so after promising to take care of the matter, he hung up. The sun was fading to memory outside the windows, darkening the shadows of the room, so I flipped the switch and stepped inside, looking at the hap-hazardous stacks of pages lying about in seemingly random disarray.

Glaring at them so hard I wouldn't have been surprised if they caught on fire, I resisted the urge to grab every last stack, every last bit of paper, and carry everything down to the back-yard and light it on fire.

Rage burned inside me once more. At Kitt, at Karl, at Anne for being so blind. At Anne for dying. The rage sank its claws deeper and deeper until I was shaking with it and the temper threatened to rage out of control.

"Stop." I shoved off the wall and turned, striding out of the library and down the hall. Taking the stairs at a jog, I strode to my room and grabbed the key, then hunted through the house until I found a large plastic bin in the children's playroom. There were toys inside, and I dumped them on the floor with a mental note to tell Guillermo to find more of the bins because we'd need them for packing up the children's toys.

Back inside the library, I dropped the bin on the pool table and started grabbing stacks at random, dumping them next to the large plastic container.

Once I had everything collected, I shuffled the pages into a neater pile and began to go through it. Within a few minutes, I deduced one thing. My brother-in-law had been a packrat.

There were menus from restaurants, receipts, playbills, movie tickets, things that couldn't have held any value for him, but he'd kept them anyway. All of those, I moved into one stack while attempting to make sense of what remained.

A picture fell out of the stack, and I stopped, laying the pages down to pick up the picture.

A knot rose to my throat as I stared at the image.

It was Anne and Karl, his arms wrapped around her as he

held her close, her feet lifted off the ground. Their faces were close, foreheads touching as they stared at each other.

It was a familiar pose, tickling a memory at the back of my mind. Flipping the picture over, I looked at the back and saw the date.

Paris. Five-year anniversary.

I dropped the picture and shoved the heels of my hands against my eyes. That would have just been last summer. I wished I hadn't even seen the damn picture, but it was too late now, emblazoned on the backs of my eyelids.

They looked like they had at their wedding. Karl had told me that day that he was so in love with my sister, it made him stupid.

How did a man go from being so in love it made him stupid, to having an affair with the au pair?

I couldn't wrap my mind around it.

"Your Highness?"

The sound of Guillermo's voice had me tensing, and I turned to find him in the doorway, Bennett, another member of my security team, standing behind him.

Both of them carried oblong brown slabs of cardboard. Frowning, I beckoned for them to enter.

"We found a store that sells boxes and such just a few kilometers away," Guillermo said. "They were running low on supplies, but another delivery is expected tomorrow. This should be enough to get started with."

Both of them looked around, uncertain.

"Put them in the hall," I said gruffly, turning the picture face down and moving to join them.

The three of us stood there, an odd, awkward silence filling the air. Guillermo cleared his throat and asked, "If there is a lot of paperwork, I can find some file boxes. That would work better than boxes like this."

"Yes." With a nod, I turned off the light, no longer in the mood to go back inside the room, unwilling to see the picture of Anne, unwilling to face my memories of Kitt. "That's a fine idea."

He nodded and glanced over at Bennett, something unspoken passing between them. Bennett gave me a polite nod and left, while Guillermo lingered.

"Something is troubling you," he said quietly.

"My sister did just die," I pointed out.

"No." He shook his head slowly. "It's more than that, and losing Princess Anne is quite enough. But there's an even heavier shadow on you now. Is it the children? They are safe, I assure you. I've got—"

Waving him off, I said, "I know. Nagel is watching the minister's house tonight?"

"Yes." Guillermo crossed his hands at his back, his expression still troubled.

I managed a tight smile and waved him off. "Go on, get some rest. At least one of you go to the hotel and sleep. No reason for all of you to stay in that car and watch over from the street."

None of them would stay in the house. It was my own fault. When we'd been traveling to the house, I'd told them I'd want time alone, and they all took me at my word. Even now, they waited outside the house after cursory checks of the interior and exterior. One patrolled the backyard while two more watched the front. And I stayed inside alone.

Under most circumstances, I'd be pleased with the time to

myself, but no sooner had Guillermo and Bennett left than it felt like the walls of the house were closing in on me.

The house had never been so quiet.

Such a house should *never* be so quiet.

Behind me, the silence of Karl's library awaited, but I didn't return to it, or the mess that still needed to be dealt with. I walked down the hall, pausing in the doorway of first Karol's room, then Josef's, thinking of my niece and nephew, worrying for them, and fighting the guilt I couldn't banish.

How would I explain to them...?

The truth wasn't an option. It wasn't like I could say Kitt had been sneaking behind their mother's back and fucking their father, now could I?

Even *thinking* it felt wrong.

Stomach churning, I shoved off the door frame of Josef's room and headed for the staircase. By Anne's room, I stopped and walked inside, drawn despite my best intentions. The room smelled of orange blossoms, the fragrance she'd always loved. There were portraits and pieces of her life scattered all over the place. The tightness in my chest returned, stronger than ever.

I'd have to pack up every picture, all the jewelry, every precious thing that the children might want.

Guillermo's voice came back to me, reminding me that I didn't have to do this myself, but there was no way I could turn this task off to somebody else. Anne had been my sister, and this was the last thing I could do for her.

Feeling helpless, I wandered around the room. A picture on the bureau caught my eye, and I stopped, picking it up. It was Kitt, the children, and Anne. I suspected Karl was on the other side of the camera. He'd always been fond of photography.

Anne was holding Josef and laughing into the camera's

viewfinder while Kitt made faces at Karol, who eagerly played along and did the same.

Just looking at the picture made a knot settle in my throat.

Walking over to the bed, I sat down, still clutching the frame.

"I don't even understand how any of this is happening, Anne."

But the dark-haired woman in the frame didn't answer.

TWENTY-ONE

KITT

For the past few days, I'd been staying at a hostel close to the city center, but far enough away from the police stations that I felt mostly secure. The hostel owner took cash and promised me I'd be safe at her place, giving me a sympathetic look.

The second day I was there, she'd brushed my hand and told me that if there was anything she could do to help me in my situation, all I had to do was ask, all the while promising my presence there was completely confidential. It wasn't until later that afternoon that I realized she must think I was fleeing an abusive boyfriend or something. That only made me feel even worse, but I couldn't exactly tell her I was hiding out from the Crown Prince of Monaco and maybe the police because they thought I'd had an affair with the prince's brother-in-law and maybe, just maybe, was involved in the murder of Monaco's Princess Anne and her husband.

That wouldn't go over well.

Even though the hostel was clean and well-cared for and only cost 25€, I'd woken up feeling uneasy that morning. I even knew why. Three backpackers, roughly my age and American, had checked in the night before. One of them had overheard me talking to a Canadian couple, two recently married college students who were spending the summer traveling Europe.

After hearing me speak English and realizing I was alone, they'd done little more than hassle me. The owner of the hostel was off, and the man covering the desk had spent most of the evening with his nose in a book. While I knew I could have asked that the police be called, I was reluctant to draw that much attention to myself, so I'd just gone to my assigned unit, one of the few same-sex ones available.

They'd come downstairs while I was pouring myself a to-go cup of coffee, hoping to escape their notice. One of them had barred the doorway, only stepping aside after another guest at the hostel had called him on it. When they'd tried to follow me, that same guest, as well as a friend had blocked them.

My stomach was uneasy at the idea of having to go back to the hostel later that day, even for a little while. Aside from the bag still locked away at the train station, everything I owned in the world was stowed in a locker back at the hostel. I couldn't leave without it.

Determined not to think about it for the time being, I went over my plan in my head.

I'd been putting this off, but I couldn't do it any longer. I had to find out if I was right about Karl. Despite my need for answers, I hadn't used my ATM card or checked my account online, because if I was right, I'd need to know more, and I couldn't put it off any longer. Wallowing in despair and self-pity could only fill up so much time.

It was a long trip. Normally traveling from Mitte to Charlottenburg via the train was a fast jaunt, but I went out of my way to take a long, confusing route, doing everything I could to avoid the closed-circuit cameras that recorded so many things in Europe. Wearing the oversized hoodie and a baseball cap I'd bought from the pharmacy across from the hostel, I kept my head bent, so my hair fell, obscuring my face.

I didn't know if it would fool anybody actively looking for me, but all the spy thrillers I loved to read always seemed to have an underlying theme when it came to escaping detection in the modern era—don't use credit card or ATM cards, avoid sites on the internet that you normally frequent, avoid using cell phones, and try not to get your face captured on camera.

Normally, I'd think it was insane to even worry about something like that—boring, lonely Kitt Bocho, rarely noticed by anybody, on the run. But if the police *did* think I was connected to Anne's death, they'd put out all the stops, including facial recognition software, surely.

ATM cards, careless internet usage, being caught on camera, any of that stuff could supposedly help locate or identify me.

I took the train halfway, then hopped off, backtracked and took a bus in another direction then dropped into a café for a quick bite that I didn't really want. There were TVs, though, and computers with internet service.

That was what I wanted.

Articles about Anne and Karl dominated the media. Nobody had any real info. The police were investigating all leads. No solid motives—at least nothing they'd made public. I breathed a sigh of relief each time I didn't see any mention of my name, but at the same time, my tension soared.

Were they looking for *me*? Was that why there was no mention?

What exactly had the lawyer told Aeric?

Why did they think I'd been having an affair with Karl?

Why wasn't there mention of such an affair anywhere?

I couldn't find any answers.

After twenty minutes in the café, I left. Even though I'd surreptitiously obscured the computer's camera, I didn't trust that other cameras hadn't picked me up, and I was too paranoid to linger. Besides, it had taken me almost two hours just to make it this far across town, considering how careful I was being. I had to get to the bank before they closed.

Panicking that I might not make it, I took fewer precautions this time, and in just over an hour, I pushed into the bank. Butterflies winged inside my belly like they'd taken speed, fluttering like mad. Keeping my head cast at a downward angle that still allowed me to look up—and *hopefully* didn't look like I was hiding, I made my way to the cashier I was the most familiar with. She had two people already in line, but I stood patiently, not letting myself fidget. I probably already looked suspicious, with my baseball cap, backpack, and baggy hoodie. Once it was my turn, I approached, tugging at my hat just as I reached the counter and forcing a smile. I knew it was strained, but I couldn't help it.

"Hi, Giselle."

She blinked at the sound of her name, then focused on me. "Oh, my goodness. Kitt..." Her hands fluttered.

Panic rose inside me, but her face collapsed into a sympathetic grimace as she reached for me, her fingers twining with mine.

"You poor thing. I've worried about you ever since I heard the news about *Frau* Weiss and her husband. Are you all right?

The children? There hasn't been any news about the children or you...well..."

"We're fine." I cleared my throat and jerked a shoulder in a shrug. "We stayed here in Charlottenburg. I..." Feeling self-conscious, like a hundred people watched, I lowered my voice and leaned in closer. It also allowed that raised barriers to better block my face from the cameras behind the counter. "I don't think I'll be able to stay in Germany, though."

"Oh, no!" Giselle looked crestfallen. "You love it here! And we love you."

"Thank you." The honesty in her voice and the genuine sympathy struck me right in the chest, and I had to clear my throat to keep speaking. "I...Giselle, can you check on something for me?"

"Of course." She gave me an encouraging smile. "Just name it."

"I need to know how much money is in my account."

She laughed softly. "That's an easy enough thing to do. There should be more than enough, Kitt." She darted a look at me even as her fingers flew over the keyboard. "You've been quite responsible with your money. Several friends of the Weiss family use au pairs, and I must say, I've never seen anybody quite so..." She frowned, the words trailing away. After a moment, she looked at me. "Have you made a withdrawal lately?"

My belly sank. "No. Well, nothing unusual. A few hundred euros maybe three weeks ago. We were going to a street festival, and I wanted some cash on hand for that and for a music festival I was thinking of attending. Other than that...? Nothing."

"Hmmm. Give me a moment." She focused more intently on the computer, her fingers flying.

With every passing second, I could see her frustration grow-ing, just by the faint narrowing of her eyes, then by the slight flush that appeared and grew until her entire face was suffused with it.

The notebook tucked into my front pocket seemed to weigh more and more. I had to fight the urge to scream, *Just tell me how much money is left!*

"Let me get my supervisor," she said, looking at me with a guilty expression.

I reached for the edge of the counter. "There's a problem, isn't there?"

I should have been more careful. I knew it the moment the last word left my lips. Head cocked, she eyed me. "You don't sound surprised."

The laugh that escaped me was bitter and hard.

She winced and looked around, then stepped back from her window and came out from behind the counter. I stared at her, feeling a little empty inside now.

"Come on." She gave me an encouraging smile as she took my hand. "I'll show you to one of our meeting rooms and have my supervisor come speak with you."

I knew the supervisor. Not as well, but I knew her. She gave me a sympathetic smile and offered her condolences about my employers as she led me to her office and gestured to a chair in front of her desk. I glanced at the computer, but it had a privacy tint that made viewing the information on it impossible.

She glanced at it before folding her hands on the table in front of her. "Do you have an idea how much money should be in your account, *Frau* Bocho?"

"Roughly twenty-three thousand euro," I responded as Giselle hovered in the doorway behind me.

"And you had no large withdrawals planned? No electronic transfers arranged?"

"No." Hollow inside, I had to fight the urge not to snap at her. "The few bills I have are already on routine withdrawal—the largest is my student loan payment, and that's two hundred dollars, withdrawn every month. I'm sorry...I can't think of the euro equivalency right now. My mind is..."

"I understand. And yes, I've noted that. The latest payment just went through a few days ago." She cleared her throat, then asked, "What was the payment to Spielbank Lux for?"

I blinked at her.

"*Frau* Bocho?"

"Excuse me? What?"

She pursed her lips and the smooth skin of her brow furrowed as she studied me. Her skin, a warm, unlined brown that gave her an appearance of agelessness, paled faintly, and she leaned back into her plush, luxurious office chair. "Spielbank Lux?"

Automatically, I translated it in my head to English, and without thinking, I responded in that language. "Luxury Casino? What are you talking about?"

Schmid looked past me, then shifted, clearly uncomfortable.

Just when I was about to ask again in German, she responded in an accented but flawless English. "Yes, it's a casino. A rather new one. Very upscale, popular. It's maybe thirty minutes from the Weiss's home. Are you familiar with it?"

"I...no." Bewildered, I looked at her before swiveling around to look behind me. A slim, refined man strode past me, olive skin glowing against a slate-gray suit, a polite smile set firmly in place. He gave me a short nod as he glided over to Schmid's side, bending down to look at the screen.

They murmured softly, but I heard only snatches of conversation.

I wished they'd speak up. If I didn't get answers soon, I'd break. Trying not to think of the book in my pocket, or the pack of matches I'd found—the deep, glossy burgundy with *Lux* scrawled across in lavish, silver font.

I tried not to think about the slip of paper with the initials *K.B.* scrawled across it, right next to a sum and a date. From five days ago.

Twenty-three thousand.

I tried not to think about Karl and his kind smile as he offered to help me invest my money, *twenty-three thousand euro*.

Sure, it was more than a lot of people had, but I didn't have a place to live, a car...nothing.

They continued to speak in low, hushed voices, and it was getting on my last nerve. Frustrated, I leaned forward, catching Schmid's eyes. "What's going on?"

It was obvious by the look on her face that she didn't want to say, but finally, she exchanged a look with the man next to her. He made a vague wave in my direction then fell back to watch.

Schmid cleared her throat. "*Frau* Bocho, our records show you to be in the negative. You're overdrawn by almost two hundred euro. Your routine payment to the creditors holding your college loan hit the other day. And you only had fifty euro in your account."

Fuck. I'd known...I'd thought I'd been prepared.

But I wasn't.

My head went light.

My belly went hot.

Bending over, I started breathing in fast, ragged pants.

"JUST CALL me in a few days, *Frau* Bocho." The bank manager gave me a solemn look as he tucked a business card into my hand.

He'd introduced himself as Arjun Singh and had been kinder than I'd initially assumed he'd be. His dark eyes focused on me, and I was able to meet his gaze.

After a brief struggle, I nodded and smiled. "Thank you, Mr. Singh," I said wanly, not realizing I'd lapsed into English until I'd already finished. "I..." Wracking my brain for the right words to apologize, I stared at him, horrified to realize I couldn't even do it in my own language. I was numb, frozen by this new curveball life had thrown at me.

"It's no trouble," he responded in the same language, his accent a charming patois of German and what I assumed might be some language from his native India. Kindness radiated from his eyes as he patted my hand. "Are you sure you do not wish to stay here and let me contact the police? They'd have better resources to track this."

"No." I managed, barely, not to shout it. Squeezing his hand, I looked over at the car he'd called for me. "You've done more than enough."

With a pained expression, he shook his head. "I feel we've done *nothing*, Ms. Bocho." He'd insisted earlier that he write a check for several hundred euro which he'd cashed and turned over to me, insisting that he'd smooth matters over with the bank as they investigated my missing funds. I'd warned him that I had a bad feeling the withdrawals might stem from the ISP of the Weiss family, but for some reason, he'd believed me when I told him I hadn't arranged for the withdrawal.

Actually, there'd been a grim sort of knowledge in his eyes as I said that and it had me wondering just what I'd been missing about Karl, and for how long it had gone unnoticed.

Now, both he, Ms. Schmid, and Giselle watched me with concern as I swung the door shut, sealing myself inside the Uber. Even though I had no reason to suspect Arjun Singh, Silke Schmid, or Giselle might be trying to lull me into a false sense of complacency, I gave the driver an address several kilometers from where I was staying and sank back into the seat, mind whirling and stomach churning.

The driver wasn't taking me to the hostel.

I had one more place I had to look into.

Wiggling around, I tugged out the matchbook and studied the glossy print across the front.

The matchbook, with its swirling, imprinted logo, *LUX*, scrawled over the front. Using my thumb, I slid the top of the matchbook up and read.

T.D. *1,175,000.*

Those initials, that number, and a date.

The date, coincidentally as one day before the check that had drained my account had cleared.

TWENTY-TWO

AERIC

HER MOUTH WAS OPEN ON A BROKEN CRY, HER NAILS biting into my shoulders. Her heels dug into my ass as I rode her hard and rough.

Kitt cried out my name, but I covered her lips, swallowing the sound down, greedy, empty, desperate.

She started to convulse under me, her body shuddering as she came.

Then I realized she wasn't in the middle of a climax.

She was crying.

Horrified, I jerked awake, and in the blink of an eye, we weren't in my bed but in her room. She was dressed in one of her foolish, silly shirts and jeans, her mouth still kiss-swollen. All around her were messy piles of paper that didn't make any sense.

"What are you doing?" I demanded, my head still spinning. I looked down and saw that I was naked. Feeling exposed, I looked for something to cover myself with, but there was nothing. Just stacks and stacks of paper.

"I was just looking for some sort of custody paperwork," Kitt said, her voice shaking.

Trepidation ticked at the back of my mind, the words nudging something loose. Shaking my head, I crossed the floor. "I don't want to talk about that." I caught her arms and pulled her up against me. "Come here."

She was docile as I pressed my mouth to hers, but as I started to kiss a path down her neck, she was already crying again. "They took the kids. Ask when they'll give them back. They're right there, Aeric. Make them tell you."

Frustrated, with that sense of uneasiness growing, I lifted my head and saw that she was pointing.

I followed her hand and saw that the room had changed around us again.

I was still naked, and now I was standing in the police station with Feidelberg, Lieberman, the chancellor, and my parents, all of them glaring at me in disapproval.

Haas walked into the room and gave both me and Kitt a dismissive look and shook his head.

"She's involved with your sister's death," Haas said, pursing his lips in an arrogant smirk that infuriated me.

"Your sister loved Kitt," my mother, Valentina Nicolai, said, her hands folded in front of her. She looked from me to the crying woman next to me and shook her head. "And your sister wasn't stupid. Are you, Aeric?"

"*Maman,* I—"

The phone in my hand started ringing.

Frowning, I looked down, surprised to see I even held it. When I looked back up, it was to see that everybody in the room was gone, save for Kitt. And we were back in the library where I'd found her, right before I threw her out of the house.

"You should answer that," she said, her voice husky. "It could be important."

It rang again as she walked out of the room.

"We're talking," I called out to her.

"I have to pack. You only gave me fifteen minutes."

I started to go after her.

But the hall stretched on endlessly, and the more I tried to catch up with her, the farther away she seemed.

The phone rang again. And again.

Awareness slammed into me, and I opened my eyes, looking around the room with confusion. The ceiling was all wrong. The scent...I dragged in a deep breath and immediately grew aware of two things. The scent in the room was perfect... lavender and verbena. And I stank. I smelled of booze and two days of going without a shower.

The phone went silent as I sat up and looked around. Something rolled and bumped into my thigh, and I looked down, head aching, to see a bottle of whisky lying there. An empty bottle. It had been more than half full the last time I remembered seeing it.

And that had been shortly before I stumbled into Kitt's now vacant room.

Groaning, I rubbed at my eyes with the heels of my hands. My head sloshed and churned, the result of too much drinking and far too little food, too little water. My stomach wasn't precisely steady either, but after I considered things for a few moments, I decided it wasn't the worst hangover I'd ever had.

Dragging myself out of bed, I took another slower look around the room, wondering why I'd ended up in here. My phone was on the nightstand, next to a picture of Kitt with the children. Picking up both, I headed out of the room.

In the kitchen, I drank down a full glass of water, then chased it with a few anti-inflammatories I found in a cabinet. That done, I made some toast and started the coffee, thankful that Anne insisted I learn on a previous trip to visit.

It came out too bitter and too strong, but the caffeine was a necessity. After forcing down a piece of toast, I took the too-strong coffee and headed off to my room for a shower. Ten minutes of steaming the toxins out, and I felt somewhat better. Maybe sub-human even.

I had just pulled on a pair of trousers and an undershirt when the doorbell rang. It rang a second, then a third time before I remembered there was nobody here to answer the door. The fourth and fifth ring made it obvious that my visitor was persistent, and my headache wasn't in the mood to see if there was a seventh or eighth ring.

There was a seventh ring. I opened it a few seconds after, already irritated.

The sight of Lieberman and Feidelberg annoyed me, but I tamped down all signs of it and nodded at them. "Gentlemen. Have you learned anything new?"

As before, Feidelberg took the lead. "Possibly." He glanced past me, not bothering with subtlety. "Would it be okay if we came in? We have some questions."

My impulse was to say no.

I wasn't in the mood for questions and looking at them had my mind drifting back to the odd dreams about Kitt.

But these were the men investigating Anne's death. As much trouble as I'd had getting Kitt out of my head, I'd have to face reality sooner or later, and it was best that it happen *sooner*, for everybody involved.

Giving them a curt nod, I stepped back and let them come in.

They looked around, Lieberman moving deeper into the house, clearly on the lookout for something.

"My family isn't here," I told him. I wasn't sure if that's who he thought he'd see. "It's too complicated a matter for them to travel when my country is in such crisis right now."

Feidelberg gave me a measuring look. "It must be hard, being torn between the duty to one's family and the duty as a reigning monarch."

"Yes." My father had called every day, sometimes several times, and the frustration, the grief both of my parents felt was a palpable thing.

We stood in the foyer. I was oddly reluctant to invite them to sit, quite content with the idea of them spilling whatever questions so I could answer them and send them on their way.

Feidelberg clearly recognized this and smiled a fraction. "We won't take up much time, Prince Aeric. Actually, it's Kitt we need to speak with. As she lives here, she likely has better insight into the avenue we're looking at, and...what is it?"

I stared at him, hard. "You want to speak to *Kitt*?"

"Yes." Feidelberg drew the answer slowly, his eyes narrowing slightly. Smoothing a hand down his tie, he studied me.

I could all but see the wheels turning, but there were wheels turning in my head as well.

"She no longer *lives* here," I said bluntly, although saying the words out loud was like spewing up acid.

Both cops went strangely still. After an awkward silence that seemed interminably long, Lieberman cleared his throat, drawing my gaze to him. "Your Highness, may I ask why?"

"Because she was fucking my brother-in-law," I snapped. Immediately, I regretted the loss of control.

"I beg your pardon?" Lieberman said, the words coming out in a mix of incredulity and what sounded like irritation.

Asshole. However...*fuck*, she'd messed with my mind. The dreams that wouldn't leave me alone. Now this, my utter lack of control.

It's not her, I told myself. *It's the circumstances. It's Anne, it's Karl. It's the children. It's everything* but *her.*

Feeling a flush creep up the back of my neck, I pinched the bridge of my nose. "Forgive me, gentlemen. The past week has been hard. But upon finding out that you suspected her of having an affair, I confronted her and threw her out. She's no longer employed as the au pair for the children. She no longer lives here."

Although I didn't feel more composed, I felt I could give the impression, and I shifted my attention back to them.

They were still staring at me, and this time, they both looked very troubled.

Lieberman started to speak, but Feidelberg held up a hand. "Prince Aeric, could we please sit? I think this conversation might be complicated."

I almost snapped—again. But the rules of decorum and proper public bearing, drilled into me so often as a child, finally won out, and I nodded. "Of course. Forgive the rudeness."

We moved into the next room, the wide, open area that had likely once been a formal receiving room but had clearly become the family room for Anne and Karl. Taking the seat nearest the fireplace, I sat and tried to give an air of calm. It was far harder than I would have liked, almost impossible really with the hangover still pulsing inside my skull and the nausea churning my belly and all of it amplified by the overly stoic expressions of the men now sitting across from me.

Neither of them seemed interested in broaching whatever complicated conversation we needed to have, so I took the initiative. "Perhaps you could help me understand just what's complicated about my request that Kitt leave this household, considering her betrayal of my sister."

Even as I said it, the stricken look on her face flashed through my mind, and the nausea in my stomach worsened. I steadied myself with a reminder of what I'd learned. Anne had loved her, and Kitt had stabbed her in the back. So had Karl. Anne had deserved better.

"Where did you hear that Kitt had been having an affair with Herr Weiss?" Feidelberg asked, his voice filled with an uncharacteristic courteousness.

"From the police." Inclining my head, I watched as a scowl took his long face and made it even longer. "What precisely is the issue here, Feidelberg?"

"I don't believe either of us mentioned anything about an affair."

No. They hadn't. That had come from the lawyer. He'd spoken with the police while looking into matters. Irritation reflected in my voice, irritation I couldn't control as I snapped, "Semantics. The lawyer my family hired to handle the custody issue of my niece and nephew told me. He'd been speaking with the police and relayed that information. Her affair was a possible motive. I don't believe she was involved in their deaths, but that's irrelevant. She betrayed my sister."

Feidelberg dragged a hand down his face and looked at Lieberman.

A grim expression replaced the normally stoic set of his

features as he leaned forward to study me. Elbows braced in his knees, he said, "Prince Aeric, there are no indications that Frau Bocho was engaged in an affair with Herr Weiss. None."

I stared at him, waiting for him to finish.

After several seconds with no response from me, he cleared his throat and did indeed continue. "Early in the investigation, we did consider whether your brother or..." he winced but forged on, "or your sister might have been involved in an affair. It's just standard procedure, but there is absolutely no indication that was the case. And there was *never* any hint that Frau Bocho might have been involved."

Blood started to roar in my ears.

Both had somber expressions as they waited for a response.

The churning in my belly grew more intense and sweat broke out across the back of my neck.

For one awful moment, I feared I'd vomit.

That look on her face. How she'd stared at me, tears in her eyes.

Rising from the chair, I moved on stiff legs to stare out the window. But I didn't see the lovingly landscaped garden, the trees, the blue sky that seemed a mockery of the storm now churning inside me.

I saw Kitt, standing in front of me, fighting tears, her shoulders straight and proud...and her hands trembling.

Lieberman cleared his throat. "Do you have any idea where she might have gone?"

"I told her she had twenty-four hours to make arrangements to leave the country, or I'd look into having her visa revoked," I said, my voice as hollow as I felt.

Until I said that, all I'd sensed from the men was frustration, but now that tension in the room changed, taking on an edge of anger. Turning to face them, I let my arms fall to my sides as I met their gazes. "Out with it."

Feidelberg gave me a dismissive look. Lieberman's expression was one of contempt. Neither was enough. I wanted anger. I deserved it.

What had I done?

Instead of either of them giving me anything that might serve as a punishment for how badly I'd fucked up, they looked at each other.

"We'll check with the airlines, see if she's booked a flight," Feidelberg said as he rose from the couch, clearly ignoring me. "You're friendly with that officer in financials still? Ask her if she can run Bocho's credit cards and banking information so we can get an idea of where she might be."

Lieberman was already on his feet, his powerful frame tense, and I had little doubt he was angry.

They both were.

I'd threatened a person living in Germany, legally, causing no harm.

I'd threatened *Kitt*, a sweet, stubborn young woman who'd done nothing but make it clear that she'd adored my sister, and my niece and nephew.

I was a complete bastard.

"We need to take a look at your sister's bedroom. An office if Karl had one." Feidelberg gave me a hard look, cutting through the morass of self-loathing and rage.

Thrown off-balance, I shook my head. "Why?"

"So far, everything points to your brother-in-law having a gambling problem." Feidelberg jerked irritably at the sleeves of his suit jacket, like he was pissed off he even had to wear it. Or maybe it was talking to me. "Too bad that bit of information wasn't passed around like yesterday's news. Perhaps *Frau* Bocho would still be here where we could speak to her. If anybody would have some insight into Weiss's pattern of behavior over recent months, it would be somebody who lived in the house with him. Sir, may we look around and see if we can discover anything of use?"

"Yes." Numb inside, I pushed myself into motion, going first to Karl's office on the lower level.

A gambling problem.

Thinking again of all the papers she'd been going through, that troubled look I'd seen on her face. I'd assumed it was guilt.

Maybe it was, because she'd been rifling through an employer's possessions. But maybe it hadn't been *guilt*...but regret. Had she *found* something?

And did it *matter* now?

I'd thrown Kitt out of a place she'd called home for almost two years...because my brother-in-law had a gambling problem.

TWENTY-THREE

KITT

Jerking upright in a panic, I sucked in a breath. Disoriented, I looked around, not recognizing where I was. A tangle of dreams and memories pushed through the terror, and I covered my mouth with my hands, acutely aware of the five other people sharing a room with me. Slowly, I slid my legs over the side of the bed. My fingers trembled. Curving them around the edge of the bed, I stared at nothing as I tried to work through the mess in my head.

Standing in the office, clutching those pages and trying to make sense of what I was looking at—and failing—then shoving everything that looked important into my pocket so I could try to find more.

Then, oddly, I heard Anne talking. None of her words made sense. She was upset, scared, then angry...screaming. Silent.

In the silence, I heard Aeric talking.

You have fifteen minutes.

Unable to tolerate it any longer, I shoved my feet into my shoes and stood. I had to get out of here, get someplace where I could breathe, maybe even scream.

As I walked, I patted my pockets to make sure I had my keycard. Cutting to the left, I moved toward the small patio. I'd avoided the area, for the most part, wanting to stay away from any place where there might be other people. People *grated* on me right now. But it was just after three in the morning according to my phone, and the entire hostel was quiet, that hushed sort of silence that told me everybody was resting.

Except me.

I'd been so jumpy, I couldn't lay down until well after eleven, the small confines of the bunk closing around me like a coffin.

Now, even the entire building felt too small.

I wanted so badly to run, just to get away. The best I could do was shove through the French doors that opened onto the small patio. It was closed in, protected by four stone walls that had been designed to match the aged appearance of the attached building. In the daylight, the little patio with its garden boxes and climbing, vining flowers that spread over the walls came off as quaint and charming.

But now, it was just another small, shrinking space. I dropped down on the nearest bench and lifted my face upward so I could stare at the sky. With the lights all around me dimmed, I could see the stars.

Now, I heard another voice, Josef's, as he talked about the stars and being an astronaut as he looked up through the skylight over his bed.

The memory hurt. But at the same time, the pressure squeezing in and choking me eased.

I thought of his sweet face, thought of Karol.

Bit by bit, the panic faded.

I wanted to run, no doubt. But I couldn't. Running away wouldn't solve anything or find answers.

I wasn't giving up.

Just acknowledging that, reaffirming it made me feel better.

I closed my eyes and slumped more comfortably back on the seat, the tension from the nightmare draining away.

Over time, drowsiness overtook me, and my lids grew heavier.

The sound of the French doors opening had roused me just before I might have slipped off, and I blinked, reaching up automatically to rub my eyes.

"Well, well, well..."

The sound of that voice had me freezing, but the fear only lasted for a minute, adrenaline flooding me and bringing me to my feet as the three Americans who'd been hassling me all weekend spilled out of the hostel onto the patio. They all stumbled, leaning heavily on each other, although the one in front looked to be steadier than the other two.

He was also the one who'd been leading his friends in their torment of me, egging them on every time we passed by each other in the hall, and every other time I saw them.

His name was Zach—I'd heard all of their names. The other two were Tate and Phillip, but I didn't know which was which.

Zach was the one who concerned me.

Even now, Tate and Phillip were snorting and more amused with their inability to stand up straight than anything else.

But Zach looked at me with a predatory light, the kind that made my blood run cold.

As they drew nearer, I cut to the side and circled around.

Zach's smile widened, and he sidestepped, moving in sync with me.

I didn't let myself fall into the pattern he clearly wanted, which would have been to lurch to the side, farther from the door, and closer to his drunk friends.

"Will you please excuse me?" I said tightly.

"You don't have to run off, ya know. We won't bite," he said, slurring his words only a little. He let his eyes slide over me, and a smile tugged his lips up. "Much. You can, though. Matter of fact, I got something you can wrap your lips around right now."

He reached down and rubbed himself through his pants, and my stomach twisted while fear turned into a pulse inside my veins. Doing my best not to let it show, I stared him down. "I'll pass. Excuse me, please."

He didn't move, but I wasn't going to stand there and wait, either. Not while he continued to smirk and his smile grew, and his eyes glinted with meanness and a hungry light that made me feel dirty.

Moving forward, I turned sideways, fitting my body into the narrow space he'd left between himself and the wall, scraping against the rough surface to keep from touching him.

Or I tried.

He grabbed me and ground against me, smirking. "That's nice...damn, you got some tits on you."

Horrified, humiliated, I shoved at him. It caught him off guard, and he stumbled backward, falling into his friends. Taking advantage, I lurched toward the French doors and jerked them open.

He pounced, crashing into me from behind, and over the roar of blood in my ears, I could hear the rising laughter coming from Tate and Phillip. "Get her!"

Zach grabbed my hair and smashed my face into the door frame. Pain exploded, radiating out from my forehead, and for a few seconds, everything grayed out. I could feel him jerking at me, and desperately, I clung to the door frame.

He gave another jerk, and I let go with one hand, swinging backward. The wild punch didn't do much more than smack him in the mouth and surprise him, but his grip loosened and I half-ran, half-stumbled into the communal area of the hostel.

I heard him snarling behind me.

My head spun, something wet running down my face. I could all but feel him breathing down my neck. I opened my mouth, a scream already swelling inside. He crashed into me yet again, slamming me into the wall right by the computer room where I'd been headed. It was private, with a door that locked and a telephone—I'd call the cops. That was the only thing I could think of. Zach clapped his hand over my mouth and used his free hand to jerk at the waistband of my yoga pants.

"You're going to pay for that, you cunt," he rasped.

I shoved against the wall, but he was too strong. Flailing, I reached out, searching for something. Anything.

My fingers touched metal.

The table set up for the continental breakfast offered by the hostel. Silverware, bowls, plates, all lined up at one end. Something stabbed into my hand, and I grabbed it, panic stuttering, screaming in my head, so loud it drowned out the pain and even the roaring caused by all the blood pounding in my ears. I fumbled with the fork until I had it in my fist the right way, then swung down and back.

He pulled back at the same time, and I could feel him jerking at his pants. He continued to snarl and threaten me, but I couldn't make sense of the words. Then, he was howling, screaming...and I was free. I half fell into the computer room, Shoving the door closed just as Tate—or maybe it was Phillip—

pulled himself out of his drunken stupor and started to come for me, I locked the door and fell back against it, struggling to pull my yoga pants back up.

While they pounded on the door and threatened me, I grabbed the phone from the desk and sank to the floor, shaking.

THE DOOR SWUNG CLOSED behind the doctor, and I sagged into the mattress. The pain medicine the nurse had given me had kicked in, and the throbbing in my head had faded. The ice pack the paramedics had applied to my bruised cheek had been swapped out for a different one, but the nurse had taken that with her when she left, along with the doctor, telling me she'd return in a short time with another.

There was also bruising and tenderness on the left side of my head, hidden by my hair, but the CT scan hadn't shown any internal swelling.

You're lucky, they'd told me.

I didn't feel lucky, although the logical part of me knew it could have been worse. Zach was looking at charges for aggravated assault, and I was told they'd update me on the status of the other two, although all three had been arrested and taken into custody. Zach had still been pounding on the door and shouting when the police arrived at the hostel, only a couple of minutes after I'd called.

It wasn't until after I'd made that call that I'd realized I might have made a mistake. If Aeric had notified them or if they suspected me of being involved with Anne and Karl's death, then I was screwed, and there was nothing I could do but wait because Zach kept me trapped in there.

But the female cop who'd arrived on scene at the hospital had shown nothing but sympathy throughout. When I gave her my name, she'd recognized it and asked about the Weiss family. I'd nervously confirmed they'd been my previous employers, but I'd been released from the job of providing care for the children the week before.

"That's rough, losing your employers and your home all in such a short time. Is that why you were staying at the hostel?"

She'd accepted a vague answer and moved on, asking more about Zach and his friends, the attack, before offering her card and promising to check back in on me in the morning after I'd had some rest.

Now that I was alone in the room, even as exhausted as I was, the thought of sleeping seemed impossible.

Zach's voice was a mocking echo in the back of my head, and everytime I closed my eyes, I was transported back to the patio, with him looming over me, watching me with predatory eyes.

The effects of the pain medication proved impossible to fight, and darkness swam in, pulling me mercifully under.

"...WAKE her, but there's no harm in us waiting..."

I stirred at the sound of that voice, familiar, gruff. It sent a shiver of foreboding up my spine even as I tried to place it. I'd been trying to slip back into the dark veil of sleep, but I hurt—bad—and the pain made it hard. The voice pushed that veil farther away.

As I drifted closer into wakefulness, the pain grew and grew until it was almost vicious.

"She had quite an ordeal, Inspector. She needs rest."

The familiar, gruff voice came again. "I understand."

"I'm already awake," I said, opening my eyes, then flinching as the bright light singed my corneas. I lifted my hand to shield my eyes, and that just made everything hurt *more*, the movement sending shockwaves through me as my muscles reacted and sent protests screaming along the nervous system up to my brain. *OUCH*!

"What the hell happened?"

The nurse, bless her heart, came into the room and adjusted the lights so the only one on was the softer one that angled up, away from my eyes. "*Frau* Bocho." She spoke in thickly accented English. "You don't remember what happened?"

I did, of course. Almost as soon as I'd said the words, I remembered.

A cold sweat broke out over my flesh, and I shivered, instinctively drawing the blanket up despite the pain the movement caused. "I...yes. Brain was a little sluggish there," I responded in German, and proved exactly what I'd just said by fumbling the translation so badly, I sounded like I was still in high school.

But the nurse patted my hand. "It's understandable, *Frau* Bocho. Are you hurting? Should I get another dose of your pain medication?"

"I..." Nervously, I glanced at the two men standing at the foot of my bed. Swallowing the knot in my throat, I pushed on. "I'm not sure. The medication knocks me out." Directing my question to the policemen, I asked bluntly, "Am I going to be leaving here sooner than expected?"

They didn't pretend to not know what I meant, which wasn't reassuring. "You're not leaving until the doctor discharges you. If you're hurting, please take the medication. You look like you've had quite a very rough few days," Lieberman said in a surprisingly gentle voice. He came closer and gestured to the chair. "May I sit?"

Warily, I nodded, then looked at the nurse. "I'll take the medicine."

As she left, I braced myself, knotting my fingers in the blanket nervously. Finally, I looked over at Lieberman, then at his partner, the grim, stern-faced older man, Feidelberg. He watched me with an expression that took a moment to place —sympathy.

"I guess you've been looking for me," I said, pleased at how steady my voice sounded.

"Yes." Lieberman studied my face, frowning. "I've read the report on your attack. You were lucky, it seems. But quick-thinking too. And brave."

"Mostly lucky." I'd been scared shitless, but I wasn't going to tell him that, especially since he was probably here to tell me I was being arrested.

What happened when Americans were arrested in a foreign country for involvement in a murder case? What was I supposed to do? And *how* was I going to pay for a lawyer? Calling my mother for help was out of the question. We hadn't spoken since the day she'd informed me it was best for me to move out so I could adjust to my upcoming life as a college student—at sixteen.

I had the fleeting thought that maybe I could call my father. I'd never met him—he hadn't wanted me. Mom had made *that* painfully clear. A rich businessman who'd enjoyed a hot, torrid affair with a beautiful young artist studying in France, but once she got pregnant, the allure wore off, and he'd abandoned her.

Curiosity had driven me to look him up, and he still lived in Paris, was beyond well-off, but that meant nothing. He probably didn't want me any more than anybody else did.

Tears blurred my eyes, and I looked down for a moment of privacy as I got my emotions under control.

"We put a flag in the system, so we were alerted if your name came up," Lieberman said, still speaking in that soft, patient voice.

Passing a hand in front of my eyes, I focused on him. "Inspector Lieberman, I'm tired, and I hurt. You don't need to beat around the bush with this. Whatever you need to say, just say it. I have a good idea why you're here anyway."

"I don't think you do." He smiled again, but it was tinged with sardonic cynicism this time. He glanced at his partner again. Feidelberg offered a shrug and Lieberman sighed, then leaned forward. "May I call you Kitt?"

"Ah. Sure, I guess."

"Thank you. Since you're clearly not in the mood for the subtle approach, I'll be direct. We went to the house Saturday to speak with you, and Prince Aeric informed us that he'd terminated your employment because he'd been led to believe you were engaged in an affair with *Herr* Weiss." Under the straight fall of his brown hair, his hazel eyes held mine.

Something about the way he'd worded that statement made my heart skip a beat, but I didn't let on. "That's correct." I braced myself for the questions that had to be coming.

"We know you weren't involved in an affair with your employer, Kitt."

"I..." Blinking, I looked from him to Feidelberg. "I'm confused. Aeric had gotten the information from the lawyer. The lawyer—"

"The lawyer jumped the gun," Feidelberg said in a flat voice. "We've already figured out what happened and who was involved in this miscommunication. He's been reprimanded, and we also advised the lawyer. He's..." He paused and tugged his glasses off, reaching in a badly-fitting suitcoat. As he drew a handkerchief out, he glanced at Lieberman.

The two of them managed to carry on an entire conversation in the span of seconds, and while Feidelberg put his glasses back on, Simeon shifted his gaze back to me. "Haas comes from an old family here in Berlin. German nobility. Both he and his father are...." He paused, brow knitting. When he spoke again, it was in English. "I believe you call their sort *ass-kissers*. They're rich, with specific ideas about the place people like you and me hold. He heard what he chose to hear and moved with it, regardless of what it might mean to you, what it might mean *for* you."

"It won't change that you lost your job, but he was...advised of how bad a fuck-up this was."

My head was still spinning. The nurse came in while I was still processing. Grateful for a distraction, I took the medication she offered and let her look over the bruising on my face. A few minutes later, she left, and I still didn't know what to say to either of the men in front of me, but I felt like there should be... *something*.

"I guess this means I'm not being arrested?"

"No." Simeon's wide, stern face softened with a faint smile, one that made him look far less fierce. "You're not. We went to the house because we needed to ask you some questions...about *Herr* Weiss."

At that, I reacted. I couldn't help it.

Simeon noticed, as did Feidelberg. "You don't seem surprised, Kitt."

Nerves rose inside me once more, drawing my shoulders and neck tight. It didn't help the pain in my head. "I..." Licking my lips, I looked away and willed myself to relax. I couldn't do it. With sweaty palms, I steadied my breathing. "I'm not. Not exactly."

"Why is that?" Feidelberg's voice was brusque, but I decided that was just him, not anything about me.

Still, it was nerve-wracking to meet his eyes and fumble out what I hoped was a plausible response. "My checking account." Puzzled looks from both had me continuing. "I went to my bank. I...Ae—" I flushed in remembered embarrassment at his outburst over how I'd called him by his name. "The prince was angry and made it clear I needed to get out of the country. I went to see what would be needed to transfer funds..."

A sharp, wild sound escaped me. The broken laughter that echoed around the room sounded nothing like me, and I covered my mouth with my hand to silence it.

"There *aren't* any funds, Inspector Feidelberg. It was all withdrawn, the funds sent to Spielbank Lux," I said once I'd controlled the laughter. "The casino. I...I don't gamble."

Both men shared a look, both growing more alert.

When Simeon directed his focus back on me, the gentleness had faded from his eyes, although his tone remained easy. "Tell me, Kitt. Whatever you know, whatever you share, tell me."

TWENTY-FOUR

AERIC

"Mama isn't coming back, is she?" Josef asked, his voice soft.

He'd always had such a soft, dreamy light in his eyes.

That was gone now. When I'd arrived at the minister's house, she'd greeted me with polite respect, but there was concern in her eyes, and once we'd had a moment where the children weren't in earshot, she'd told me the children would benefit from receiving counseling as soon as possible, especially Josef.

The harsh way he'd learned of his parents' death had been brutal. He was too sharp, saw things too easily, even with those dreamy eyes. Or perhaps that was *why* he saw things so easily.

Out in the yard, Karol played with the minister and Mila, along with Conrad and Darrick. She looked tiny compared to the two boys, who were clearly going to be tall like their parents. But although she was smaller, she easily kept up with the two older boys.

Today, though, her happiness appeared to be dimmed.

Perhaps things were becoming more real to her.

She had asked several times if her mother and father were done being dead. I was so out of my depth. Give me an international crisis to deal with any day.

I wouldn't hide from this, though. Folding my hand over Josef's, I said, "No, Josef. She's not coming back."

"And Papa? He's gone, too. Because they're both dead." He blew out a hard breath, and his thin shoulders rose and fell with it, trembling slightly. He sniffed, and as I watched, he swiped a hand under his nose. No tears fell, though, and that tore gouges into my heart. "What about Kitt? You call, and you come to see us, but she hasn't. Why hasn't Kitt come to see us? Why hasn't she called?"

Setting my jaw, I tried to come up with something that would pacify a child and make sense, but wouldn't hurt his feelings, all while trying to think through the choking fury in my head.

I wasn't used to feeling guilt, self-doubt, to questioning myself—or mentally castigating myself for the majority of my waking hours. Ever since Lieberman and Feidelberg had left the house, giving only a terse reference to being in touch as needed, I'd felt every single one of those feelings. Now, they ramped up yet again, like the rising tide.

"Kitt is...trying to deal with things too," I said, taking the coward's way out. I tried to convince myself it was for the best that I not tarnish Josef's faith, and I didn't want to do that for selfish reasons, although I deserved the pain after what I'd done.

In the end, I didn't tell him because I didn't know if he could handle another loss, another uncertainty in his life. I had to find Kitt and make this better, at least have her see the children. I wasn't sure where things would go from there, but she couldn't just disappear from their lives.

I didn't know why I hadn't seen the sense of that before. A life of considering what was most important to me, my own needs. I'd always thought I was doing as I was expected, focused on living a life in service to others, to my country. Certainly, I was an entitled, rich prick, but I should have been able to *think*.

"Kitt must be really sad." Josef sniffled again. "She loves Mama and Karol and me so much, and she's all alone. She needs to be with us."

I stroked a hand over his soft hair, while razors dug deeper into my heart.

"Your Highness."

Guillermo's voice cut through the noise in my head. I hated that I welcomed an intrusion on my time with my niece and nephew, but I did. Hugging Josef, I nudged him up off the bench. "Go. Go play with your sister and friends."

He stood and took a few steps but stopped and looked at me. "You're not going to take us with you today, are you?"

I wanted to tell him I would.

But it wasn't the wise thing, or the responsible thing. Here, the children were safe. Once my parents made arrangements for Josef and Karol to safely be taken to Monaco, it would be easier.

Now, though...I couldn't risk them. There were people out there who had killed my sister and brother-in-law, possibly over money. In my mind, that meant one thing. Josef and Karol could also be in danger, just as the police, just as the lawyer had insinuated. Only not from Kitt.

From those cold enough to shoot unarmed people, including my sweet, loving sister, shot in the back while on her knees by the bed. Such an action took a deliberate sort of coldness.

I thought of that as I turned to the house where Guillermo waited with the inspectors from the German police. Both

Feidelberg and Lieberman watched with the same expressions of *fuck-you* politeness they'd worn at our last meeting.

I didn't blame them.

If anybody deserved a good, old-fashioned *fuck you* without the politeness given only because of my title, it was me.

Grimly, I approached, maintaining an expression of stoic detachment. It wasn't always easy to present that façade to the world, but there were times when it was necessary, like now. Neither of the cops needed to know what a wreck I was inside, and it wouldn't help my niece and nephew to know either.

On a political front, while Mila Kelly wasn't a player when it came to the field of world politics and government, she did have the ear of powerful people in Germany and likely other contacts in neighboring countries.

The last thing I needed was for her to see how much of a wreck I was inside.

"Inspectors." I nodded at each of them, folding my hands behind my back. "I'm hopeful that you have some information for me."

"Little to nothing at this point." Lieberman paused, drawing it out several seconds before adding coolly, "Your Highness."

There were some people who could make almost anything sound like an insult, but the words were all so proper, even the gestures and facial expressions, there was nothing you could actually do or say to highlight the disrespect without being an ass.

And what had I done to earn this man's respect at this point?

One could always point out that it translated to no respect for my title, and therefore no respect for the country I represented, but wasn't that my fault?

I studied him for a long moment, and he blandly returned my gaze, unperturbed.

Guillermo observed everything, and as the tension climbed, he cleared his throat. "Perhaps I could fetch beverages, Prince Aeric?"

"Not necessary," Feidelberg said brusquely. "We won't be staying long. If you could give us a few minutes?"

The words were directed at Guillermo, but Feidelberg's eyes never left my face.

My aide ignored him, keeping his gaze on me as well. "Your Highness?"

I nodded at Guillermo, aware of his suppressed anger. In French, I said, "It is all right, my friend. Why don't you go inside and call home? Perhaps you can speak to Gustave or Madame Laurent and see how my parents are?"

"Of course." He gave both officers a look of warning, but if they noticed, they weren't concerned.

Once we were alone, Lieberman looked at the children. "I imagine it's been hard on the boy and girl, losing their mother and father, then having their au pair disappear, all within a few days. Did you tell them you thought she was sleeping with their papa?"

Anger burned in my veins—at him, at me. The glint in his eyes served a warning, and it was the only reason I was able to temper my response. "I suspect that's something they're too young to understand."

"They understand she's not been to see them." He shrugged, tugging at his tie, gaze still on Karol and Josef. "As upset as she was? And I heard the reports about the kids too. Little Karol kicked and fought the workers from the Ministry of Youth who collected her, insisting she wasn't supposed to go with strangers. It wasn't until *Frau* Kelly arrived that she calmed, from what I've heard."

"Are you here to remind me about the trauma your government has inflicted upon my niece and nephew?" I demanded.

"I'm just concerned for their well-being." Lieberman finally looked at me. "It's simple concern...Your Highness. Please don't misunderstand."

"Thank you for the concern...Inspector. Now, please tell me why you are here."

Feidelberg took that one, scratching at the stubble already darkening his jaw. "We were just wondering if you could tell us something about your brother-in-law's gambling debts. The money he owed Spielbank Lux, for example."

That came as a surprise. Mind blank, I stood silent, unable to offer any response.

What response *was* there?

"If I was a betting man, I'd wager you didn't know anything about those debts," Feidelberg said, a broad, unpleasant smile spreading across his face. "That's weird. Isn't that weird, Lieberman? You'd think his sister would have said something about it, wouldn't you?"

"As close as they're supposed to be...? You'd think."

"What are you talking about?" I asked, taking a step closer to them, forgetting about the children behind me, and everything else as my mind whirled with what they'd said. They'd said a gambling *problem*—but money owed? "How much money?"

"I'd say more than twenty-thousand euros. Pocket change to you, right?"

Twenty-thousand euros? I almost laughed at them. Of course, it was pocket change. It was pocket change to Anne—or it *would have* been. But the amount, and how the inspector had worded it, had me eyeing him in speculation. "If you know it was more than twenty thousand, surely you have a few details you can share."

"Not much." Lieberman slid a look toward his partner. Feidelberg shrugged, then nodded, and the younger inspector met my gaze once more. "We're still working the angle. We left the bank after confirming a transaction, and origin, twenty-three thousand euros sent to Spielbank Lux, paid from Kitt Bocho's account just over a week before your sister and brother-in-law were murdered."

"That doesn't make any sense. Money from..." My throat knotted up as her name formed, resisting, and I had to force the words out. "Kitt's account? It should be her debt then."

"We've verified that she has no account with the casino." Feidelberg smirked.

I wanted to plant my fist in his face more than I'd wanted anything.

"They won't tell us who *owned* the account, but after the appropriate paperwork and legal squawking that took place yesterday after we received our information about this payment, the casino's financial department did confirm that she didn't, and had never had, an account there. And...we have confirmed via banking and credit card records that Karl Weiss *was* a frequent patron of the establishment."

The breath gusted out of me, and I turned, staring blindly at the fountain on the far edge of the stone patio. "How did you come across this information?"

"*Frau* Bocho told us."

Something about the way Lieberman said her name annoyed me enough that I swung back around. He'd reached into his jacket, and I watched as he pulled out a notebook, flipping it open. Eyes narrowed, he skimmed something noted there and looked up. "Twenty-three thousand, to be exact. That's how much was missing from her account when she went to inquire about the process of transferring funds once she got back to the United States. Since you made it clear you planned on having her permanent resident permit revoked, of course. But while she was there, she learned she had nothing in her account, that it had been emptied down to nothing more than a few euros, and when her college loan payment went through, it put her in the negative. Her life savings, completely gone. From what we can tell, your brother-in-law stole everything from her just days before you tossed her out into the streets."

"Poor woman." Feidelberg grunted, his long face softening slightly. "Having a rough time of it, I'd say. Loses her employers, ones she considered friends. One of them stole from her, then she loses her job and home. She loses the children she loves so much."

He gave me an ugly look, and the guilt I felt was so intense, I thought it would choke me. If the guilt didn't choke me, the bile churning up my throat surely would.

I wasn't sure if I'd mind.

If Feidelberg recognized that his words had impact, he wasn't concerned, continuing on his rough manner. "Then she gets roughed up by a couple of punk tourists and ends up in the hospital."

"What?"

I didn't remember moving. One second, I'd been standing there, swimming in a sea of guilt and anger, then I was only a foot from Feidelberg and reaching for him.

Feidelberg stepped back, face hardening. "Watch yourself there, prince."

The back door opened. Footsteps came rushing at us, and I heard Mila calling out, her voice commanding and calming at the same time. I yanked myself under control as Guillermo and two of the minister's security guards reached us.

"What do you mean, Kitt's in the hospital?"

Feidelberg arched thick brows. "You don't need to concern yourself, Prince Aeric. She's in good hands."

Mila reached us. The expression on her face was one I recognized—brisk, optimistic, confident, and competent, something unique to good leaders. She rested a hand on my upper arm, a calming gesture I doubted she would have used under other circumstances.

I didn't entirely welcome it now, but I didn't reach for Feidelberg again, the way I was tempted. I wanted to grab him and slam the asshole up against the nearest hard surface until he told me every damn thing I needed to know.

He must have seen something in my eyes because his narrowed once more, giving me a long, incisive study. After a few moments, he snorted and shifted his attention to Lieberman, one of his thick brows lifted in question.

Now the focus of men, I glared at them. "What the—" I sucked in a slow breath and tried to calm the rage inside, then tried again. "I feel like there's something I'm not being told. Please enlighten me."

"Nice manners," Feidelberg muttered.

Mila sent him a hard look, which I pretended not to notice as I stared Lieberman down. He'd be the one to talk. I already knew that.

"Kitt was attacked. She was admitted to the hospital for

observation," the big, broad-shouldered man said, tone implacable and eyes cold, sharp as jagged glass. "She'd been staying at a hostel. She didn't say it in so many words, but I had the impression she was afraid to go to a hotel because they'd ask for ID and such, and she worried the police would be looking for her. She made it clear that she felt she might be forced out of the country, despite having a legal permanent resident permit."

A muscle pulsed in my jaw as I stared at him. I couldn't say anything.

What was there *to* say? I'd been the asshole to make Kitt think she had to leave in such a rush, and we all knew it.

"Is she...how badly was she hurt?" I managed to ask, despite the knot that had seemed to secure a permanent resident permit of its own, right in the middle of my throat.

"She came through with mostly bumps and ugly bruises. And some uglier memories, I'd imagine." Lieberman's eyes took on a cold glint. "But only because she's a clever and courageous young woman."

The hard, angry glitter of his gaze didn't make me feel any better, but I knew better than to ask anything else. If I dared try, he'd just take more pleasure out of hanging whatever knowledge he had over my head.

To my surprise, Feidelberg offered more information, although maybe it shouldn't have come as a surprise. He got some sick pleasure from twisting the knife. "She'd gone outside at the hostel where she stayed. A safe place in general. But a couple of troublesome tourists decided they'd have a go at her."

My stomach twisted into hot, savage knots, but before I even voiced my frustration, Feidelberg continued. "She got away, likely because they were intoxicated. After locking herself in a room, she was able to call for help. But she was injured. The doctors mentioned keeping her another day, I believe."

AS GUILLERMO ESCORTED the cops back inside, I was acutely aware of the children watching me—and Mila. She paced back and forth by the stone fence, talking quietly on her phone as she shot furtive glances my way.

"Why were you mad at them, Uncle Aeric?" Karol's words were somewhat muffled as she spoke to me around her thumb. Mila told me she'd started sucking it sometime in the past couple days.

Kneeling in front of her, I tugged on her wrist and folded my hand around hers, wet thumb and all. "I was mad at myself, Karol."

She watched me with a solemnity that didn't suit her young, sweet face, her mouth screwed up in a pucker that made me think of Anne while she watched me with her father's eyes. Finally, she blew out a rough sigh and practically fell against me.

"I've been at myself for days and days and days, Uncle Aeric," she whispered against the front of my shirt.

"Have you?" I closed my arms around her and pulled her in close. "Why is that, baby?"

She sniffed. "You might get mad at me too."

"No." I stroked her soft, downy hair. "I won't. I love you, Karol. You know that."

She sniffed, then hiccupped. "I got mad at *Maman* for not taking me with her and *Papa*. I yelled at her and told her she was mean. Then I yelled at Kitt. Maybe it's my fault they can't come back."

"Karol." I closed my eyes, misery twisting through me at the anguish in her voice. "Sweet, sweet Karol...it isn't your fault. You're just a sweet girl who wanted to go on a trip with her *maman* and *papa*. I used to get mad when I couldn't travel with my parents all the time."

She went still, then slowly lifted her face to study me. "You did?"

"Yes." I brushed her hair back from her face and tried to coax a smile from her. I wasn't successful, but the puckered, angry set of her brow faded, and she looked at me with exhaustion.

"What if *Maman* is dead and thinks I hate her and I'm mad? I can't tell her I'm sorry until she comes back."

The simple innocence in those words tore through me, and I hugged her again. "Your mother *knows* you love her, Karol."

"Even if she's dead?" Karol whispered the words against my chest. "The twins said *dead* is forever, and I can't tell her anything ever again."

A sharp gasp alerted me to the presence of another, and I looked up to see Mila standing there, her mouth going tight while her eyes sought out her sons.

I already knew why, even without asking. I lifted a hand in wordless understanding and shook my head, still hugging my niece.

"Everything's wrong," Karol whispered, thin shoulders shaking. "*Mama* is gone, and *Papa* is going, and *Kitt* is gone...*why* is Kitt gone?" Abruptly, she shoved away from me and glared. "Is Kitt dead too?"

"I..." Thrown off-guard, I looked at Mila dumbly. "No. No, Karol, she's not dead."

"Then where is she!" Karol slammed her small fists against my chest, her face angry and red and miserable. "I want Kitt!"

So did I.

Catching her hands, I brought them to my lips.

"I'll find her, darling. I promise."

TWENTY-FIVE

KITT

Save for the few things I still had stashed in a locker at the train station, everything I owned in the world was shoved into my pocket, my purse or into the backpack I clutched against my chest as I looked out the window of the S-Bahn, the world speeding by.

After my discharge that morning, I'd gone back to the hostel to get my things and had all but run away when the owner kept apologizing. I couldn't have gotten away from there fast enough, but once I'd gone a few blocks, I realized I really had *nowhere* to go, and I had next to no options left to me.

The crushing despair was overwhelming. Logically, I knew I needed to figure out something, plan something. Do something.

But I was still in that odd, frozen state, and I couldn't engage my brain.

I'd spent most of the afternoon traveling the rails, either on the S-Bahn or the underground version, the U-Bahn. Maybe I should have just gone home after Aeric had thrown me from the house.

Not that I would have had the funds to do it.

I did have a credit card I could use, but what was I going to do if I flew back to the US? Where could I possibly go?

The only thing of real value now in my possession was the annual ticket provided to me by Anne and Karl back in January. I stifled a hysterical laugh. I had enough money to feed myself for a little while, thanks to the kindness of Herr Singh, the bank manager who loaned me a few hundred euros while the theft of my funds was investigated. I could always find another hostel, but if I did that, my dwindling funds would dwindle far faster. And even the idea panicked me.

A surge of helplessness and hopelessness rose up yet again, and I closed my eyes, blocking out the view beyond the window. Evening had fallen, and my belly was a cold, empty knot, but despite the pangs of hunger, I couldn't have eaten, even if the most tempting meal were to appear in front of me that very moment.

A low noise escaped me before I could stop it just as the train started to slow, the automated voice making its announcement. Without thinking, I bolted upright, one arm looped through the straps of my backpack while I used my free hand to grip the handle overhead.

When the doors opened, spilling me out in the fading light of day, I sucked in a breath and moved forward automatically to stay out of the flow of people. But there weren't more than two or three others exiting with me. Frowning, I looked around, not even entirely sure where I was.

It took two seconds for that to change, and I spun back around, ready to lunge back on the train, but the doors had already closed. Groaning, I swung my backpack into place and squared my shoulders.

Without even realizing it, I'd exited at the station right

around the block from my favorite coffee shop—which was exactly a kilometer from the Weiss's estate. The shop, tucked into a trendy new little area, was next to the bookstore I liked to peruse.

With a groan, I looked at my watch and tried to decide what to do.

I was tempted to just swipe my ticket and get back on the next bus headed for Mitte, Berlin's center, but that wasn't going to work for the long term. The trains didn't run all night.

I needed to figure out where to go, where I'd sleep. And beyond that.

I needed to figure out a plan, *period*.

I needed to do...*something*.

So, I did. I walked to the coffee shop, went to the counter and ordered the strongest tea I could stomach. The man working the counter didn't recognize me, but I usually didn't come in so late. Taking my drink, I sat down at a small table by the front and curled my hands around the cup, letting the warmth seep in. It felt good, and I was dimly aware that I was cold, despite the balmy temperature outside.

My mind wouldn't settle. It kept spinning in endless circles, bouncing from one thought to another seemingly at random. Squeezing my eyes shut, I lifted the tea to my lips and sipped. The strong brew hit my stomach like a punch, and I immediately put it back down.

"Kitt."

I jolted at the sound of my name and looked up to find Miriam, the assistant manager of the shop, standing at the side of my table, her face pale, hands knotted at her waist.

Dread crept inside me, and I braced myself for her to tell me to leave.

Instead, she slid into the seat.

"Hi, sweetheart," she said, her English touched with the lightest accent. She'd been born in Germany but had moved to America with her mother when she was five. Ten years ago, she'd told me, she moved back here after her mother's death, and she'd been working here at this shop ever since. She planned on buying the owner out eventually, she liked to say. A coffee shop with a bookstore next to it—heaven on earth—and she'd laugh. But there was no laughter on her face now. She reached out and covered my hands with hers. "How are you?"

"I..." The obvious compassion in her eyes almost broke me. Blinking the tears back, I looked away. "I'm fine, Miriam. How are you?"

Instead of answering, she squeezed my fingers. "Be honest, Kitt. I read about Mr. Weiss and..." she colored and laughed self-consciously, "Princess Anne. I never realized you worked for the Princess of Monaco."

Tears rushed to my eyes at the mention of Anne.

Remorse immediately lit the other woman's expression. "Oh! That was so thoughtless of me. Damn it, Kitt, I'm sorry."

"It's okay." Pasting a smile in place, I tried to reassure her.

"I...well, it was thoughtless." She rushed to smooth it over. "Are you hungry? Can I get you some soup? It was potato and leek today."

My belly surprised me with a greedy growl, and I hoped it was too loud in the shop for her to hear it. "No. I'm not hungry."

"You need to eat." She rose and pointed a finger at me. "Stay there. It will be my treat. You've clearly had a rough few days, and it's the least I can do."

I wanted to argue, but she moved too quickly, and my belly

gave another rumble. I could pay for the soup—I did have some money after all. And she was right. I had to eat.

A dull ache pulsed at my right temple, and I told myself not to worry about it for now. After all, there were more than enough things knocking around in my head. Why add something so inconsequential?

Ten minutes later, as I spooned my way through the soup, I caught sight of Miriam looking my way. Already feeling a little better, I offered a weak smile, but she'd turned her back on me before it even formed.

Weird...

Pushing the thought aside, I finished the soup, working away at the problem in my head—where to go. What to do.

"...of Monaco has been seen in Berlin."

I'd been lost in my own thoughts, but at that, I came flying back to awareness and looked up. The TV mounted in the corner was on, the local news playing. A glossy PR image of Aeric flashed across the screen while the reporter talked about reports of the young royal being seen in the country, amidst speculation that he was there because of his sister's murder.

Intent on that, I was unaware of Miriam approaching until she cut between me and the television. Biting back a curse, I smiled and hoped it didn't look like I was baring my teeth in a snarl.

"Where are you staying?" She settled in the seat across from me, two mugs in hand.

I started to argue as she slid one to me, but she shook her head. "You're not drinking your tea. I bet your stomach is all a mess from the stress. This is chamomile. It will help."

"You don't have to do this," I told her. I suppressed the urge to sigh, straining to listen to the reporter. I gave the TV what I hoped was a casual glance, but the report had already changed.

Damn it. Having nothing else left to do but be social, I took my tea and met Miriam's curious gaze. The mug was warm in my hands, and still struggling to find an answer, I lifted it to my lips. The familiar herbal taste of chamomile, offset just a bit with honey, hit my taste buds.

"Mmmmm." Giving her a grateful look, I said, "Okay. I'm glad I didn't keep trying to argue."

Miriam laughed, her eyes crinkling at the corners. "I'm just being a friend, Kitt. I know we only talk casually, but it's okay to let somebody help." She paused a moment, and when I didn't say anything, she arched her brows. "So, does this mean you'll answer when I ask if you have someplace to stay?"

Guilt flooded me, but I lied anyway. "I'm...ah...I'm staying with a friend."

"Good." Doubt flickered in her eyes, but she didn't push. "Do you know what you'll do now? Go home? Look for another job?"

Another job. I cringed internally but managed to keep my face calm. "I'm still trying to decide."

For several more minutes, the casual questions came. My unease started to grow, and when rain began to fall outside, that unease when from a steady stream to a flood. All the worst shit happened in my life when it rained, and I wasn't exactly getting good vibes right now.

Miriam paused to take a drink, and I darted a look at the time. "Oh. It's getting late. I have to be going."

"But—"

"Really." With a fake, plastic smile, I shouldered my backpack. "How much for the food?"

"I already told you." Her smile softened sadly. "It was my treat."

"Thank you." Passing by her, I rested a hand on her shoulder, then hurried out into the night, instinctively swinging east. The rain came down harder still. Within half a block, my hair was soaked, but I didn't stop. Even when the chilly wet penetrated my hoodie, I kept going.

I was soaked in under five minutes, and judging by the way the downpour picked up, it wouldn't stop anytime soon. I couldn't go back to the coffee shop, though. I didn't know where *to* go, but I had to go somewhere.

That sense of helplessness returned, and I collapsed against a light post, the pressure of my backpack digging into me. Covering my face with my hands, I struggled to breathe, the weight of everything building inside, a silent scream that didn't want to stay trapped another second.

The quiet purr of an engine was almost inaudible over the rain. I sensed it more than heard it, and looked over, apprehension tightening my muscles as a black car pulled up next to me.

Shoving off the light post, I started to walk. Manic despair rising, I realized I was heading right back toward the Weiss house. The last place on earth I could go.

But behind me, a car door opened, and it wasn't like I was going to turn back.

TWENTY-SIX

AERIC

"Your Highness."

I'd come outside to hide away from everything, but it seemed impossible. Half the day had passed since I'd learned about Kitt, and I felt like I'd traveled throughout all of Berlin searching for her, to no avail.

Just over an hour ago, I'd come back to the house, thinking I'd look through her room for some hint as to where she'd gone, and Guillermo had been waiting, springing his well-laid trap. "Wait for her here, Your Highness. I've requested help from the German government. The police are looking for her now. They'll let me know if she's seen, and we'll go once she's located."

But staying *here* was driving me mad.

The low, soft sound of Guillermo's footsteps had been hidden by the rain, and I hadn't realized he was approaching until he stood at my side. Not looking at him, I stared out into the rain, watching as an empty swing on the elaborate play set moved back and forth slightly.

"Yes?"

I had no real belief that they'd have any luck locating Kitt. She'd left the hospital, had collected her things from the hostel and effectively disappeared off the face of the earth.

I had no way of reaching her since she'd left her cellphone behind, but even then, I'd called her number frequently, just listening to her voicemail greeting like a love sick puppy.

Shit.

"*Frau* Bocho is in a coffee shop just a kilometer from here."

I went rigid and stiff from shock. Grabbing his arm, I stared at him. "What?"

"I sent the team out to ask questions in the local shops and stores." A faint smile ghosted over his face. "There's a coffee shop and a bookstore in a little shopping area near here. She visits both frequently, and the employees said they'd let us know if she stopped in."

I was already heading for the car, not thinking about anything but getting to her.

"You'll need these." Guillermo's voice stopped me just a few feet away, and I looked back to see him holding the keys. He tossed them into my open hand and then gestured at me. "Do you wish to put on your coat?"

I looked down, taking in my shirtsleeves. "No. I'm not on my way to a dinner. Where's this coffee shop?"

"I've already texted you the address. You have your cellphone?"

I touched my pocket and nodded. It had buzzed earlier, but I hadn't bothered to check the message. I'd given up hope that Kitt would reach out, and my parents would have called. Nobody else mattered enough at this point.

Once in the car, I pulled up the directions, heart racing at the thought of how close she was. Minutes away. Just minutes.

I pulled out onto the street, the rain coming down harder with every passing moment, but I didn't care. Vaguely, I was aware of the car following me, my ever-present security team, but I tuned them out of my mind.

The headlights cut across the gloomy night, and I checked the directions once more, then focused on the road, already composing my apology. I'd come up with a hundred versions. None seemed right. This one didn't either. But I'd find the right thing to say, find some way to fix this. I had to.

Movement on the side of the road caught my eye, and I glanced over, then focused back on the road. After a split second, I whipped my head back and stared.

Had it not been raining so hard, I wouldn't have been driving so slow, and I never would have noticed her. But the deluge required it, and although I couldn't clearly see her, I knew in my bones that it was Kitt.

My heart clenched as she sagged against a light post, then brought her hands to her face. Every line of her body, the tilt of her head, the slump of her shoulders, all of it shouted despair.

I did this.

The bitter, vicious twist of guilt grew sharper, but I shoved it down. I'd have to find a way to deal with this, a way to accept it. But not now. Pulling to the side of the road, I climbed out of the car.

She'd noticed and had already shoved away from the light post, walking away, all but *running*.

"Kitt."

It came out a bare breath of sound, completely lost to the rain pounding around us. My hair was already plastered to my face, my shirt glued to my skin as I slammed the door closed.

"Kitt!"

She froze.

She didn't *stop*—she *froze.* And even though I couldn't see her face, I already knew she'd be sheet white and her eyes filled with terror. Swallowing the ugly, bitter taste of guilt, I walked to her. She still didn't move. I half-expected her to take off running, but she was still in that odd, petrified state when I circled around to stand in front of her.

Her blue eyes were dull as she stared at me. She sighed, her shoulders rising and falling as the spell holding her still shattered. Tears burned her eyes, and she lifted her face to the rain.

"Of course he's here," she said bleakly. "It's raining, so who else would show up?"

I didn't even try to make sense of that odd comment. I couldn't. I needed every bit of sense I had to get through the next few moments.

"Kitt..." I lifted a hand toward her.

She flinched.

"I wasn't trying to come to the house," she said, her voice harsh and tight. "I was just *walking* and not paying attention, and I ended up here. But you aren't going to believe that. Go ahead. Call the cops. They can arrest me, and hell, that's fine. At least I'll have some place to stay tonight. Maybe I'll get lucky, and they'll deport me. That's the only way I'll be able to get back to America anytime soon anyway."

Each word was like a kick to my gut. "I..." I cleared my throat. "No, Kitt. I'm not calling the cops."

She was staring at my extended hand as if I had shoved a venomous snake at her. Slowly, I pulled my hand back. "I...Kitt, I was wrong. I'm sorry."

She blinked, but there was no other response.

She hadn't backed away or run off, though. That was something, wasn't it?

"I spoke with Inspectors Feidelberg and Lieberman."

She looked away, and I saw the bruising that darkened the left side of her face, from the edge of her cheekbone, stretching up and out until it disappeared into her hairline. Rage blasted into me, and I almost welcomed it—so much better than guilt. But I had to fix this before I did anything.

She sensed what I was looking at and dipped her head so that her wet hair fell to hide her face.

"Look, we need to talk. Come with me. Please."

"No." Gaze swinging back to mine, she gaped at me then shook her head. The word was just a ghost of sound, and she cleared her throat, then tried again. "No. I'm...I've got a friend waiting for me."

The lie was written all over her face, but I wasn't going to call her on it. I'd done enough damage as it was. "Then let me drive you. Kitt, you're shivering."

"I..." She clamped her mouth shut and glared at me. "I'm fine. Go home, *Your Highness*."

I just waited.

"Are you just going to stand out here in the rain?"

"If you won't let me give you a ride, I don't have much choice. I can't just leave you standing here."

I was surprised when she huffed out a breath and went to the car. I tried to get there before she did, but I didn't and had to watch as she fumbled her backpack off, her body language very clearly communicating that I was *not* to assist. That helpless sensation spread, and I did nothing, just watching as she slid into the car and slammed the door shut.

No words of wisdom struck on the short circuit around the

car, and when I settled in the seat next to her, I wasted far more time than necessary adjusting the climate controls. She still shivered next to me, and I asked, "Should I make it warmer?"

"I'm fine."

I had a feeling she could turn into a frozen statue and would still find a way to mumble out, "'m 'ine."

And I couldn't blame her. At all.

Gripping the steering wheel, I stared into the driving rain. "I'm sorry for what I did, Kitt, and for how I acted. I was completely in the wrong."

She said nothing.

I feared what I might see on her face, but it was sheer cowardice to not *look,* so I forced myself to do it. She sat there, staring straight ahead through the window, drops of rain rolling down her nose, clinging to her eyelashes. She shivered and hugged her backpack and sat there like I hadn't spoken.

"Kitt, I made an awful mistake. I—"

"I heard you." She looked away as she spoke, her voice small, quiet, and weary. "I assume you spoke to the cops before you came to this grand realization."

"Yes." I wanted to lie, but that, too, would be an act of cowardice. "I think...No, never mind. That isn't important. I was wrong. That's all there is to it, and I'll never be able to explain how much I regret it, or how sorry I am, or—"

"I heard you the first time." She continued to stare outside.

I had a feeling nothing I'd said had penetrated, not really. And it was nobody's fault but mine. Grimly, I gripped the steering wheel. "Where does your friend live? You must be exhausted."

"There isn't a friend," she said dully. "But you probably already knew that."

I didn't respond to that. "Would you like me to take you to a hotel?"

"A hotel." She said it slowly.

When she started to laugh, it surprised me, the sound brittle and sharp, jagged bits of glass that hurt to hear. The laughter stopped almost as soon as it started, and she turned her head, staring at me with overly bright eyes. "There's no money to spend on a hotel, *Prince Aeric*. Your brother-in-law emptied my checking account, using the money to pay off a gambling debt. I have *nothing*."

She covered her face with her hands, and that helplessness and rage swam back up, nearly overwhelming me.

"I..." Without thinking, I reached out and touched the back of her hair.

She tensed. Then she shuddered and started to cry.

"I'm taking you home," I said quietly.

Kitt said nothing. I wasn't even sure if she'd heard me.

I put the car into drive and pulled away from the curb, acutely aware of each soft, muffled sob. I felt each of them, like a rusty blade tearing at my flesh. But this went far, far deeper.

The drive to the house seemed like it took hours, although it was only minutes. Certainly, it seemed as though I'd listened to her sobs, unable to do anything to comfort her.

She'd still been weeping when I turned onto the drive, even when I put the car in park next to the side door. But by the time I rounded the car to open her door, she'd gone silent. I crouched down next to her and found her staring once more out the windshield, face still damp with tears.

"Come inside," I said, reaching for the backpack she clutched like a lifeline.

She didn't resist, but her reluctance to let it go was obvious.

I have nothing, she'd said.

"Come, Kitt. I'll just put the bag in the house on the bench where you keep the rain boots for the kids. It will be safe there. You can dry off."

She let go slowly, and I swung it awkwardly up onto my shoulder. She slid from the car but froze as she realized how close I was.

I backed up, giving her the room she clearly needed, even as I thought about how she'd cuddled against me as she slept. Her eyes darted to my face, then away as she sidled out from between me and the car, arms wrapped around herself.

I had a hundred things I needed to say to her.

A thousand.

I couldn't think of the first one.

Leaving her standing in the kitchen, I went to my bathroom and grabbed a couple of towels and a shirt.

She still stood, wet and bedraggled in the middle of the kitchen, looking lost.

I offered her the towel.

She took it slowly, her eyes locked on the refrigerator. The towel fell from her loose grip as she took one step, then another toward the refrigerator. Bewildered, I tried to figure out what was wrong, but then I realized.

The pictures. Artwork by kids, showcased as if on display. A picture from Josef in a magnetized frame, and another from Karol. They were both placed in positions of honor, drawing the eye of whoever might walk into the room.

And they'd definitely caught Kitt's eye. As I watched, frozen, she clapped her hands over her mouth, and her shoulders jerked, a strong, sudden movement so erratic it caught me off guard. A second later, the movement came again, then again.

No longer trapped by my own feelings of impotent anger, I moved toward her.

She tried to jerk away, but I ignored her, pulling her up against me. "Go ahead and hate on me, Kitt. Hit me if it will make you feel better. But you've grieved alone too long, and there's nobody else here to help you through this. I can't do anything else to undo what I've done but this."

I half expected her to shove at me again, and I'd have to let her go, but to my surprise, her arms came tight around me, clinging desperately. Not giving myself a chance to think it through, I swept her up into my arms and carried her into the front parlor. She was too caught up in grief to feel the cold, but I grabbed the blanket and tucked it around her, then held her as close as I could.

The tears she'd cried in the car were nothing compared to this. A spring rainstorm. This was a hurricane, and it wanted to level and destroy.

I lost track of time. Other parts of my clothing had dried haphazardly, but the material of my shirt where Kitt had her face buried was wet with tears, and still, she shuddered. The sobs had grown weaker, hoarse now and quiet, but the tears fell relentlessly.

I'd helped add to this. Hell, I caused a great deal of it.

I wanted to go to my knees, beg for forgiveness, but she didn't need to hear from me right now. What she needed was time to grieve without me intruding, and that, at least, I could give her.

The storm outside had long passed, and the only sounds in the house came from Kitt, and the low, quiet sounds of my breathing. Then, even the broken noise of her grief faded and the silence around us grew weighted.

I'd never felt so useless, so impotent, in my life.

All the words trapped inside me would have to stay, because I'd come to realize they were meaningless in the face of the pain I'd inflicted on her. Nothing excused it, not even my own grief, because while I could always claim that grief had clouded my thinking, that hadn't been entirely true when it came to what had happened the day I forced her from this house.

Some ugly part in me had latched onto the possibility of getting away from her. She had already slid under my guard in a way no woman ever had, and that scared me.

Then the thought of her lying in that simple bed in her room with Karl...that had maddened me in ways I couldn't describe.

Maybe that was what temporary insanity was—only I'd given into it willingly. I'd welcomed those ugly doubts, all so I could force distance between us.

And all I'd done was hurt a woman who'd done nothing to deserve it.

"If you keep thinking so loudly, my head's going to explode," she mumbled.

She stirred, then lifted her head, careful not to look at me. I braced myself for the loss of her warmth, but after a few seconds, all she did was let her head fall back down.

Not quite daring to breathe, I closed my eyes.

She sighed, her body all but sinking into mine, the pause between breaths stretching out.

Stunned, I realized she'd fallen asleep.

Sliding my hand up her back, I combed my fingers through her messy, damp curls and closed my eyes.

There had to be some measure of trust still in there. How

could she have fallen asleep so easily if she had no faith at all in me?

Although I was exhausted myself, I had no intention of falling asleep. I'd enjoy this, every second of it. Until she woke up and realized what had happened. Once that occurred, this would end.

I had no doubt of it.

So I'd enjoy it...while...

TWENTY-SEVEN

KITT

Heat seeped into my bones.

A hard, strong body pressed to mine. Stirring, I cracked open one eye and caught sight of a chiseled jawline, Chris Evans's level of perfect.

Dreaming, I decided, and I was quite content with the idea. Wiggling closer, I curled my arm around his neck and flung my leg over his hips.

He made a low noise in his throat, and the arm he had around my back moved down. As he cupped his hand over my butt, I shivered and instinctively pressed closer.

All that did was make me aware of a few other rather specific details. Like how his other hand hooked over my knee, holding me close against him. The uncomfortable but intimate press of my breasts pushing into him, my nipples tightening despite layers of clothing separating us.

His hand roamed restlessly over my butt and hip, as if seeking, and I pressed more firmly into him, hoping to relieve the ache that had centered squarely between my thighs. But nothing helped.

Frustrated, I climbed on top, thighs spread to accommodate his hips and that...*that* helped.

I felt the hard jut of his cock pulsing against the sensitive space between my thighs, just as his hands closed over my hips.

"Kitt..." The raw, hoarse rumble of my name against my lips seemed a little too...*real*.

I didn't want *real*. Shoving my hands into his hair, I pressed my mouth to his, determined to block out the memories, the hurt, the loss...*everything* that didn't relate to this—heat and want and desire and his hands on me, mine on him.

His mouth didn't part right away, but as I licked at his lips, his chest shuddered against mine. In the blink of an eye, he shoved a hand into my hair and moved, flipping us so that I lay under him and he settled between my thighs. Almost all his weight centered between my thighs, and I moaned, instinctively bringing my legs up and curling them around his hips so I could grind myself against the solid, thick brand of his cock burning through my clothes and his.

"Kitt," he muttered against my lips. He shoved the other hand into my hair and cranked my head back, deepening his access to my mouth. At the same time, he thrust up against me.

Pleasure blistered, tore and destroyed me. I fell apart in his arms, crying out against his mouth, and in mere seconds, that brutal, unending climb to nirvana started all over again.

Panting for air, I shoved at his shoulders and sucked in a breath.

He let go, only for a second.

But it was long enough for me to look into his eyes.

It was a span of heartbeats...*one...two...three*...

That was all it took for me to come to stark, staggering awareness.

"Aeric!"

I had no idea if he'd respond.

Seconds passed. The pulsing weight of his cock between my thighs made me question whether I even *wanted* that. I felt more alive now, more aware... and not at all concerned about loss or grief or emptiness.

But...

In the end, that *but* was too strong, and I locked my elbows when he would have gone to kiss me again.

He didn't, though. Not after the first few seconds. Aeric started to pull me close once more but his eyes locked on mine as if he, too, was just now becoming aware of what was going on.

Five seconds.

That was all it took, and we were several feet apart, staring at each other as if we had no idea how we'd come to be in this position.

This position, one that had our hunger raging in a rhythm so perfectly choreographed, we could see the beat of it just by looking at each other, only served to jack up the intimacy of the moment.

My breasts rose and fell against my shirt, my nipples stabbing into the material. Between my thighs, I was wet and aching, the emptiness inside me a living, breathing thing.

I *hurt*. For him.

I hurt for him, and there was no denying it.

Flustered and embarrassed, I swallowed, trying to find some way to handle this that didn't involve running screaming from the room.

Aeric beat me to it.

"I apologize," he said in a stiff voice, his cheeks red. He stood with both hands clenched at his sides, and his muscles were stone-tight with rigidity. "That was appalling, Kitt. I have no excuse."

"I wasn't exactly unresponsive." Blood rushed to my cheeks, but there was a two-party mess-up here. I had no idea who'd made the first move, but I was just as guilty as he was.

"That doesn't—"

"Stop."

He looked slightly surprised at the hard, firm tone of my voice—or maybe it was because I'd interrupted him. Princes probably didn't get interrupted that often. But I wasn't too interested in courtesy at the moment. No, I was focused on—

Stop it, Kitt!

"I'm an adult, Aeric, and capable of taking responsibility for my actions. Maybe I don't have the experience behind me that you have, but I was very much into what was going on there, and you weren't taking advantage of me, so please don't insult me by acting otherwise."

"I wasn't..." Aeric sucked in a breath and gave me a look that, although it wasn't a glare, it wasn't precisely a happy expression either. "You make it difficult to know how to handle you at times, Kitt."

"I don't need *handling*. I was involved in..." I looked over at the couch and motioned vaguely, "that."

It sounded juvenile, and at odds with the casual demeanor I struggled to maintain, but I couldn't exactly say, *I was two steps away from jumping your bones.*

Why not? The part of me that wasn't in the mood to be courteous asked, making it so simple.

I silenced the voice.

"That." A ghost of a smile lurked around Aeric's lips as he glanced at the couch.

I couldn't decide if he was laughing at me, but I didn't care. Shoving my tangled hair from my eyes, I said, "I need a shower. Am I okay to use my old one?"

While in there, I was going to indulge in some self-satisfaction techniques just to relieve the ache still pulsing inside.

I must have broadcast the thought all over my face because Aeric's lids drooped. He didn't move a muscle beyond that as he watched me, several long, taut moments ticking away. Finally, he said, "You're more than welcome to do whatever you like in this house, Kitt. It is your home. Use the shower."

A band loosened around my chest at those words because I knew he meant them.

But a new sort of band immediately took its place as he took one slow step after another toward me, eyes lambent and intent, hot on my face. "You could, if you so choose, even use mine."

My breath wheezed out.

The invitation was clear.

He wanted me.

He knew I still wanted him.

But he wasn't going to make a move.

Maybe I shouldn't have been so blunt in making it clear that I was such a mature woman because I'd much rather he just kiss me and let our bodies do the deciding like they'd done before.

But...that wasn't being mature.

A wild, crazed need hit as we continued to stand there, staring at each other, our hunger a palpable thing.

I listened for that rational voice to speak up and tell me to walk away.

It was silent.

"You told me that if we ever..." I hesitated, then forced

myself to take the bull by the horns. "If we ever had sex again, I could tie you up. Did you mean that?"

I'd surprised him. It was obvious by the way his eyes widened, the way his lips parted. And once more, a dull, ruddy flush settled over his cheekbones, although this time, I knew it wasn't caused by embarrassment.

"Yes," he said, voice little more than a growl. He moved closer, reaching up to put one fingertip under my chin, lifting my gaze to meet his. "You can do whatever you want to me, Kitt. I'm your servant."

I was going to self-combust. Or melt. Or explode. Something. All this heat wasn't good for a woman's health. It couldn't be.

He dragged his thumb over my lip. I felt it straight down to my core, my clit pulsing in outraged envy.

"I think I'd rather use your shower after all."

Backing away, I turned and started for the door. Halfway there, I looked back at him. He remained where he'd been, motionless. "Are you coming?"

I wasn't quite sure how to handle the *I'm your servant* thing, but one thing was obvious—Aeric was clearly intent on *serving*.

When we first got to his bathroom, far more elegantly appointed than my own and mine was pretty damn nice, the first thing I'd done was look in the mirror.

The second thing—aside from a mental cringe—was to look for a brush. My hair was a catastrophic nightmare.

"What's wrong?" he asked, moving up to stand behind me, hands on my hips as he nuzzled me, burying his face in that catastrophic nightmare.

Maybe he had a serious vision impairment that I was unaware of, because I couldn't imagine him *seeing* my hair and not cringing in fright. Or maybe a hard-on, like the one nudging me in the ass, affected a man's judgment more than I'd ever realized. Regardless, I'd keep it cool, so I didn't alert him to the disaster. "Ah, nothing. I just...um. My hair. I always brush it before I shower. The curls and...tangles."

"I don't have a brush. Is there one in your room?"

"Yes, I'll go get it." I leaped at the idea—or I was ready to—but he beat me to it, striding out of the bathroom.

"I'll be right back," he said over his shoulder.

The second he left, I attacked my hair in desperation, using my fingers to smooth it down, although I might as well have been trying to smooth a poodle's coat after she'd been electrocuted—twice. Hearing the steady, decisive tread of his footsteps in the hall, I gave up and wrapped my arms around myself and looked up to meet his gaze in the mirror as he came back into the bathroom.

The boar-bristle brush I'd left behind was in his hand, but when I reached for it, he shook his head.

"Let me."

I hesitated, uncertain, but then nodded and held still. Before he'd even finished the first stroke, I knew he'd done this before. I said as much and watched a faint, sad smile curl his lips. "I used to comb Anne's hair when she was younger. She'd have nightmares, and it was something that always calmed her. Her regular nanny was hurt one summer when Anne was six. The woman broke her leg in a fall—nasty break. Needed surgery and several months off to recover. The woman my parents initially hired to replace her had come highly recommended, but she wasn't the nurturing sort, they later learned. Anne would wake up crying, and this woman would ignore her. At that time, I still had the rooms across the hall, and I went to the nanny's room the first night and told her that

Anne was crying, thinking perhaps she just couldn't hear. She'd heard, she assured me. But children didn't learn to confront their fears or overcome them through coddling. I had no idea what coddling meant, but I knew she wasn't going to comfort Anne. So, I did. I went into Anne's room and sat with her. She asked if I'd brush her hair. That was what Andrea always did. She'd brush Anne's hair until Anne fell back to sleep."

"You must miss her terribly," I said softly.

"Right now, I'm still working on accepting and struggling not to implode from the rage inside me." He moved to another section of my hair, eyes focused on that task, and that task alone. "But for now...I don't want to think about it or talk about it. I just want to think about you. Can I take your shirt off before I finish this?"

The rapid change of subject was enough to give me whiplash.

"Ah...what?"

"I want to take your shirt off and stare at your lovely tits while I finish brushing your hair." When he looked up, his hot gaze all but scorched me. "May I do that?"

My throat was so dry, I couldn't speak. My self-consciousness had me wanting to say no, but raw heat and naked desire filled his eyes, and it was contagious, flooding me. I had no defense. With a single nod, I gave him my permission.

He tucked the brush away, into his pocket, I assumed, then reached around, his fingers going to the top button. He took his time with each one. Undressing had never been so sensual, but he treated it like a reveal, a striptease, but I was the one being stripped and teased...with my own body.

Finally, he reached the last button and smoothed the shirt

down off my shoulders. "Look at you," he murmured, voice guttural. "Your cheeks are flushed, and that soft pink runs straight down your neck over your breasts. And your breasts..." he cupped them through the plain cotton bra, plumping them together and circling my nipples with his thumbs, "so fucking gorgeous."

I couldn't think of a single response. I couldn't even think. I just wanted. Shoving myself into his hands, I whimpered.

I did it again when he let me go, although when he reached behind me to free the catch on my bra, I decided that maybe it was okay.

He didn't go back to touching me though.

Instead, after tossing the bra on the floor with my shirt, he pulled the brush back out. The disgruntled look I gave him made him laugh. "I told you I wanted to do this. You said I could. Have you changed your mind?"

"No."

"Good. Your nipples are so tight and swollen. Do they hurt?"

"Yes." And just having him *ask* that made it even worse.

He moved to another section of my hair. "Are you wet?"

"Yes." Without thinking, I reached back and clasped his hips, pulling him up against me. His cock nudged my ass, and through my clothes and his, I felt him pulse. Longing ripped at me, vicious and feral.

He tossed the brush onto the counter and reached around me, arms going under mine. "Can I?" He tapped the button of my jeans.

I nodded, and he stripped them off in a brisk motion far at odds with the manner he'd used earlier, taking my panties down as he went until I stood there completely naked with him kneeling behind me.

Hands gripping my ankles, he pressed his mouth to the dip in my spine, then moved lower. His hands moved upward, tracking along my calves, thighs and upward. In a smooth motion, he came to his feet, hands now gripping my hips. He pulled me tight against him, and I groaned as he thrust his cock against my ass. My knees threatened to melt when I heard the rasp of his zipper.

"Maybe we can do the tying up thing later?" Aeric asked.

I whimpered, intent on soothing the ache inside. But then the words penetrated. I tugged away from him and turned, shaking my head.

Even as aroused as I was, as needy, I was driven by something I couldn't describe, and I needed more than just sex. "Get undressed. I want a shower...then we can do the tying up...and other things."

Part of me thought he'd tried to change my mind.

He took my hand and bent over it, pressing a kiss to the back. "As I said...I'm your servant."

I'd just gotten my hair wet when he joined me and took over the task. "Allow me," he murmured.

"You're enjoying this *servant* thing," I said, sinking into him as he massaged shampoo into my hair.

"I think I could get used to serving you." There was an odd note in his voice, but he stood behind me, and I couldn't look into his eyes, or even see his face to search for clues. "Maybe you could get used to relaxing and enjoying it. For now, at least?"

It was hard not to enjoy it, the hot, pulsating water pounding down on me while he took care of my hair, rinsing away suds, then working conditioner through the curls, tackling each step as if he'd been trained to do so.

"You're an expert at this kind of thing. Is there a school for it, or do you just enjoy providing this service to the women you sleep with?"

He brushed his lips over my shoulder then slicked me down with a thick liquid cleanser that smelled of him. "I'm afraid to answer that. It's not considered good form to discuss one's previous lovers when you're working on seducing the woman you want to spend the night with, after all."

"Oh. I guess I never read the rule book. You were my first and all..."

His hands stopped moving.

I winced, realizing what I'd just let slip. I'd thought maybe he hadn't realized, and I'd been fine with that. It's not always as obvious as books make it out to be, and I knew that. Now, face heating with embarrassment, I didn't know what to do or say as he urged me to turn around.

It wasn't like I could take the words back.

"You're first," he said slowly, as if measuring each word. "Are you...you hadn't been with anybody before me?"

"Ah. No." Clearing my throat, I shrugged. "I didn't think it was a big deal, and I didn't want you changing your mind or anything. I mean...we both needed to not think, right?"

He cupped my face in his hands and dipped his head. "Kitt..."

I thought he'd let it go at that.

I was wrong.

He lifted his head, eyes still reflecting shock. "I can't...I would have..."

"Don't." I touched his mouth. "I don't regret it. Well, I kind of did for a few days, but...I don't now." Shame flashed across his features. "I don't deserve the truth you're giving now."

Taking a deep breath, I smiled, just a bit. "Well, you're supposed to be letting me tie you up, right?"

He laughed, and something inside me unclenched.

TWENTY-EIGHT

AERIC

It was a good thirty minutes before she had me where she wanted me.

I hadn't been content to just let her dry her hair with a towel, instead digging out the hair dryer I'd never used. Combing my fingers through the silky-soft curls, I dried them until they framed Kitt's face in tousled waves.

Then, while she'd waited with a towel wrapped around her, I fetched the lotion I'd seen in her bathroom. It was erotic torture and untold pleasure to slick and spread and smooth it into her skin.

Another torture was watching her watch me. I hadn't bothered dressing or grabbing the robe hanging outside the shower, and it had been so she would do just that—watch me, as I watched her.

Her eyes followed me hungrily, and what I'd wanted to do was lift her onto the counter and take her there. But she'd made her choices clear, and now, after she'd tortured me with her breasts swaying inches above my face as she tied my wrists, she knelt between my thighs and licked her lips.

"If you keep looking at me like that, I'm going to lose it." My cock pulsed in agreement.

"I'm just wondering where to start." She smiled, and it was clear she'd made up her mind. I hissed out a breath as she dragged one finger down the length of my cock. "I'm starting here."

As she bent over me and took me in her mouth, I closed my eyes.

Immediately, I opened them, straining to see her through the fall of her hair. The few glimpses I got were just enough to tease, and I clenched my hands into fists.

She was a bit awkward at first, and it was obvious she was trying to learn her way, but every move, every drag of her wet mouth over my swollen flesh was sweet. By the time she found a rhythm, I was already thrusting up to meet her mouth, swearing and pleading for more.

She paused and looked up at me, a faint smile appearing.

"You're enjoying this." Panting, I jerked against the tie and craned my head to stare at my bound wrists before focusing back on her. "Aren't you?"

"It seems you are, too." She licked swollen lips.

"I'd enjoy it more if you swung around and sat on my face."

She blinked.

"Do it, Kitt. Let me eat that delicious pussy while you suck my cock."

She shuddered. It was a visible reaction, and the thought that I'd caused it made me even hotter, needier...desperate.

But she shook her head. "Maybe next time."

"So, you want to torture me. Is that it?"

"Maybe?" She cocked her head, as if considering. Then bent back over me for more erotic torture.

A strangled noise left me as she slid back up, then slowly repeated the move. I hit the back of her throat, and as she started to pull up, I said, "Don't stop...please...fuck...a little more..."

She tried to move deeper, and I felt her tighten, then she jerked up. "You're too big."

"No man ever minds hearing that." I smiled, although what I wanted was to be back inside that mouth of hers. "You can take more...just...breathe...go slow. If you untie me, I can help."

"No." She bent back over, taking me at my word, going *slow*...so slow, I was shuddering, every muscle rigid by the time the head of my cock nudged the back of her throat again.

"There, Kitt..." The words came out a growl. "Right there... just...relax your throat. *Swallow* me..."

It took several more tries, but then, something changed, and she *did* relax. When she swallowed, brilliant bursts of light exploded in front of my eyes as she did it a second time.

"That's it...damn it, Kitt..." Arching into her, I begged and pleaded. "Untie me, damn it. Let me fuck that pretty mouth... that's it...don't stop...again...oh, hell...just like that..."

Abruptly, she stopped and crawled up my body so fast, I was still mid-plea when she straddled my hips, mind struggling to catch up. Then she was sinking down on me, her wet pussy slick and hot, her muscles squeezing, and squeezing...

"Kitt!"

Her eyes were wild, locked on me as she fell forward and started to ride me. A low, ragged moan escaped her as she moved harder, faster.

"Kiss me, Kitt."

She bent down, and I licked at her lips, stabbing at them until she opened for me. While I dominated that kiss, she rode me, her pussy milking me, her breasts rubbing over my sweat-slicked chest.

Time faded away.

The only things I could hear was the roar of my blood, pounding in my ears, and her ragged moans, breathy pleas.

Her climax started to build as I fought mine off, determined not to come before she did. Her muscles clenched, every part of her tightening in readiness.

And then it was there, ripping through her, and I couldn't hold back any longer.

I groaned her name against her lips, the sound almost broken, desperate and soft, at odds with the vicious hunger over-powering me.

TWENTY-NINE

KITT

I woke up to find Aeric propped up on his elbow next to me, staring at me with dark eyes, his face unreadable.

"Did I wake you?"

"No." I frowned, then shook my head. "I don't think you did."

The look on his face left me with the urge to squirm. "What's wrong?"

Instead of answering, he reached up and traced his fingers over the bruising on the left side of my face. When gravity wasn't working against me, as it was now, my hair hid much of the bruising, but I had no doubt he could see the ugly discoloration in all its hideousness now.

"How did this happen?"

I should have expected the question. Swallowing, I tried to find the right way to explain.

He must have taken my silence for something else because he started speaking. "I know you were hurt, that you were in the hospital. Feidelberg told me, seemed to take a great deal of pleasure in watching me squirm." He scowled, then sat up, facing away. "Not that he was happy you were hurt. Neither of them are very happy with me, not since I told them I'd thrown you out of your own home, then threatened you. Police officers don't like it when some foreign national comes into their country and makes threats against legal residents of that country. I should know that. It's happened in Monaco a time or two and the police don't care for it there either."

I reached out and put a hand on his back.

He turned and met my eyes. "Will you tell me?"

"I was staying at a hostel. A couple of tourists were drunk, and one of them tried to put his hands on me. I ran and was trying to get into a room where I could get away from him." My throat tried to tighten up, but I kept going, recounting it as best as I could.

By the time I was done, his jaw was clenched, fury etched into every part of him.

Sitting up next to him, I took his hand. He clutched at mine, and I leaned against his arm. The silence was taut and growing heavier by the minute. "I've been thinking I should go back to America."

He tensed but said nothing.

"I haven't figured out how yet, considering the status of my bank account, but I don't know what reason I have to stay." I squeezed his hand, then got up. It wasn't until the sheets fell away that I realized I was naked. I looked down at myself and blushed. "Um."

He cocked a brow, but even the smile he gave me was bleak. "If you must dress—and I'm not insisting you must—you can grab a shirt from my closet. I think I'll enjoy seeing something of mine on you."

Not sure how to parse that, I went to the closet and grabbed the first thing I saw, shoving my arms into the sleeves and buttoning it before turning back to him.

He'd risen and pulled a loose pair of pants up over his hips. Turning, he met my gaze.

"The inspectors working the case have talked to me. They know I'm not involved. So, I don't need to worry about that. And I..." Sighing, I shoved a hand through my hair. "I don't know what's left for me. You'll go to Monaco soon and take Josef and Karol with you. Maybe it's best if I just go back now rather than wait and let it drag out."

A muscle pulsed in his cheek.

I waited for him to say something, although I didn't know what I expected.

The phone rang. Flustered, I reacted out of habit and went to answer.

"Ah...*Frau* Bocho?"

The voice on the other end of the line was familiar, although I couldn't immediately place it. "Yes. May I ask who is calling?"

"It's Simeon Lieberman, Inspector Lieberman. I...well, I suppose Prince Aeric managed to track you down."

Flushing, I shot a look at the man in question. "Yes. We spoke last night. I assume you wish to talk to him?"

"Yes, please."

I turned the phone over and ducked into the bathroom as much to give him privacy as anything else. After taking care of matters, I stalled a few minutes longer by gathering up clothes and tidying the room.

He knocked on the door. "Are you stalling so I could talk freely?"

"Guilty." I winced as I opened the door to find him waiting.

"It wasn't necessary," he said softly. He traced the bruise on my face once more. "It enrages me to see this, even more to know I put you in the situation by my actions."

"You're not responsible for what they did, Aeric," I told him.

He clearly didn't agree but let it go. "The police are being careful with the children since we don't know what led to...the attack on Anne and Karl. I visit them daily but only after security measures are cleared. That's what the call was for. I'm cleared to visit, but I have to leave within the next thirty minutes, or we'll have to do another security check which means waiting a few more hours. Do you wish to come?"

"Yes!" There was no question.

A smile softened his face, and he angled his head toward the door. "Then go get dressed. We have to leave soon. As charming as you look in my shirt, I'd rather nobody else see you that way."

I rushed from the room, grateful for the distraction—not just from the way my heart sped up at his final comment, but from everything weighing on me.

I did have a new concern, though. Several of them, really. What would I tell the kids when they asked why I'd been gone so long? And should I tell them I might be leaving them again too?

THIRTY

AERIC

"She's very good with them," Mila said, sitting next to me in the shaded area of her back yard while Kitt raced around with Josef, Karol, Conrad, and Darrick. The shrieks of laughter coming from the children as they tried to catch her, only to have her catch them, was the best sound I'd heard in days.

Well, save for the sounds of her in my bed last night. Her sighs and moans...they were a music I'd never forget.

"Yes, she is," I said, realizing that Mila seemed to be waiting for some sort of response. "She adores them. And it's clear the feeling is mutual."

Just watching the three of them filled me with an ache I couldn't quite define. It was separate from the grief, an emptiness I'd never known before.

"Yes, Kitt and those children are quite close."

I couldn't miss the subtle undercurrent in the woman's voice this time. Turning my head, I met her gaze. When I'd arrived at the house with Kitt, both women had greeted each other with tearful hugs, and it had become obvious in that moment that Kitt had met Mila more than once. Although the woman was easily a good ten years older than me, she must have been more than just a casual friend of Anne's for her to be so comfortable with Kitt, and for Kitt to be so comfortable with her.

Now, as I looked at her, I could see the concern in her eyes and an uneasy feeling settled inside, rather like when I'd been a child and had been caught doing something I shouldn't.

"Anne was very fond of Kitt," Mila said in a matter of fact voice. "And I'm...aware that Kitt has already been through an ordeal since your sister and brother-in-law passed."

There was nothing untoward about the way she delivered those words, or even in her expression. Her face was calm, her dark skin smooth, a faint half smile on her lips while her brown eyes held mine steadily.

Yet I felt as if I'd just been scolded by my mother.

I had no idea how to respond to her since I wasn't about to start babbling out an apology. I had no problem of apologizing endlessly to Kitt—not that she was giving me many chances to do so. Every time I brought it up, she changed the subject or brushed it off.

I had no desire to discuss it with somebody else. Unless, of course, that person had a magic wand that would turn back time and let me undo every fucking mistake I'd made, and I doubted Mila had one handy.

"I think all of them have been through an ordeal," I said finally, as it was clear that Mila wasn't going to move on until I responded in some way.

"You as well, Your Highness," she added, the proper amount of deference in her voice, along with a polite nod of her head that conveyed true respect, not the sarcastic mockery like the inspectors gave. But again, she went silent, watching...and waiting.

Frustrated enough, tired enough, I blew out a breath and rose, pacing away a few feet, acutely aware of Guillermo and my other security men watching from within the house. On the far end of the yard, one of Mila's guards patrolled the interior perimeter, and I knew another was on the opposite side, doing the same.

All these people made me feel claustrophobic in a way that made me want to grab Kitt and the children, throw them in a car and just start driving—fast—until we were very, very far away.

Instead, I just paced to the end of the cobblestone patio before returning and meeting Mila's level gaze with my own. "You clearly have something you want to say. And you're an observant woman. You've likely noticed that I'm tired, frustrated, and you are already aware, I'm grieving. Would you please save me the trouble and just say what is on your mind?"

"May I be blunt?" she asked after a moment, her full lips, painted a deep shade of red, curving up.

"I just asked you to do that very thing."

She laughed, the sound full and bright and warm. "Not precisely...and this isn't related to the matters weighing on my mind, but...still, I'd like to say it. You are quite like your sister, you know. So very regal and proper." She pursed her lips and looked me up and down before adding, "Royal. So very royal. Until you're done with it and then you're very blunt, and you have no problem dropping *regal* and *proper* by the wayside."

The humor faded from her eyes, and she looked back over at the children. At Kitt.

"Americans do not understand the nuances of royalty the way Europeans do, Prince Aeric. And Kitt is...young. Innocent, even. I won't say naïve. I think she's faced some cruelties in her life that stripped that away some time ago. But she is innocent. She sees the good in people, and it can blind her to reality."

Giving me a weighted look, she arched her brows.

"I'm sure you have a point to this."

"Very much so." She glanced over at the children—and Kitt —playing in the yard, a warm smiling curving her lips upward. "A person would have to be blind not to see it, you know. The way she watches you. And how you watch her. But this isn't fair." Mila swung her head back around and pinned me with a hard look. "Surely you're aware of that."

"What are you suggesting, Frau Kelly?" A muscle pulsed in my jaw and that sense of vague discomfort vanished, lost in a rush of anger.

"She's their caretaker. Their nanny, for all intents and purposes. *A servant*, which is how the world would view her. Are you planning to take her back to Monaco? Install her in the Princely Castle so she cares for them during the day and services you at night?"

"You overstep," I said, fury biting into me.

"If I do, I do it out of respect for your sister," Mila responded calmly, unintimidated. "What would *she* think of you turning her friend, the caretaker of her children into your bed partner?"

"It's more..." I went silent as the impact of that hit me. *It's more than that.* Swallowing, I swung my head around and watched as Kitt let the children tackle her finally, taking her to the ground. She shrieked as they pounced and started to tickle.

The emptiness I'd been trying to understand suddenly made sense.

That emptiness was *her*. It was a void—one only she could fill.

"It's more than that," I finished gruffly.

"You're in line to become the next Prince of Monaco, Your Highness," Mila said gently. "She was hired to take care of your niece and nephew. How much *more* can it become? Where can this possibly lead?"

Kitt called out in a breathless voice, "I yield! You win! I yield!"

So do I, I thought, dazed.

The children around Kitt broke out into whoops and cries, falling away and she sat up. When she did, her eyes sought me out, and my heart clenched.

Without even giving any real thought to the consequences, I simply said what I was feeling. "As you said, I'm in line to become the next Prince of Monaco. I think it's up to me to choose where this leads. Well, me and Kitt. Personally, I'm of a mind that it shouldn't lead to her simply being their caretaker."

I'D GONE MOST of my life without being a fool. I hoped that would incline my parents to give me the benefit of the doubt if my reckless words from earlier managed to work their way into the mainstream media before I had a chance to talk to my mother and father, but I wasn't going to hold my breath.

It had been nearly an hour since those few tense moments with Mila, and now the minister and Kitt were exchanging hugs while Mila's husband distracted the children. Both Josef and Karol had been in tears when Kitt explained she couldn't stay, and no, she couldn't take them with her, but unlike when I'd been in a similar situation, she hadn't frozen in panic.

She'd sat down and explained in a calm, simple voice that there were things she needed to take care of, because their mother and father would want it that way.

Even though they weren't here where the children could see them, their parents still loved them, and Kitt very much loved them, and making sure they were taken care of was the thing that mattered most. Soon, she'd promised, things would be settled, and they'd be able to go home and sleep in their own beds again.

She'd given me a level look when she'd said that, making it clear I'd have to honor that promise. They'd need that bit of normalcy for a time, even if it was just for a night or two before they moved to Monaco.

I'd already hugged each of them and kissed them goodbye. "Just for now, right, Uncle Aeric?"

Karol had made me promise I'd come back, and I'd done so.

Mila had told me she was having a friend come over for dinner—a child psychologist, somebody the children could talk to, just a casual matter, but she was concerned that Karol, especially, was developing some separation anxiety issues.

That filled me with guilt. I should just grab the children, and Kitt, and go to the airport, leave this country and return to Monaco. Once they were safe within the Princely Castle, I could come back here, bring my own security and intelligence people to start looking for answers—unofficially, of course.

The idea settled in the back of my mind and started to grow, like an ember.

I'd have to think on that with some consideration.

Kitt came toward me, her eyes overly bright, but while the

tears looked close, she didn't let them fall. I took her hand, and we quietly slipped from the house, surrounded by my security detail.

Once we reached my car, I looked at Guillermo and held out my hand. "The keys. I'm driving. You can ride with the men."

Guillermo frowned, his lips compressed tight as he glanced at Louis, the head of my team. Before either of them could argue, I stepped between them both. "This isn't a matter for debate. I need a few minutes to think without you breathing down my neck, and I think Kitt could use the privacy. She's not used to having so many people hover around her. There are two other cars, and you'll be with us the entire way. Now, hand over the keys."

"Your Highness, I do not like this idea," Louis said, his deep voice thick with disapproval. "It was one thing when you first arrived and nobody knew you were in Berlin, but over the past few days, you've been seen by too many people, and you no longer have that protection. We had two reporters snooping around outside the house this morning. This is unwise."

"I agree." Guillermo's hazel eyes held mine as he proffered the keys.

"Your concerns are noted." Taking the keys, I nudged Kitt toward the car, guiding her to the passenger side while my men gathered around, providing a barrier between us and the clearly empty street. I understood their vigilance, and normally, it didn't grate on my nerves, but normal had long since gone by the wayside. I was hard-pressed not to growl at them in a demand for breathing room as I circled around the car.

"You're going straight to the house," Guillermo said, hesitating close enough to the car that it kept me from opening the door, unless I wanted to hit him with it. I wasn't that annoyed. Yet.

"Straight there." Not bothering to offer anything else, I gave the door a pointed stare, and he stepped away, although I was fully aware of his displeasure. He rarely let such emotion show, and I lingered, giving him another look. "It will be fine, Guillermo."

With a stiff nod, he backed away, and I climbed into the car. The moment the door shut, some of the tension fell away, a sigh escaping.

"You too?"

I started the car and looked over at Kitt.

Her brows arched over her soft blue eyes, a rueful smile on her lips. She nodded to the car in front of us as Guillermo climbed in. "Do they hover like that all the time?"

"In Monaco, not so much." After checking the mirrors, I pulled onto the street.

It was quiet, but Charlottenburg almost always seemed to be rather quiet. The lunch hour had passed, and it was too early for people to be traveling home for work, so the residential streets were fairly empty.

"When I'm out of the country or when there are...other concerns? They are more alert."

"Other concerns. Like...Anne."

From the corner of my eye, I saw her shiver.

"Yes," I said, knowing there was nothing else I could say to lessen the fear she had to be feeling. I'd had some of it myself, although it was more for my niece and nephew. There was rage, though. So much rage.

The quiet, tree-lined streets where Mila lived gave way to

more open property as we drove, the tracts of land becoming larger and the houses more exclusive.

Our next turn came into view, and I blew out a sigh. My exhaustion went so deep it made my bones ache. I wanted to lay down with Kitt in my arms and sleep a solid twenty-four hours. But that was a luxury I didn't have. It was time to move the children—and Kitt—out of Germany and into Monaco where my people could protect them.

Unease pricked at me, and I glanced in the rearview mirror as it occurred to me that I'd left Kitt very vulnerable over the past few days—Kitt, and myself.

"What's wrong?"

The tension in her voice had me unclenching my jaw.

Lovely. She'd picked up on my unease. And I could well be reacting to what I'd sensed from Louis and Guillermo. This was why leaders were pressed not to convey emotion—it was too easy to convey the wrong one.

"Nothing, beloved," I said, the endearment coming easily, with no conscious thought. "Other than the stress and worry we all feel right now, at least."

She squirmed in the seat. From the corner of my eye, I saw her hands twisting in her lap, and a few seconds later, she burst out, "I saw you on the news yesterday. I'd been at the coffee shop, and they had a picture of you...you were trying to keep it quiet that you were in Berlin."

"I was, yes." Shrugging as I pressed on the brakes, slowing behind the car in front of us, I added, "We knew it wouldn't last forever."

"Now that more people know you're here, you're in danger, aren't you?"

"No." Instinctively, I laughed the idea off and responded with my trademark arrogance, but not even thirty seconds passed before I made myself step back and view this from her eyes and take her into consideration, then forced myself to answer as the Prince of Monaco—not as Aeric. "That isn't entirely honest, I suppose, Kitt. I'm likely not in any more danger now than I would be had I been visiting under other circumstances. I just need to—"

The screeching tires split through the relative quiet like an eerie scream. It was the only warning we had as the black delivery van that had been driving at a normal speed in the opposite lane suddenly veered and gunned for us.

I saw him coming, and although instinct demanded I do something, for a few taut moments, I had no reaction. At all. I could only stare at the van racing in our direction.

Kitt cried out, startled.

That sharp sound of feminine distress snapped me out of my fog, and I punched the gas, wrenching the wheel just as the van slammed into the car behind us—the one driven by Louis. Some part of my mind—the part that still worked—took in the fact that the van had slammed into the car exactly where Louis would have been sitting.

Louis had already taken action. I saw the car jerk backward, then wheel left, minimizing the impact, but what would that mean, really?

I heard a car horn, followed by another, then again, the screeching of rubber on pavement.

"Aeric!" Kitt's panicked voice had me bracing myself, and I looked to see her staring out the window as two more black vans appeared.

"Fuck," I muttered, whipping the wheel to the right. The pricy, boring vehicle Guillermo had rented for me reacted swiftly, and I punched the gas. The first van slammed into the car carrying Guillermo, and a mix of panic and rage blistered, threatening to explode.

It didn't have a chance.

Kitt screamed.

I saw the third van now, no longer hidden behind the one that had rammed into the security car in front of me. It had slowly, almost lazily rolled around the second one, coming to a halt, blocking me in and preventing me from peeling off to the right so I could drive off.

"Why the *fuck* did I insist on driving?" I muttered, clenching my hands tight around the steering wheel.

Kitt reached for my arm, gripping it silently. Although she said nothing, her fear came through loud and clear, and I reached over, covering her hand with mine.

"It's going to be all right, Kitt," I told her. "I don't know what's going on, but whatever it is, it's going to be—"

The impact came from behind, hard, merciless, and unforgiving.

Kitt screamed.

I shouted, swearing in French, then in Italian. Then the car hit us again, hard enough to leave my ears ringing.

I was only dimly aware when somebody jerked open the door, even less aware when something sharp penetrated my arm.

"I'm sorry, Your Highness," a low, soft voice said. "This isn't how I prefer to do business, but your family owes me a debt."

THIRTY-ONE

KITT

"She's waking up."

The voice was low and annoyed.

Excuse me for not responding appropriately to being kidnapped. The thought popped into my mind, and in that moment, likely hysteria-induced, it struck me as absurdly funny.

There was *nothing* funny about what was going on, though. Not from where I stood.

Or where I sat, rather.

I wasn't *waking* up. I'd never really been asleep—or drugged and unconscious like Aeric had been. When a big, bulky sedan had slammed into the right rear fender, I'd smacked my head on the window, and temporarily, I'd faded in and out, but by the time they'd thrown me into the back of the third van, I'd been awake—instincts bellowing at me to be quiet.

Over the past few minutes, the voices around me had risen, a woman, arguing with a man and telling him to stop fretting like her grandmother, while another man offered to *wake* me up —which had Aeric biting out cold, cutting threats.

At one point, one of the men must have made some move

toward him, because the woman had inserted herself as the leader. "You are not going to strike him, Pierre. We have time."

I'd spent what felt like hours buying time and trying to figure out what was going on. I'd once heard somebody say that if you were ever kidnapped, it was important to stall for time and gather information, if you could. I'd done my best, but then Aeric woke up and one of the men left, fetching the woman.

Now, feeling the weight of her presence once more, I knew I couldn't fool her into thinking I was still struggling to wake up, not the way I'd fooled the two men.

Dragging my head up, I blinked and looked around.

I didn't have to feign the fear, though, and the suspicion that had been forming in her eyes leaked away as she studied me. "*Bonjour, Mademoiselle* Bocho."

Acutely aware of everybody watching, I nodded awkwardly. "*Bonjour.*"

"You speak French."

Guardedly, I nodded, fully aware she was thinking back to the conversations they'd had—and considering whether there was cause for concern.

"My...my father is French. I learned it because of him," I said, tossing it out there for no other reason than as a distraction.

A slow, cool smile curled her lips. "You've never even met your father."

The certain way she spoke those words had my gut going cold. It wasn't a guess. She *knew*.

"How do you know that?" I asked, shrinking back from the predatory look in her eyes.

"There is very little about the home and household of Karl Weiss that I do not know." She blinked, a slow, lazy dip of long black lashes over dark, liquid eyes. "You're twenty-two, a graduate of Texas A&M, and the bastard daughter of a rich Frenchman who tossed his American mistress out on her ass after she told him she was pregnant. She went back to Texas, disgraced and disgruntled and had you. When you were eight, there was a barn that caught on fire at the ranch owned by your grandfather. He told the sheriff you started it. That's noted in the police report, but the investigation reveals that a new employee had admitted to smoking in the barn. When you were fifteen, your grandfather died in a crash during a thunderstorm while coming to pick you up. After you graduated high school at age sixteen, you sought emancipation and left the ranch and haven't been back since."

I felt stripped bare by her cursory summary of my pitiful life. Face hot with humiliation, I forced myself to meet her gaze. "Yes, my childhood sucked. I thought meeting my father might give me...something. But he never responded when I reached out to try and arrange a meeting. All those years spent learning French were wasted. Why am I here?"

She pursed her lips, still watching me pensively. But after a moment, she straightened and turned to Aeric.

He hadn't spoken a word in the past several minutes although I'd been acutely aware of his intense stare.

If looks could kill, this slim, dark-haired woman with her vaguely Asian features and exquisite beauty would be dead, blood oozing from a hundred small wounds.

"Oh, Your Highness." She huffed out a small breath. "Don't look so angry. I think I've been quite reasonable. I haven't harmed a hair on her head, or yours."

"Reasonable." Aeric's voice dripped with scorn. "And that is why my sister is dead."

I tensed, but nobody reacted, all of them focused on Aeric.

"That was an error," she said calmly. "And it was made by two of my men. I assure you, they've suffered for their missteps. The princess was never meant to come to any harm."

"Harm?" Aeric's rage and grief came through in that single word, his eyes lasering on the woman. "*Madam* Danett, my *sister* didn't come to *harm*. She's *dead*."

She sighed and walked over to a couch I didn't even notice until that moment. "Benny, I want some wine."

From the corner of my eye, I saw a man spring into motion, moving for the bar tucked against the wall on the far side of the opulent room. She sat there, legs crossed, feet clad in sparkling, strappy heels as she studied Aeric. Her complete lack of denial slapped me in the face. *She's dead.*

"You killed Anne," I whispered, horror flooding me.

She glanced at me and offered a liquid shrug. "Not personally. But the men who went after her and her selfish, arrogant husband were mine, so her death is on my hands."

She said it so *coolly*, so matter-of-factly, like we were discussing a carton of cracked eggs or a glass of spilled milk—not two living, breathing people.

Something of what I felt must have shown on my face because she kept her attention on me, head cocked, eyes narrowed and lips pursed. "You look so surprised, *mademoiselle*...Kitt. I'll call you Kitt. You may call me Tam."

There was something almost friendly in her voice as she spoke, and it sickened me. I didn't want to be *friendly* with the woman who'd killed the closest friend I'd ever had, or her husband.

"Why did you kill her?" I demanded.

Tam sighed again and shook her head. "You're upset. Both of you. I expected no less, but the two of you do not understand my world." As she spoke, there was a knock at the door. Without looking away from me, she called out, "Come in."

A thin, elderly man with a shock of white hair crowning his head came in, eyes on his feet. He turned over a file to Tam, then left. After a few more seconds of her weighted stare, she shifted her attention to Aeric.

"Your brother-in-law owed me money. A great *deal* of money. At one point, it was almost three million euros."

I blanched, feeling sick to my stomach.

A muscle pulsed in Aeric's jaw. "Is that why my sister died?"

"No. Dead people can't repay debts, Your Highness." She sounded annoyed. Leaning forward, she put the file down on the table in front of her, flipping it open and removing something. I only caught a brief glimpse as she turned the items over to one of the men who carried it over to Aeric.

Pictures, I realized.

Aeric's jaw tightened as he looked at them for a brief moment. "What's this?"

"The punishment they received for your sister's death. Princess Anne was never meant to be harmed. My men overstepped, and they were dealt with for that mistake. The younger man had only been with me for a few months, so I was lenient. He lost two fingers on his left hand, and he's... providing service elsewhere to show me that he wants to earn my trust back. His partner is dead. He was older and had worked for me for nearly twenty years. He should have known better."

"That mistake...I assume you mean my sister's death." Aeric gave her a bored look that didn't seem possible considering how he sat there, bound. But he pulled it off. "Am I supposed to believe that my sister's death was a mistake and that you killed one of the men responsible and maimed the other?"

"In my world, Your Highness," she said coolly, "debts must always be paid. Five years ago, in a run of bad luck, Karl Weiss ran up a considerable debt to me at the casino in Monaco. I marked it down considerably after he moved to Germany and helped me establish my business presence there. At one point, his debt to me was *three* million euros. I marked it down by more than half and gave him a time frame. He failed to meet it."

She waved a dismissive hand. "All he had to do was go to you or your father. What is a million or so euros to Monaco's Royal Family?"

"That's why he's dead," I whispered, feeling sick.

Tam sneered dismissively. "He's dead because he's foolish and prideful. While he wasn't to be killed, I can't say I regret it. I *am* sorry for the death of Princess Anne, so I'm providing you, Your Highness, with a choice."

The way she delivered those words filled me with a slick, oily sense of fear, and I closed my hands into fists, panic rising in me, the urge to *run, run, run* suddenly overwhelming.

Wheeling my eyes around, I looked over at Aeric, but he was focused on Tam.

"The debt still remains, Your Highness," she said softly, her face remote and calm, her eyes unreadable. "Over the past two years, he's made payments, but he still owes nearly two hundred thousand. One of you are going to settle it."

*Two hundred thousand euros...*my brain went numb.

Her dark eyes flicked in my direction, and I realized I'd said something out loud. A cool smile twisted her lips then she swung her head back around to study Aeric once more. "How do you propose we settle this matter?"

THIRTY-TWO

AERIC

ALL HE HAD TO DO WAS GO TO YOU OR YOUR FATHER. WHAT IS a million or so euros to Monaco's Royal Family?

Tam's offhand comment circled through my head, as well as her dismissive attitude about my sister's *murder*. She thought *maiming* some fuck would make up for what we'd lost?

In my world.

Her world.

She was a criminal. She'd been operating a casino in Monaco, and through that casino, she ran drugs, money, and flesh—something we'd yet to be able to pin on her, but the pressure had been enough that the woman had diversified out of my country.

And moved to Germany, I reminded myself.

With Karl's help, because he'd owed her a rather obscene amount of money. How had my brother-in-law gotten in so deep with her?

Why hadn't he come to me?

I could understand why he wouldn't have gone to my parents, but he could have come to *me*.

And now this woman wanted to know how we would *settle* this?

Her brows arched as if she knew exactly what I was thinking, and a faint smile curled her lips. "I understand you're upset, Prince Aeric. But you must understand, I'm a businesswoman."

"You're a criminal," I bit off. "And you're the reason my sister and brother-in-law are dead. You sell drugs, you sell flesh. You're not a businesswoman."

Her eyes flashed, but other than that, she showed no reaction.

"You have your ways of doing business, Your Highness." Tam lifted a shoulder, her long, dark hair sliding silkily down her arm. "I have mine...and right now, I'm in charge at the negotiating table."

I snorted. "Am I to assume you're going to kill *me*?"

"Of course not. There's no profit in ending a life. But there *is* profit to be had here." She slid a look toward Kitt, gaze lingering.

"Don't," I bit off. "Don't even consider it."

"As I said, I'm giving you a *choice*." She leaned forward. "But I'm running low on patience. Every moment I spend addressing this debt of Karl's is a moment I'm not tending to other business. In the end, that's more money he's cost me."

"You can shove that debt up your ass."

"You should have a care, Prince Aeric." Tam leaned back in her seat, assessing me with a shark's predatory gaze, then, without blinking, she recited off an address.

My blood ran cold.

Across the room, Kitt tensed, and I knew she'd recognized it as well.

Mila's home. Where the children were.

"Leave them alone," Kitt said, her voice a combination of harsh and pleading.

"It's not the way I care to do business." Tam pursed her lips in mock consideration as she looked at Kitt. "Children too often become pawns to those around them. But it's up to you. Either one of you will handle this debt or—"

"I will."

"No!" I jerked against the ties that held my wrists together as Tam turned to look at Kitt. "Kitt, be quiet. Just...sit down and be quiet. I'll take care of this."

But Kitt's soft blue eyes never wavered from Tam's. My heart clenched, and although I wouldn't have thought I could feel any more anger, any more fear, a new well of it raged inside. I knew the kind of shit Tam had been running inside Monaco—that was likely why she'd shifted her base to Germany. A larger country meant it was much easier to hide the sort of unsavory business she'd indulged in.

And Kitt was blindly throwing herself into that with no idea of the ways Tam would expect her to *pay* that debt back.

Tam circled around Kitt, giving her a measuring look. Once she stood behind Kitt, she flicked a gaze at me, and I saw the appraising interest, the faint smile. "You could be very popular, *mademoiselle*."

"Stop it," I said, so furious I was shaking with it. "She's not going anywhere with you. She's not doing anything *for* you."

"I think the decision has already been made." Tam finally looked at me, then nodded.

But the nod wasn't for me, and although I tried to move, there wasn't enough time to evade.

The blow came from behind, a black starburst blinding me.

Then everything went dark.

SOMETHING cold and hard pressed against my cheek. Pain pulsed in the back of my head, growing more and more real as I drifted closer to wakefulness. It was so intense, I didn't want to wake at all, but a gut-deep sense of wrongness settled over me.

Something was wrong.

What was it?

What was wrong?

Fighting past the fog, I forced my eyelids to lift, and I shoved upright. My tongue was glued to the top of my mouth, and my limbs didn't want to move. The stiffness, combined with the obscene pounding in my head made me think I'd been hitting the bottle, except I knew that wasn't right.

I'd been visiting Karol and Josef...and Kitt had been with me.

Kitt.

My mind snagged on that detail, and the sense of alarm, of *wrongness,* flared once more. What was it? What was wrong?

Swearing, I lurched to my feet and shoved the heel of my hand to my temple. Dizziness crept in, but I swallowed and focused, staring at a vase of flowers on the table in front of me. They were dead. I hadn't noticed before, but now their withered blooms struck me as obscene.

Kitt wouldn't have let them die.

Anne wouldn't have let them die.

Kitt. Anne. Karl.

"Fuck!" I shouted.

Memory slammed into me, hard and fast, filling in those fogged, empty spaces with brutal, cutting efficiency. Tam Danett. The national police's criminal investigations unit had been looking into her for several years, but she had been able to elude arrest—and prosecution. There were worries about a corrupt official in the unit, and in the back of my mind, I was already planning how I'd deal with that. *If* it was true...

But I'd deal with that later.

Tam Danett had killed my sister.

Tam Danett had made threats against my niece and nephew.

And Kitt...

"Kitt!" I shouted, although I already knew the house around me was empty. The only other sounds in the house were those of my footsteps and voice, growing ever more furious and panicked.

After going through the house a second time, I came to a stop outside my bedroom and sagged against the wall. Listlessly, I stared at the antique mirror on the far wall. Solange had given that mirror to my sister and Karl as a wedding gift. It had been in Solange's family for almost two hundred years, a token of her affection for my sister.

Staring at my reflection, I felt my rage growing ever brighter, ever hotter, and without thinking, I lunged forward and grabbed the mirror, yanking it from its moorings. It came off the wall easily—too easily—but in my rage, I didn't notice. Not until I spun and threw it, watching as it crashed against the wall where I'd just been standing.

Immediately, guilt and disgust rose inside me. A piece of the carved, decorative wood had broken off, and I could hear Solange's voice in my ear. "Such a fine piece...dates back to the 1700s. They don't make them like this anymore, Prince Aeric. She can give this to her daughter when she marries."

Kneeling by the broken piece, I scooped it up, running my

thumb over the jagged edge absently and straightened. I stopped and looked back at the broken piece in my hands. "Dates back to the seventeen hundreds?"

The exposed wood was a soft, mellow gold.

Unsettled, I hunkered by the mirror and righted it, studying where the ornate, decorative piece had broken off. The churning in my gut grew as I saw pieces of exposed wood far too pale, considering the mirror was supposed to date back to the 1700s. And the 'gold' leafing that made the piece shine so subtly, so exquisitely even after hundreds of years? I picked at an exposed fleck and rubbed it between my thumb and forefinger.

"Fake," I murmured.

If I knew much of anything, it was that my mother's beloved *Dame d' Honeur*, Solange Laurent, would have *never* given my sister something covered in cheap, imitation gold leaf. Or perhaps not so cheap, considering this mirror had hung in Anne's home. I hadn't even noticed.

But Solange would have.

Antiques had never held much interest for me unless they fell into a few specific areas...and one of those areas happened to be automobiles. My father had given Karl a 1966 AC Cobra 427 Roadster for Christmas the year after Josef had been born.

Although it hadn't been my favorite from my father's collection, I'd teased him about it good-naturedly, and my father, in the same manner, had replied, "Had you been the first to give me a grandchild, the car would have been yours."

I'd pointed out that *Karl* wasn't his child, which was when Anne had opened the small gift box that matched her husband's and found the keys to the 1965 Aston Martin DBS. That *had* been a favorite.

"No. But Anne is," he'd said, chuckling at my look.

I burst out the back door, running for the garage just as a pair of lights spilled across the driveway. I ran across their path and heard somebody shouting, then recognized a voice. Guillermo.

In the back of my mind, there was relief, because I'd remembered the accident too. But I was intent, focused on my destination. I jerked at the doors, but they didn't open.

Guillermo drew even with me and caught my arm. I spun to face him, and he flung himself at me. "Prince Aeric," he said, voice choked with emotion.

The vans, all of us surrounded. I closed my eyes, hugging my friend and aide briefly before nudging him back. He cleared his throat and adjusted his shirt—one that had blood splashed across it. There were other men around us, most of them strangers, and I ignored them. "How bad was it? My security team?"

His gaze fell away. "Louis didn't make it. He took the brunt of the impact. He realized something was wrong before any of us, it seems. He'd shouted a warning at the others in the car, pulled his weapon. He'd gone to lean out the window..."

At his pause, I squeezed his shoulder. He covered my hand with his.

But I didn't give myself more than that brief moment, turning back to the garage. "I need these doors open."

Voices rose behind me, but I tuned them out, and Guillermo asked no questions. He pulled the keys from somewhere, and seconds later, the doors opened. Only two cars were inside—a nice SUV and a simple sedan. The SUV was a BMW, but there was nothing remarkable about it. The sedan was a Ford and looked to be several years old.

Turning on my heel, I headed for the house, pushing through the throng of people, my mind whirling. He'd sold the two cars, the mirror. What else? I tried to remember other gifts or things of value that Anne would have had, but I'd grown up surrounded by luxury.

The incessant chattering coming from behind me fell on deaf ears as I strode through the kitchen and down the hall to the formal parlor, the large room Anne rarely used.

Too stuffy, she'd told me. *But Karl likes it this way for when he has business partners he wants to impress.*

Flicking on the lights, I looked around, gaze landing on a Ming vase that stood on a table near the mirror. I picked it up and studied it, but I had no idea what to look for.

"Your Highness, what are you doing?" Guillermo asked, his voice cautious.

"I'm looking for fakes," I said shortly. Pinning him with a hard look, I repeated myself. "I'm looking for fakes because I think Karl sold off almost everything of value to pay that fucking gambling debt."

One of the men separated himself from the group, and I blinked, surprised to see who it was.

He held out large hands and offered a faint smile. "My mother is an antiques dealer, Your Highness. I'm no expert, but I know a couple of points to look for...and I can do that while you advise us as to what is going on."

THIRTY-THREE

KITT

A HARD SHAKE ROUSED ME FROM A DEEP, DREAMLESS sleep.

Confused, I opened my eyes, only to immediately close them and shield my face as light splintered in, threatening to damage my corneas in brutal fashion.

"That's enough, Benny," a soft, feminine voice said.

I recognized neither the name nor the voice—at first.

"You might as well open your eyes, Kitt. I have a painkiller to help with the headache, but you can't see it or the breakfast and coffee if you lay there, hunched over like a drunken lout with a hangover."

"I'm not..." I had to stop and clear my throat, but it was so painfully dry, it didn't help. "I'm not drunk."

Even as I said it, I did a mental recount because the pounding in my head did sort of feel like a hangover. Coffee, she'd said. And something for the headache.

I sat up, the feel of the bed beneath me unfamiliar. Squinting, I looked around, avoiding the direct source of light coming from behind me as I let my eyes adjust. I saw a tray of food on a nightstand by the bed. There were also a couple of plain white tablets, a glass of water, and a steaming cup of coffee. I grabbed the pills without thinking and popped them into my mouth, washing them down with the water.

"You're a trusting sort, aren't you?"

"What?" Confused, I looked up and finally saw her, the woman who'd been speaking. She looked familiar, but I couldn't place her.

"Taking pills offered by a woman you don't really know." She lifted a shoulder. She sat with legs crossed, her other arm draped over her lap, her fingers tapping out an idyllic rhythm on her knee. "Who knows what those pills could have been."

I blanched.

She tossed her head back, laughing. "Oh, such a look. Relax, darling. They are exactly what I said, a painkiller for your headache. Nothing more."

I swallowed back the nausea, still uneasy. Memory had started to return, and I looked around. The last clear thought in my head had been the sound of my own voice, rising as I shouted for them not to hurt Aeric. Then something had jabbed me in the arm.

"You drugged me."

She lifted a shoulder. "We had to bring you to the casino, and as it happened, the German police were already looking for both you and Prince Aeric." She paused, then added, "That search has already been called off."

"Why?"

"Prince Aeric returned to Monaco with the children." She smiled, looking pleased. "And a woman fitting your description, with your passport, boarded a flight for Heathrow, with a continuing destination onto the United States. As far as the German police are concerned, you are no longer in Germany, and thus, none of their concern. Happily for me, you were cleared of all involvement in the deaths of Princess Anne and that useless fool she married."

Hot rage burned within. Clutching the edges of the mattress, I fought to hide it, but I didn't do that good of a job because a small smile curved her lips.

"Why be angry at me, Kitt? It wasn't *my* actions that brought you here. I'm not the one who stole the money *you* earned. I'm not the one who sold two classic cars, gifts from the Sovereign Prince of Monaco, to pay down an obscene debt incurred because of a weak will and inability to cut my losses. That was all because of Karl...a useless fool."

"Karl isn't the one who drugged me or offered me the choice between paying off *his* debt or letting you take it out on his children," I bit out. "That was *you*. But, of course...there's no reason for me to be angry with *you* for kidnapping me, drugging me, sending the men who killed not only him but Anne as well. How silly of me not to see that."

Something flashed in her eyes, and the lazy tapping of her fingers stilled.

Taut silence passed.

I counted a beat of ten, then twenty. Then her fingers started tapping again, and a smile returned to her face, still cool, but holding a far sharper edge to it.

"You're not quite the meek little thing I'd expected. That may be a good thing...and it may be a bad thing." She rose and gestured to the tray. "You should eat. Food will help flush the drugs from your system more quickly. You have thirty minutes to eat, shower and get dressed before you're needed downstairs."

Anger still burned inside, a hot little ball that grew and grew, storming and swirling with other emotions.

Part of me was relieved to hear that Aeric had gotten the children safely out of Germany. Another part felt...empty, aching with the loss of him already, even though we barely knew each other.

Of course, I wanted him to take care of Josef and Karol. They were children and had already suffered so much.

But the hurt, lonely girl inside me felt lost, cut adrift once more.

Don't think about that, I told myself as I watched Tam cross the room toward the door.

"Downstairs for what? And what am I supposed to wear?" I looked around the elegant suite. "It's not like I packed my overnight bag."

"There are clothes in the closet. The uniform is...tightly regulated, but you can mix and match the basic pieces. As to what you're needed downstairs for?" She smiled. "You're working off the debt, as we discussed. You'll be serving drinks, food...or anything else my guests in the high stakes lounge require. And should one of them decide they require *you*, you'll provide that service as well."

My blood went cold. "I don't recall agreeing to that."

"Your agreement isn't necessary." She shrugged, clearly unconcerned. "My security team alone will decide if somebody is out of line. This room is yours, for now, so if somebody wants to bring you back here, that's permissible. And you're allowed to accompany guests from the high stakes lounge. They've all been adequately screened to provide for everyone's comfort."

"*I'm* not comfortable."

"Well. You'll have to work on that." She left then, the door closing behind her with a final, doom-inspiring click.

I dropped down on the bed and stared at the tray of food.

What had I gotten into?

THIRTY-FOUR

AERIC

THE ASSAULT VEST WITH ANTI-RIFLE PLATES WAS INSANELY hot, but the only way I'd even been allowed to participate had been if I'd agreed to wear it. News of Louis's death had gotten back to my father, and although he'd been adamant against my returning to Germany at all, when I told him who'd been involved—and *why* Anne had been murdered—he'd seemed to understand it was something I had to do.

And he was right, although there were more complicated reasons for my involvement than Anne alone. I would have insisted on being there just for her, so one day, I could look my niece and nephew in the eye and tell them that I'd made sure that the people responsible for the deaths of their mother and father didn't get away with it. It would be cold comfort, but it would be closure, and we all deserved that.

But Tam Danett had taken Kitt, and I'd hunt her across the earth.

Of course, instead of hunting her across the earth, I was stuck in the security room that had been taken under control by

Germany's elite tactical unit, the Grenschutzgruppe 9—the GSG 9.

There were three different teams involved, all from Germany but an elite tactical unit from Monaco was also involved.

My security team was with me as well. Guillermo, my personal aide and bodyguard, had been chosen from that detail, partly because we'd gone to school together and partly because we'd always gotten along together.

Louis had been in that detail, and I'd never forgive myself for not listening to him. If I had, perhaps he'd be alive, and perhaps Kitt wouldn't have been taken.

There were also men from my father's personal detail, since half my team was in the hospital dealing with injuries. They'd wanted to be discharged so they could be here. Their need for vengeance was riding them strong. For Anne, for Louis...and for not protecting me, I had no doubt.

We all had a stake in this.

But none of them had the same driving need pushing at them like I did.

I stared at the security monitors, searching for a sign of Kitt.

She hadn't been on any of the gaming floors. Two of Danett's men had been inside the small security and tech serve room when it was taken over, and now they were restrained and sat glaring at us.

Frustrated, I turned and looked at the one who looked the most nervous. "Where else would one of the women Tam offers her guests be?"

"Don't say anything," the bigger guard said belligerently. "Tam will have us out of this in a few hours."

"Is that so?" I paced over and bent down until our faces were on level.

"Yeah." He sneered at me. "You've got no idea how many people she knows, how high her connections go."

"Really." I smirked. "Is one of her connections the chancellor?"

He frowned.

"You're German, aren't you?"

"Damn fucking right." He puffed himself up, lifting his chin as he sneered at me.

"For a man with his hands cuffed behind his back and looking at charges tied to human trafficking, drug trafficking, conspiracy related to both, and that's just to start, you look incredibly arrogant and smug," I said, straightening. Looking over at Guillermo, I asked, "Did you check his travel records?"

Guillermo gave me a thin smile. "I did. He's on the list for extradition."

Germany had agreed to give us that, considering how entangled all of this was in my sister's death. Anybody who'd been employed in specific positions in Danett's casino in Monaco would be on the list.

Guillermo likely already had the list memorized.

"Extra..." He blinked, looking back and forth between Guillermo and me, before shifting his attention to the three remaining members of the GSG-9 team. "What the fuck are they talking about? I'm a German citizen!"

None of them even bothered to look away from the bank of monitors. One even leaned forward and tapped a screen on the far left, murmuring to one of his companions.

"You're a German citizen who committed crimes in *my*

country," I said softly, catching his gaze once more. "And those crimes led up to the death of my sister."

The man's eyes widened, and some dull spark of recognition hit.

"I see you finally recognize me." Hate and rage burned inside, stronger than anything I'd ever felt. It wasn't even directly focused on *this* man—he was just handy. A target. Somebody who worked for Tam, the woman who was responsible for the death of my sister, for Karl. The woman who'd taken Kitt. "Where is the woman Tam brought in earlier?"

Despite the uncertainty in his eyes, he curled his lip in a sneer. "Which woman? There's about two dozen whores running around just in the high stakes area alone, and you think I'll remember *one* of them?"

"You—" I leaped for him.

Guillermo caught me. "Don't." I still struggled, and Guillermo put more effort into holding me back. "Prince Aeric. Don't. Look!"

Look. Look away from this fucker I wanted to kill?

But the urgency in Guillermo's voice nagged at me, and I listened, giving in and following his subtle guidance.

One of the members from the German GSG 9 team pointed at a camera, a picture of Kitt in his hand for reference. "That's her. Right there. I think that's..." He frowned and checked something on the tablet in front of him. "Yeah, that's Henreich Fuchs. He's a registered guest, staying in one of the penthouse suites. He's a sadistic prick—"

The man with him shoved a hard elbow into his side, but it was too late. I'd seen. I'd seen the big bastard all but hauling Kitt down a nearly deserted passageway toward an elevator.

"How do I get there?" I demanded.

"Your Highness..."

I gave Guillermo a cold look. "Find out, or I'll tear this entire building to the ground and find out for myself."

———

"REMEMBER," Guillermo said, his voice low and intense. He stood in front of me, partially blocking my body with his. "*We go in first.*"

"I remember."

I'd never agreed, but I remembered.

I had the assault vest and the same drab uniform worn by my men, as well as an AS 600 Armorsource Ballistic Helmet, the same gear worn by elite tactical units across the globe. In my hands, I loosely gripped a Glock 17 Gen 4, a weapon I was more than marginally comfortable with, thanks to training from Guillermo and Louis.

And I wanted to rip off all the gear, throw the pistol down, and barrel down the hall and through the double doors at the end, all so I could tear the man in that suite limb from limb.

He'd been inside the room with Kitt for less than two minutes.

It had taken us almost ten to get where we were. A tech team had come in after GSG 9 had cleared the main level, and thanks to several clever maneuvers by one of the team members, and a woman by the name of Ilse, the elevator had encountered a brief power malfunction.

I'd hope they could just stall the elevator, but one of the GSG 9 operators shot the idea down, saying if he was in the small space with Kitt for too long, he might grow impatient and turn on her where she'd have limited space to protect herself.

Now, Kitt was in that room, alone with a man who likely had no qualms about doing whatever he wanted, whether she agreed or not.

I'd tear him apart if he hurt her.

A low, angry yell came from behind the door in front of me, and I tensed.

Guillermo shot an arm out in front of me.

"Just the two of them in the room," Jerome Schneider, the team leader of the GSG 9 unit, said, lowering a small device and tucking it away. He said something else, but whatever it was, it fell on deaf ears.

It didn't matter.

I'd heard what I needed to hear.

There was nobody else in the room ahead of me—just Kitt, and the man who'd forced her into the elevator just as the raid on the casino floor was taking place.

Slowly, I secured the Glock at the drop holster on my right thigh, gaze locked on the doors.

There was another yell.

Guillermo gave me a questioning look. *Are you good? Can you handle this?*

I nodded shortly and stood stiffly as the team conferred, speaking in low, harsh voices, using terms that made no sense to me.

And as soon as they were distracted, I bolted.

One of them reached for me, but it was too late.

I was tall and long-legged and fast. And more than that, I was furious and the woman who mattered more than my own life had just cried out from behind those doors a third time.

I slammed into them, driving my shoulder into the seam of the two double doors where they'd be the weakest. They gave way with what felt like ridiculous ease. I pitched forward, hit my knees and rolled, coming up in a crouch, eyes already scanning the room.

Kitt was on the far side.

The big man I'd seen on the security feed had a dumbfounded look on his face, but it had nothing to do with me. I saw that right away.

Kitt had the heavy, silver-plated ice bucket in her hands, and judging by the way she stood, she'd just swung it at the bastard. He swayed, then steadied himself at the last moment, shaking his head as if to clear it.

He never even saw me, swiping out a hand to reach for her, but Kitt danced backward out of his reach.

I lunged for him, vaguely aware of an odd noise—something reminiscent of an animal's—echoing around the room. It never occurred to me that it was my own voice, as I snarled at him.

Taking him down, I plunged a fist into his face. Once. Twice. Three times. Four. Five.

Blood splattered.

But it wasn't enough.

Somebody caught my arm, and I flung him off.

Then I heard her.

Kitt's voice, soft and pleading. "Aeric!"

Dazed, I looked up and saw her hovering there. My arm, still half-lifted, wavered.

She caught my wrist and held tight.

"Kitt," I whispered.

"You can stop hitting him." She laughed, the sound wild and watery. "He can't even feel it now."

I looked down and saw with some level of detachment that she was right.

Heinreich Fuchs was unconscious, his face badly misshapen, bruised and bloody.

Slowly, I stood, wavering a little as the adrenaline storm suddenly drained out.

Kitt grabbed me and held on, while several members of the German tactical unit edged in and caught Fuchs from under his arms, pulling him away.

"You came back," she whispered against my chest. "She said you'd gone back to Monaco with the kids, and I understood. They *needed* to be safe, but...you came back."

She hiccupped and shook her head, lapsing into silence.

My right hand ached, a dull throbbing already making itself known as I curved my palm over the back of her head. I wrapped my other arm around her waist and pressed a kiss to the top of her head. "Of course I came back. I couldn't have left you here, Kitt. Don't you know that?"

She sniffled and burrowed in deeper.

All around us, people rushed back and forth, and I cursed the lot of them because I couldn't tell her.

Not here.

Instead, I wrapped my arms around her and clung tight. "I'll always come for you, *cher*. Always."

KITT DARTED a look at the house, then at me. "Why are we here? I thought you wanted to get back to Monaco. To Karol and Josef."

"I do. Yes." Blowing out a breath, I fought to relieve the tension that held my muscles in knots. It didn't help. Raw, restless energy burned inside me, liquid lightning inside my veins, and nothing helped. "But it's late. I'm in bloody, torn clothes, and I'm tired. You must be exhausted. The children are sleeping. We don't need to arrive on the doorstep of the palace looking like we've been through a war. We need to...compose ourselves before we see them."

Kitt shifted next to me and reached out to touch my hand. I tensed, and she immediately jerked back. I caught her wrist loosely and brought her fingers to my lips, kissing them.

"Apologies," I said. "I'm...on edge."

She offered a weak smile. "I get that. Me too. You're right, really. About composing ourselves and all. I'd feel a lot better if I could get a shower, honestly. Get out of these clothes." With a questioning look toward the door, she arched her brows. "Are we going to get out or just sit here?"

"We're sitting here," I said grimly, watching Guillermo through the glass. He stood on guard just outside the car. "At least until my aide gives me the all-clear. I feel I owe it to them to behave after what happened earlier."

Her eyes widened, and immediately, I felt like a monster. "I'm sorry. That was—"

"Don't." She shook her head and turned her hand until our fingers entwined.

Such a simple act. So simple. So natural. So...right. Staring at our joined hands, I tried to come to grips with the odd ache inside my chest, but it was a struggle—one I was losing.

"Was anybody hurt?" she asked hesitantly.

Raising my eyes to meet hers, I gave a terse nod. "Louis. The head of my personal security detail. He was in the car following us and...he didn't make it."

"Oh, no." Tears flooded her eyes, and she leaned into me, wrapping an arm around my shoulders. "I'm so sorry, Aeric."

Turning my face into her hair, I breathed her in and nodded, not trusting myself to speak.

A short rap sounded on the window, and the door opened.

Guillermo discreetly cleared his throat, and I broke away from Kitt. "Come on. They've finished checking the house. Let's go inside. I'm exhausted."

She nodded, and as we walked to the door, I told myself to be patient. Calm. She'd had a rough few days, and there was no telling what had happened earlier before we got to the casino. We were both exhausted, as well.

"About Josef and Karol," Kitt said once I closed the door behind us.

Turning to look at her, I tossed the key down on the counter and dipped my hands into my pockets so I didn't grab her.

"They're at the palace in Monaco with my parents. Safe. We'll go there tomorrow. If it wasn't so late..."

A look of relief crossed her face, and her shoulders slumped, tension draining out of her. "I can see them?"

The expression in her eyes, on her face, had me scowling. "Of course you're going to see them. As I said, it's late, and we're tired. We need rest, but we're already scheduled to fly out in the morning at ten. If you can't pack everything you need, don't worry. I've already hired a company to handle that."

"Pack..." Her forehead crumpled, and she reached up, rubbing at her temples like she had a headache. The lines slowly faded away. "Do you want me to stay on as their au pair, Aeric?"

I stared at her. For a few seconds, that was all I could do.

She fidgeted, tugging at the skirted panties she wore. That and a bustier that barely went down over her ribcage was all she wore. *My uniform*, she'd told me with scorn. Under most circumstances, the outfit would have been appealing, but now I could only think of how she must have felt being told to put it on—and what she must have been told to expect.

Unable to take the sight of her in it, I unbuttoned my shirt, the fine cotton wrinkled after being stuffed inside the vest for so long. But it would cover her, and that ridiculous *uniform*.

Shrugging out of the shirt, I crossed to her. She eyed the shirt, then glanced up at me as I draped it over her shoulders. "I think we'll burn what you're wearing. Does that sound good to you?"

"Yes. Burn it to ash," she said, her voice fervent. Sliding her arms into the sleeves, she tugged the lapels closed over her chest, then reached for me before I could back up. "You haven't answered me."

"That's because I'm still struggling to get myself under control, and you've had a horrible day, and you want a shower and should get rest," I said, the words spilling out of me faster and faster. I caught her hands, braceleting them loosely at the wrists just as she started to stroke her palms down my chest. If she touched me for too long, I was going to fall on her like a madman, and we should talk first. Right? That was why I hadn't told her things I needed to tell her back at the hotel.

"I didn't realize it was such a complicated thing. I mean, if you have somebody else in mind, I understand. I half-expected it anyway. And regardless, just having a chance to spend some more time with them...after the past few days, I'm grateful even for that." She glanced at my grip on her hands, frowning.

I pressed a quick kiss to her lips, breaking it before she could deepen it.

"Does that mean you don't want to keep taking care of them?"

She frowned, her full lips pursing together. "Does that mean you're asking me to?"

"Not exactly. At least not the way you mean." I was making a mess of this. Where had the man with the silver tongue gone? Sometime in the hours since I'd been told of Anne's death and the days leading up to now, he'd disappeared, possibly gone forever, but it wasn't just the loss of my sister that had done it.

"It's you," I murmured, not realizing I'd spoken aloud until Kitt squinted at me, confused.

"What's me?"

"You. I'm making a mess of all of this, and the only thing that explains it is *you*." Bringing her hands to my lips again, I kissed one clenched fist, then the other before lowering them and letting go. *Get some distance,* I reminded myself. Falling on her like a madman wouldn't help. "Don't you want to take that shower?"

"I'd rather hear just how I'm to blame for you making a mess of things," she said, her tone caught between affronted and hurt.

"See? I'm doing it again." Turning back to her with a scowl, I slashed a hand through the air. "I just need..." I stopped, hearing the sound of my own voice, and I started to laugh. "Unbelievable. My parents raised me to have impeccable control, did you know? It's *expected*, after all. I'm going to one day be the Sovereign Prince of Monaco, and you can't lead a nation if you're constantly flying off the handle."

"You might want to work on that, then." She crossed her arms over her chest and lifted her chin. "I think I'll go take that shower after all."

She turned on her heel, walking away, shoulders a tight, rigid line under the borrowed shirt.

"Damn it, Kitt. I think I'm falling in love with you."

She stopped dead in her tracks.

But she didn't turn around.

"See? I'm making a mess of this. I can't think straight, and it's because I've got this...I've got *you* in my head. All the time. Ever since I saw you wearing that silly *Doga* shirt and you grabbed my arm and snarled at me not to wake the kids...I felt like I've been asleep all my life and you went and woke me up."

A harsh noise escaped her, a choked whisper of air, and her shoulders, still so rigid, rose and fell.

Fuck. Was she going to cry?

She spun around and stared at me, eyes glittering, hands fisted at her sides. "What?"

"I think I'm falling in love with you."

"You *can't* fall in love with me," she said, sputtering out a laugh.

"Why not?" Something in her eyes made the knot in my chest loosen and fall away.

"You...you just *can't*."

"You sound very certain of that." I closed the remaining distance between us and caught the lapels of her shirt in my hands. She remained rigid, her clear blue eyes locked on my face.

"I am certain of it. It's ridiculous. You have to know that."

"I don't think it's ridiculous."

Kitt rolled her eyes and tugged against my hold, but I didn't let go. Her expression grew annoyed, but there was something else in her eyes besides annoyance.

I wanted to think it was hope, but I couldn't decide if it was me or just wishful thinking.

"You're a prince, Aeric. You're used to people calling you

Your Highness and going out of their way to keeping you happy, and if you say *jump*, they want to know how high."

"I don't know if you could say I'm used to it." Brow arched, I added, "You clearly don't do any of those things. Although we can always give it a start now. But how about instead of saying jump, I say trust me. Will you ask how much?"

Kitt laughed, the sound strained and nervous.

And I wasn't wrong. She did have a wild, wary look of hope in her eyes.

Even as she shook her head and started to back away, I said again, "Trust me. I know I'm not the only one who feels something here."

"You...you..." She stopped and clamped her mouth shut, shaking her head.

When she said nothing else, I reached for her again, pulling her against me and pressing my hand to her cheek. "Are you going to tell me I'm wrong? Am I mistaken?"

"No." Giving me an annoyed look, she curled her hand around my wrist. But she didn't try to pull away. Her fingers pressed lightly on my pulse point, and I wondered if she could feel how quickly it raced. "I do feel something. And that's why I'm telling you how ridiculous this is."

"Clearly, I'm not the only one who is confused." Dipping my head, I nuzzled the most sensitive part of her neck. "Here I am having trouble thinking straight. But it's kind of obvious you're having the same trouble."

"I'm the *only* one who's thinking straight right now." Her tone was firm, but her body melted against mine, her head falling to the side as I sought out the sensitive spot that made her gasp when I bit her.

She gasped, shuddered. And kept being logical. "Aeric,

consider who you are, what you are, and then who I am. I'm an American au pair, and I only came into your life because of your niece and nephew. *You* are one day going to rule a country. I don't know about you, but I don't really want to walk blindly into something that can't go anywhere."

Her voice had grown breathier as she spoke.

By the time I'd raised my head to look at her, her lashes had drooped low, and her words were little more than a whisper.

"Who says it can't go anywhere?"

She swayed against me, then blinked. With a shake of her head, she pushed at my chest. "Haven't you heard anything I said? Let me go."

I wanted to clutch her even closer and tell her I'd never do that, never let her go, but how could I?

Slowly, I released her and watched as she backed away. I half expected her to take off running, but all she did was pace to the doorway before turning back to look at me, arms spread wide.

"Listen to how crazy this sounds, Aeric! This isn't a fairy tale. This isn't a Cinderella story. My grandmother and mother practically threw me out of the house as soon as I graduated. Everything I own is still down in my room here. I don't even have any money. All of that's gone. Because of—"

She stopped speaking abruptly and looked away, her cheeks flushing a dull red.

"Because of Karl," I bit off. I jammed my hands into my pockets with enough force that the seam on the left tore. The slacks I wore hadn't been tailored with such use in mind, and for some odd reason, the sound was oddly satisfying. I was in the mine to destroy something, tear something apart.

I wanted to commit bloody violence and had yet to be able to satisfy that urge. But damn it, I had ripped open a pocket.

"You told me about the money, Kitt. Did you think I'd forgotten? Or that the police wouldn't relish rubbing that fact in after how badly I've fucked things up?"

Kitt didn't look at me. She didn't say a word.

I wasn't surprised, and it made me want to grab her and pull her against me even more. She was stubborn, and proud and fierce.

Nothing would keep me from making her mine.

Nothing *could* keep me from making her mine.

Except for her. If she didn't want me...

"Do you love me?" I asked quietly.

She flinched and wrapped her arms around herself, staring intently at the refrigerator door. The two pieces of children's artwork held her attention as though she stared at Leonardo's masterpieces.

"Aeric," she whispered, low and husky.

But she said nothing else, and she still wouldn't look at me.

I closed the distance between us once more

That had her glancing at me, and she started to back away but then stopped, holding her ground as she stared back at me.

"Answer the question," I said. "After all, I'm a prince, and I'm used to having people addressed me as *Your Highness* and if I say jump..." I cupped her cheek. My gentle teasing didn't so much as elicit a smile.

"Yes. I do. I don't know how or why it happened because I barely know you, and half the time, you've been an arrogant ass. But I do." She sucked in a breath, and I thought she was done, but she kept going. "It already hurts like hell to think about not being in Josef's and Karol's life. I don't need to make it worse by thinking about what's going to happen when the time comes for me to not be part of yours."

"That's not going to happen." Still cupping her face, I lowered my head and rubbed my lips over hers. "I want you. And I love you. I'm going to have you in my life. The only thing that can stop that is *you*. If you don't love me and if you don't want me in your life, then tell me now, and we will end this."

She shuddered and reached for me, her fingers digging into my sides as she clung tight. "Yes, I want you. Yes, I love you. But of—"

"No." I kissed her, hard-and-fast. Not giving her a chance to pull away, I said it again against her lips, "No buts. You love me. I love you. We will make this work. It might take some time for my father to come around, but he keeps insisting that I marry, and this at least will satisfy him on that front."

Kitt jerked back so suddenly that I couldn't keep hold. She stumbled a few feet back, gaping at me. "Did you say *marry*?"

"Yes. What did you think I was getting at?" I eyed her and the distance between us again and shook my head. I had been wrong. I didn't need distance between us. I needed her in my arms, pressed against me, skin to skin. Right now.

Kitt leaned against the kitchen counter, hands on it as if she needed support. "You want me to marry you."

"Yes. I'm going to insist on it. Later." I grabbed the ham of the undershirt I still wore and stripped it off, tossing it on the floor.

Kitt's eyes widened, and she licked her lower lip.

"What are you...no." She held up a hand as if to hold me at bay although I had yet to take another step toward her. "Are you serious? The two of us marrying? People would have a field day with that, the Prince of Monaco marrying his sister's au pair."

"I don't care what they think." Shrugging, I undid the zipper on my slacks and pushed them and my boxers down, kicking my shoes off as I went. My cock was already hard. It had been pretty much ever since we'd exited the car. The need to touch, to reassure myself that she was unharmed in the most basic way went all the way to my bones.

Her blue eyes grew hazy and soft, and she kept dragging her gaze up from my penis to look at my face only for the cycle to start all over again. I wasn't above playing dirty, so I slid my hand down and cupped the heavy sack of my balls for a moment before sliding upward to palm my cock.

"Are we going to keep discussing this or would you rather get naked so I can fuck you?"

"We should discuss this," she said, but there was no real strength to her voice. "It's important."

"There are a great deal of important things to discuss. I fisted my hand and dragged it up, then down, struggling to keep my voice calm. "We won't be able to marry right away. There is a period of mourning that must be observed. And it will take time for people to acclimate. Things like that...we will have to discuss them. But none of that needs to be a concern tonight. Or even in the next few days."

Her lids drooped down, and she leaned more heavily against the counter, lips parted and breaths coming faster.

"Can we stop talking now?"

"I'm afraid if I say yes, you'll think you got your way and everything is settled." She wasn't even trying to look at my face now.

I wondered if she realized she'd clenched her thighs together.

"Of course everything isn't settled. I haven't even formally asked you to marry me yet. But we can get to that." I pumped my fist harder. "Right now, I'm desperate to have you wrapped around my dick, feel that sweet pussy melt for me, then tighten as you come."

Her breasts rose and fell as she pushed away from the counter. Then, eyes meeting mine, she shrugged out of the shirt and went to reach for the waistband of the skimpy garment covering her lower body.

I was on her before it had even cleared her hips. Yanking it down, I tossed it to the side, and then giving the bustier the same abrupt treatment, I tugged and jerked at the hook-and-eye fasteners until I could toss it onto the ground.

Once she was naked, I lifted her onto the counter and grabbed her knees, hooking them over my elbows.

"Hold my shoulders," I ordered her.

She did.

Blindly, I slammed my mouth down over hers just as I thrust deeply into her cunt, feeling the hot, slick glove closing around me. I shuddered and withdrew before pulling out much more slowly, enjoying every flex and every clench of her muscles. She whimpered, the hungry little noise so sexy and throaty, I thought it would burn me alive.

Her nipples were tight and hard, rubbing against my chest with every thrust, her big breasts bouncing from the impact. I wanted to catch those ripe curves in my hands, but at the same time, I had no desire to loosen my hold on her. She took me so deep this way, stretched so tightly, so sweetly around me.

The temptation proved more than I could handle though, and I turned away from the counter, setting her weight with an arm around her waist. I crossed to the table and laid her on it. Bending over her, I guided her knees over my shoulders and drove back inside, flexing my hips just as I filled her completely, letting the head of my cock stroke her in a deep, intimate caress.

Kitt cried out. As I went to withdraw again, her pussy tightened even more. I grunted and sank back in, not quite yet ready to leave, even if it was just so I could fill her again. Bracing my weight on my elbows, I shifted and arranged her until I could cover her breasts with my hands.

She gasped and arched up, then, in a move that had my balls tightening all over again, she covered my hands with hers and pressed harder, spine arching as she pressed deeper, squeezing my hands and restlessly plucking at her nipples.

I took over, pinched one, then the other, watching her face for cues until I found just the right level of pressure to have her arch up and tighten around my cock.

I moved harder, faster and she writhed under me and arched, urging me on.

"More...please...harder...Aeric!"

Always, I thought. I would always want her.

She shattered in the next moment, and I shoved upright, grabbing her hips and slamming into her, all finesse gone, nothing left but this, the need to fill her, fuck her, brand her...keep her.

Always.

I came only seconds later, and drained, empty, I went to my knees in front of her, resting my head on her leg. She slid her hand into my hair, and despite the hard tile biting into my knees, despite the light chill in the room, I'd never felt more complete.

THIRTY-FIVE

KITT

"I THINK I COULD LIVE HERE HAPPILY FOR THE REST OF MY life."

Aeric came up behind me and slid his arms around my waist. "That's not going to happen."

Unlike me, he was fully dressed.

I wore nothing more than a robe. He was staying in the suite across the hall from mine. At least, that was the official story, and nobody had questioned it.

He had come over not long after we had returned to the manor home where we were staying while in Luxemburg for his cousin Stacia's public wedding ceremony.

I doubted it would surprise anybody that he had spent the night in my room. Aeric was adamant he keep up appearances, teasing me that the world needed to believe I was making him an honorable man.

I knew why he did it. There had been a lot of gossip over the past year as our courtship went from rumor to acknowledged fact.

More than once, he'd stepped in when some of that gossip proved to be cattier than the rest. He denied it, of course. And maybe it wasn't *him* personally, but it was somebody from the Princely house. I had no doubt of that.

There had been more than a few apologies and retractions issued from various gossip rags, even though I had told him not to worry about it.

I might as well be talking to a wall as far as he was concerned. He worried quite spectacularly. In all honesty, it was flattering. Aeric and his family were the only people who had ever gone out of their way to concern themselves on my behalf.

My mother and grandmother certainly never had, although, over the past year, my mom and grandmother had started reaching out to me. I knew why. It had to do with a man standing behind me and nuzzling my neck.

My father had done the same, after he realized who I was, of course. I had no idea if I was going to even try to rebuild bridges with my mom and grandmother. I was positive I wouldn't bother trying with my father, though.

"Do you know I'm standing here nibbling on your lovely neck and your mind is a million miles away?"

I laughed softly. "A few thousand at most."

"At a specific enough guess. Just what are you thinking about?"

Turning in his arms, I looked up at him. "My parents," I admitted. "I got another email from my father."

Aeric's brows came together. "I'll have Guillermo take care of it. Or..."

I frowned at him, already knowing what he was going to suggest. I was right.

"You can do as I've asked and let me hire you an aide."

I rolled my eyes. "I don't need an aide to answer e-mail. He looked like he wanted to argue, and I covered his mouth with my finger. "I'm perfectly capable of answering my own email," I told him. "We've had this conversation a hundred times and will have it another hundred if need be. I've got it."

"I'll let it go for now. But if your father starts getting too pushy, let me know, and I will have Guillermo handle it."

I made a noncommittal noise under my breath and turned back around to watch as the sun continued its slow rise up over the mountains. "Are you sure we can't just stay here? Why can't you do what millions of people do anymore? Telecommute your job."

He ran his knuckles down my side in warning.

I grabbed his hand. "Don't start that."

"If you keep this up, I'll start thinking you don't like Monaco."

"You know better." I huffed out a breath. "I love Monaco. I just really love these mountains."

"You can come visit whenever you want. You seemed to get along really well with Stacia."

I smiled and leaned back into him. "Yes. I really love your cousin."

"Good. I'm glad. I want you to like her. I want you to like all of my family. I want you to love them. And I want you to love Monaco."

There was an odd note in his voice, and I craned my head around to look up at him. "I do love Monaco. You know that, right?"

I expected a teasing smile.

Instead, he turned me around and caught my hands and his.

When he went to his knees, my heart lurched up into my throat and started to beat hard and fast. Hard enough, fast enough that it knocked my breath out of me.

"Aeric?" It came out just a bare whisper of sound.

He kissed the back of my right hand, then my left before shifting until he held only my left.

"I've been trying to find the right way to do this for days. But there hasn't been the right moment. I guess I was waiting for now. Seeing you with the sun rising up over the mountains, with that smile on your face...I guess Luxemburg isn't all that bad." A smile crooked his lips as he peered up at me.

This was all a dream. This past year...all of it had been a dream.

That's what I told myself. But I knew that wasn't the case. I couldn't possibly imagine this beautiful man on his knees in front of me.

I couldn't imagine the cool, hard press of the ring as he slid it onto my finger. "Kitt, will you marry me? Make me and the children your family. Make Monaco your home. Not just for now but forever."

"I can't breathe."

A faint smile curved his lips. "That's not exactly the answer I was hoping for."

I tugged on his hand, urging him up to his feet as he rose. I flung myself at him, and he caught me in his arms, holding me tight.

"I can't breathe," I said again.

"Still not quite the answer I was hoping for." He was laughing as he said it and pressing kisses to my neck.

Laughing now myself, breathlessly, I said, "Yes. Absolutely yes."

THE END

Check out the other books in my Filthy Rich Royals:

1. **The Perfect Guy (Liechtenstein)**
2. **The Dukes Virgin (Luxemburg)**

ALSO BY M. S. PARKER

His Obsession

His Control

His Hunger

His Secret

Sex Coach

Big O's (Sex Coach 2)

Pleasure Island (Sex Coach 3)

Rescued by the Woodsman

The Billionaire's Muse

Bound

One Night Only

Damage Control

Take Me, Sir

Make Me Yours

The Billionaire's Sub

The Billionaire's Mistress

Con Man Box Set

HERO Box Set

A Legal Affair Box Set

The Client

Indecent Encounter

Dom X Box Set

Unlawful Attraction Box Set

Chasing Perfection Box Set

Blindfold Box Set

Club Prive Box Set

The Pleasure Series Box Set

Exotic Desires Box Set

Casual Encounter Box Set

Sinful Desires Box Set

Twisted Affair Box Set

Serving HIM Box Set

Pure Lust Box Set

ABOUT THE AUTHOR

M. S. Parker is a USA Today Bestselling author and the author of over fifty spicy romance series and novels.

Living part-time in Las Vegas, part-time on Maui, she enjoys sitting by the pool with her laptop writing her next spicy romance.

Growing up all she wanted to be was a dancer, actor and author. So far only the latter has come true but M. S. Parker hasn't retired her dancing shoes just yet. She is still waiting for the call to appear on Dancing With The Stars.

When M. S. isn't writing, she can usually be found reading–oops, scratch that! She is always writing.

For more information:
www.msparker.com
msparkerbooks@gmail.com